HOME FOR THE HERO

CHERYL HARPER

Recycling programs for this product may not exist in your area.

ISBN-13: 978-1-335-60515-3

Home for the Hero

For questions and comments about the quality of this book, please contact us at CustomerService@Harlequin.com.

Harlequin Enterprises ULC
22 Adelaide St. West, 41st Floor
Toronto, Ontario M5H 4E3, Canada
www.Harlequin.com

HarperCollins Publishers
Macken House, 39/40 Mayor Street Upper,
Dublin 1, D01 C9W8, Ireland
www.HarperCollins.com

Printed in U.S.A.

1 2 3 4 5 6 7 8 9 10 HDC 28 27 26 25

“Are we going to eat your sister’s onion rings while she’s gone?”

The warmth in his eyes delighted Lila. It was like the two of them had their own language. The rest of the world would never believe he was teasing her like this.

“Absolutely we’re eating her onion rings.” Lila took one and nodded when he selected his own. “She knows better than to leave food unattended. I’ve been teaching her that lesson my whole life.”

Trey smiled and shifted in his seat. “I don’t have any siblings. Sometimes I’ve regretted that, but I will add never having my snacks stolen to my list of pros to being an only child.”

Lila pursed her lips. “Is it theft? Or is this the ancient common law doctrine of ‘finders keepers’ at work?”

His low laugh caught Lila’s attention. Hearing it for the first time felt like winning something big.

It also caught the attention of the tables around them.

Dear Reader,

I love to meet new characters, whether they're standing next to me in the grocery store checkout line, hanging out between the covers of the new book I just bought (because there is always a new book I just bought) or waiting for me to build them in a story I want to tell.

The new police chief, Trey Douglas, is a fish out of water, mainly because he insists on doing the right thing the right way and ruffling a lot of feathers. He lacks the talent for conversing easily with others and it shows. Lila Shepard never met a stranger. Everyone in town watched her grow up, but she has a business to run now. Getting her neighbors to see her differently matters.

Trey and Lila don't want to work together, but their success will change how the people of Horizon see them. And like the best relationships, it will also change how they see themselves.

If you'd like to know more about my books and what's coming next, please visit me at CherylHarperBooks.com.

Cheryl

Cheryl Harper discovered her love for books and words as a little girl, thanks to a mother who made countless library trips and an introduction to Laura Ingalls Wilder's Little House books. Whether the stories she reads are set in the prairie, the American West, Regency England or Earth a hundred years in the future, Cheryl enjoys strong characters who make her laugh. Now Cheryl spends her days searching for the right words while she stares out the window and her dog, Jack, snoozes beside her. And she considers herself very lucky to do so.

For more information about Cheryl's books, visit her online at cherylharperbooks.com.

Books by Cheryl Harper

Harlequin Heartwarming

A Lowcountry Heroes Romance

A Hero's Rescue

The Fortunes of Prospect

The Cowboy's Compromise
Courting the Cowgirl
The Right Cowboy
The Cowboy's Second Chance
Her Cowboy's Promise
The Cowboy Next Door

Visit the Author Profile page
at Harlequin.com for more titles.

CHAPTER ONE

TREY DOUGLAS WAS battling an uncustomary tangle of nerves as he prepared for his first official appearance as the new chief of police in Horizon, South Carolina. Breaching the doors of active trap houses hadn't fazed him. Interrupting drug deals and netting dealers at all levels of their organizations had been the job and he'd done it well.

But the job in Horizon was a whole new world.

He'd promised himself it was temporary. Three years max. Then he'd go home. He could return to the Columbia Police Department, the task forces he led and the only real community he'd ever belonged to.

Even if small-town law enforcement might test his skills and his patience, he had to make this work.

The suspicion on DEA Agent Dennis Browning's face as he'd grilled Trey about his partner's illegal activities had been the final straw. Being suspected of accepting bribes by the man who'd been a mentor and led Trey to the career he loved had changed everything.

Horizon was supposed to be his lifeline.

Trey picked up the Horizon Police Department coffee mug that he'd found in the chief's desk and took a sip of black coffee. The immediate burn made him wonder if his tooth enamel was in danger, but it couldn't stop him. Caffeine was necessary that morning.

"This coffee needs something sweet," he muttered before trying another sip. It didn't improve much. He'd had worse coffee than the Horizon PD's communal pot, but not much worse. On his last assignment, they'd enjoyed gourmet roasts from South America.

That should have been his first clue that someone was being paid to look the other way on their investigations.

He still would never have suspected his right hand, the guy who'd been working next to him for years. Together they had operated targeted assignments with federal task forces, and they had been very good at it.

His whole life, he'd held himself to a high standard. As an army brat, he'd been tossed into new places and messes, and he'd worked hard to fit in. As the new kid, he was most often the odd man out, too. That gave him plenty of experience doing hard things alone. It also made it much more difficult to leave Columbia and his team behind. It had taken time to feel at home, but now that he'd lost it, he understood how much home meant.

In law enforcement, he'd built a reputation for efficiency and effective leadership, for reliable protocols that were carried out with precision.

That anyone could think he'd accept bribes himself…

The betrayal stung.

Success here would shut down any questions about his integrity or ability.

The former chief, Tom Shepard, was known far and wide in South Carolina law enforcement. If he could win Tom Shepard's approval, his career would be back on track.

Efficiency. Attention to detail. Knowledge of the law and procedures that kept the streets he was responsible for safe. Those things mattered in police work, big city to small town and everywhere in between.

Running this meeting wasn't the hardest part of this job. It could even be the easiest, if he ever got started.

"The longer you stall, the worse this gets," he muttered.

Trey straightened his shoulders.

He brushed off his uniform and adjusted his badge and brass nameplate.

Then he wished momentarily for the comfort of a tactical vest.

The clipboard Tom Shepard had left behind was centered on his desk, loaded with the day's assignments. It would be his only real protection against the unknown.

As Trey picked it up, he wished it was larger, heavier or at least more comfortable in his hands. Displaying any of this uncertainty when he stepped up in front of the squad room would be a mistake. He and his squads had always appreciated strong leaders.

As a kid, he'd learned to move through every new school lunchroom with his eyes set on a distant target, above all the curious looks. If they couldn't find his weakness, then he had no weakness.

Confident. In control.

Those were the attributes of leaders he wanted to follow.

He didn't belong here in Horizon, but he had a lot of experience with that.

Trey marched out of his office and down the long center aisle of the squad room. As he went, laughter floated through the air, and he had to wait for a rowdy conversation at the back of the room to die down to get the attention of his officers.

There, clustered around a desk in the corner, a group of his officers including TJ and Bee Shepard were gathered in a circle around a woman with a long blond ponytail. He couldn't see her face, but the eye-popping color of her pink dress made it evident that she did not belong in the squad room.

Her broad, dramatic gestures convinced him she was the catalyst of the laughter as well.

Clearly, she had to go. It was time to get to work.

"Let's get the official morning briefing started. I don't see any signs here, but this squad room is closed to the public, officers only past those doors. I will get one posted and reiterate to the front desk all policies regarding public access to police department resources," Trey said from his spot near the map of Horizon. We Serve was painted in bright blue letters on the wall above it. "This room is for police business, ma'am. Please exit to the lobby."

The group immediately disbanded. TJ and Bee gave him their attention. Officers Roberts and Rodriguez moved to take seats at their desks, and the blonde turned on her heel to give him a sharp salute with her right hand. It was perfectly executed, but her smirk changed the flavor from respect to something else.

"Of course, Chief, I would never interfere with official *police business*. Although if I did and I brought in some of my mother's banana bread for everyone in the squad room, do you think I would get a special invitation? Kay Shepard? You remember meeting her at the Shoreline Animal Shelter's Spring Social, right?" she asked.

He did remember meeting the former chief and his wife at the spring picnic—the mayor had invited him to sway his decision to accept the job. A career lawman of Tom Shepard's stature and reputation was intimidating. His wife had been lovely.

"That's my mother for you. Really friendly then, when you were introduced, and today she wanted to welcome you on your first day." Her lips curled but it wasn't an actual smile. She tapped a plastic container on the desk beside her, and Trey felt a pang of regret.

He loved banana bread. Would she carry it back out of the squad room when she left?

Didn't matter. Rules were rules, and his officers didn't need the public dropping in on a whim.

Learning the rules of every new place had been the key to his success growing up. As an adult, Trey was committed to setting them.

"We do appreciate it," Trey said as he braced one hand on his utility belt, "and you can leave any other treats with the officer in the lobby." Officers with front-desk duty were assigned to interact with the public. That was a simple solution. "Where the public is welcome."

The blonde turned to TJ and Bee and raised her eyebrows in a "can you believe this guy?" expression. TJ coughed into his hand and nodded at his K9 partner, Lucy. The yellow Lab promptly did a lap around the desks in the room to sit in front of Trey.

He studied Officer Lucy Shepard while he waited for the blonde to exit. The dog wagged her tail, and he had to cross his arms over his chest to contain the urge to introduce himself.

Since he knew very little about police K9 officers specifically—except that they took their jobs seriously—or dogs in general, Trey decided an impassive expression was best.

That could be because the blonde was still watching him.

He recognized Lila Shepard from the giant billboard on the highway right before the exit to Horizon. He hadn't done much research, but as far as he could tell, she was the town's only dedicated real estate agent. The sign had a professional headshot, where she resembled a dozen other beautiful blond agents, polished, with a careful smile.

Here, in person, she was magnetic. The flush in her cheeks did nice things for her eyes, too. The careful smile from her photo was gone. If he had to guess, he'd say she was angry.

"I'll happily be on my civilian way, Chief, back out to the lobby to join the rest of the public." Lila waved as she pressed her left hand to the double doors that led back out of the squad room. The police department was located on the first floor of the historic building that housed Horizon's Town Hall, including the mayor's offices on the top floor. Originally a hotel for wealthy tourists around the Civil War, the building had been restored and pressed into service for the city's administration.

"Ask either of those two and they'll tell you I never interfere in *police business*," Lila added, pointing at TJ and Bee Shepard. Then she shoved open the heavy wooden doors and let them close with a hard thump behind her.

That was an effect of the age of the Horizon police station. Even the slamming doors were elevated from Trey's usual experience, but he didn't have any trouble reading Lila Shepard's intent.

He had grown up with boxy base housing as a kid and worked out of utilitarian government buildings and temporary workspaces in office buildings since then—where everything had been built for economy or transition—so this place was a new and interesting experience.

Horizon's Town Hall had history and permanence in its bones.

Encountering Lila Shepard was also new and interesting.

Her dramatic departure left an uncomfortable silence in the squad room, so Trey cleared his throat. Lucy stood, and Trey glanced down to see the dog's eyes were locked on him.

He tipped up his chin. "We're running late. These meetings should be efficient, short and to the point because I do not want to take any unnecessary time from your patrols."

It was hard to ignore the uneasy shifting in the seats he observed, and it was impossible not to see the way TJ Shepard and Bee Shepard exchanged meaningful glances when Lucy returned to her normal position next to TJ's desk. Was her tail drooping? Lucy was a police dog. Surely she didn't register his getting right to work as a snub.

"By now, you've seen the overnight reports. We have one in holding on public intoxication charges, pending a bond hearing today. Officers responded to three other calls overnight, one accident and two health emergencies." Trey flipped through the pages on his clipboard to calm his nerves. "There's no alteration to normal assignments. I see a community event on the calendar for Wednesday. Rodriguez, send me the details."

The department's community outreach officer nodded. "Sure thing, Chief." His brief hesitation over the title reminded Trey that they were all in choppy waters. His squad was adjusting to a big change after years of calling Tom Shepard the chief. "We'd love to have you come out. The school district has a back-to-school event planned. We're going to have a table set up for school-supply donations. Excellent opportunity to meet and greet." He turned toward the corner of the room to address TJ Shepard. "You and Lucy will drop by, right?" He motioned with his thumb. "Lucy's our celebrity. She draws the crowds."

TJ nodded. "We'll be there." He patted Lucy's

side and met Trey's stare. "She's kind of a big deal."

Trey took that to mean TJ and Lucy were town celebrities. Was Lucy operating as more of a mascot than a K9 officer completing search-and-seizure assignments? That would be a massive waste of the department's resources.

He made a note to check into their work more closely but carefully. TJ was the former chief's son and the whole family was revered in Horizon. Changes might rock the boat, something he'd like to avoid. The last thing Trey needed was more bad press, especially coming from a man as respected as his predecessor.

Being outnumbered by Shepards three to one in this room alone would be a challenge. It was hard to pivot from the *Shepard* Horizon Police Department when the Shepards still filled the room.

Trey rubbed his chin as he read the remaining notes he'd made.

"Any other items we need to discuss before we dismiss? Concerns?" he asked. Since Trey didn't know the main hot spots, it made sense to rely on the officers who did.

When Bee Shepard stepped forward, Trey was surprised. Dispatch had not been involved in any briefings in other places he'd served. They were officers assigned to the station with no regular patrol. They took in information, yes, but how much could they observe?

"As most of you know, there will be a concert at the Battery next weekend." Bee surveyed the room before meeting his stare. From that, he surmised she was speaking for his benefit. "It's one of the town's biggest events, and it always attracts a surge of day-trippers determined to squeeze in one last party before the season ends. Patrols in and around the Battery should be on the lookout for early arrivals this week into next, kicking up sand. I told Charlene at the Sandlapper to be alert and give us a call if she sees anything to raise concern out at the restaurant. The live music there always draws a rowdy crowd."

A wave of nods swept through the room.

"Citations for public intoxication and disturbing the peace will dampen any rowdiness. All patrols around the park are authorized to skip warnings and go straight to tickets," Trey said as he made note of the officers assigned to those zones. He'd review their citations at the end of the week. It had been a long time since he'd walked a patrol and issued tickets for infractions like disturbing the peace, but it was one of the tools in their arsenal to keep Battery Park—which the locals apparently called the Battery—safe. They would use those tools. Public safety was their first duty, after all.

Trey made a note that he needed to swing by the Sandlapper to get the lay of the land. Was the old restaurant on a dock? The image was hazy in his mind, a weakness he needed to address quickly.

"If there's nothing else..." Trey waited a second before nodding. "Dismissed."

The hesitation in the room caught his attention. He'd witnessed how the Horizon PD mobilized for their shifts under Tom Shepard. There had been fewer confused glances around the room.

Unless he was mistaken, two of them were muttering about citations and tourists, but it didn't matter to him who was guilty of breaking the rules governing the park. The rules applied to the town's citizens and tourists alike.

Then he saw the look the Shepards exchanged.

One way to improve his strategic position as chief would be to lower the number of Shepards in the room. TJ and Lucy were a team, but Bee Shepard's presence was optional here.

He crossed over to where Bee and TJ were talking with Rodriguez.

The outreach officer handed him a note with an address. "That's the football stadium. The back-to-school event will be there. We'll be accepting school supplies. The fire department is doing a food drive. There's a blood drive. Food trucks. It'll be a good night to talk to your new neighbors."

"Yeah, the *public*," TJ added. His emphasis on the word suggested he thought as much of Trey's closing the squad room and inviting Lila Shepard to leave as the woman herself had. "Relating to them is part of *police business*."

Trey watched Bee stare hard at her brother, and

he figured there was some mental telepathy happening. She was trying to shut TJ's mouth with the power of her mind.

"I'll be there." Before he could second-guess himself, Trey nodded. "I wanted to excuse you from attending the daily shift change briefing for patrol officers, Shepard. I'll send you the assignments. No need to step away from the duties of Dispatch."

The temperature in the room dropped suddenly.

Then Rodriguez's eyes bugged out.

But the clearest indicator that he'd landed a blow was the way Bee Shepard's posture changed. Instead of an easy stance, her shoulders straightened, and every bit of warmth faded from her face.

Her clipped "yes, sir" was the only response he got before she stalked away.

TJ watched her go before swinging back to face Trey. He wasn't sure what TJ wanted to say, but the battle to keep it under wraps showed on his face. Every time he'd seen TJ, the man had been charming someone—old or young, it didn't seem to matter—with an easy smile. His lips were a hard line now. Finally, TJ said, "Lucy, let's go to work."

The two of them hit the doors to the lobby at a fast clip. Neither of them looked back.

That left Officer Rodriguez standing awkwardly next to him.

He'd efficiently set the tone for his morning briefings. Any irritation the Shepards experienced would fade when the meetings ran as expected.

Trey couldn't find a way to smoothly transition out of the conversation and retreat to his office, but he finally met Rodriguez's stare.

"I'm glad you're planning to attend this outreach event, sir," Rodriguez said slowly, as if he was picking his way carefully through something he had to get off his chest.

"Out with it." Trey crossed his arms over his chest. Police forces ran on hierarchy and command, much like the military. Rodriguez wanted to say something, but he was worried about breaking that chain of command.

Rodriguez nodded. "I'm not originally from Horizon, Chief. I moved here after marrying my college sweetheart, but I will tell you it's a mistake to be looking for enemies in the Shepards."

Trey frowned as he considered that. "Because they have so much power in Horizon?"

Rodriguez snorted. "No." Then he shrugged. "Well, they do, but it comes from being good people. Like the kind you want to live next door to or marry into or work for or with. Just good. You're in a tricky spot, no doubt. I didn't have the same situation. But I do know that Bee Shepard's contribution is the kind that's hard to measure but a mistake to discount."

"There's no obvious need for Dispatch in the

briefing," Trey said, "so it's not efficient to pull her from her duties. Efficiency is my goal always. The taxpayers deserve that, and so do your fellow officers. These protocols support good police work." This was technically true and sounded much better than saying he didn't want to face both Shepards if he could only deal with one.

Rodriguez rocked back on his heels but didn't argue.

That convinced Trey that his logic held.

"Anything else?" he asked to show he was open to criticism.

"Do not miss Kay Shepard's banana bread," Rodiguez said without a second of hesitation.

Trey didn't take a slice of bread, since it would weaken his position, but he returned to the safety of his desk, pleased with his overall performance. He'd conquered his first morning briefing. His logic was sound. This shift change had set the right tone. Trey treated every new assignment with the same focus, his goal to meet and exceed expectations whether they were set by the governor, the mentor who'd taken a chance on him fresh out of the police academy or his old friend, the mayor of Horizon.

He might not be planning to retire from this office like Tom Shepard, but while he was here, he'd show his new neighbors that he deserved the job. When the gossip in Columbia died down, he'd be able to go back to the police work he knew with his head held high.

He'd stick strictly to the laws that the police were called to enforce and set high standards for his officers. When he left Horizon, the police department would be stronger for his time here.

Every day would be easier moving forward.

CHAPTER TWO

LILA SHEPARD DID her best to take calming breaths as she climbed the sweeping, airy staircase that led to the second floor of Horizon's Town Hall. Today was supposed to be an exciting day for her family—the first day of her father's freedom from the demands of his career with the Horizon Police Department. Lila wasn't sure who her father would be in retirement, but she wanted to find out.

Meeting the new chief of police had shoved that excitement behind a giant chunk of irritation. Her whole life, she'd had to untangle police business to get to her family. She hated it.

The town's demands on the police chief would never have come before family for Tom Shepard, but Lila wasn't sure he understood how difficult it was to reach him sometimes. His career was his calling, but every single one of them had ended up serving along with him.

Lila knew the Horizon PD would continue to occupy Shepard dinner table discussions, thanks to TJ and Bee, but she'd hoped today would mark a change.

And it had.

She might hate being coldly tossed out on her ear even more than hearing the details of police life at every family gathering.

Lila paused on the landing as she always did to admire the columns that framed the entry to the mayor's offices. Substantial cornices and the palmetto-leaf medallions that dotted the old hotel-turned-city-offices were too beautiful to stomp past because she was angry with the new police chief. Besides, arriving at her meeting with Rainey Blackwell without clearing some of her annoyance would only lead to more questions than she wanted to answer.

The new chief was Rainey's choice, handpicked by her to take over. She wouldn't take criticism of him lightly.

Lila wasn't sure why she had gotten so embarrassed by his autocratic manner anyway. That was a police chief trait in her experience, but Trey Douglas was really leaning into it.

Enduring his disapproving frown while everyone in the squad room watched them face off had gotten under her skin. That might be because it brought up old feelings of facing her father the same way, but she was an adult now, not a kid.

Lila stared out the tall, narrow windows that lined the second-floor gallery and tried to shake it off.

"I don't want to be involved in police business anyway," she muttered. "Never have, never will."

Police business never stopped, and it didn't recognize a single boundary. Even when her father left the police station, everyone knew how to track him down. There was no quitting time.

They also knew exactly how to report back to the chief anytime his kids bent a rule. Since Lila was the single Shepard kid who occasionally colored outside of the lines, that was a problem.

Lila was always a Shepard, always the chief's daughter, and someone was always watching.

If she didn't love the place so much, it would be tempting to leave, but no one could sell Horizon better than Lila. Being the town's only local agent meant she got some after-hours calls, but there were far fewer real estate emergencies than police emergencies, so that wasn't much of a problem.

Being able to pop in to see TJ and Bee at the station whenever she wanted was one of the few perks of being the chief's kid.

Obviously, that perk no longer existed.

The next time her mother created a flimsy excuse to get Lila in front of the newest single man in town, she had a good excuse to avoid it. In the presence of a handsome man like Trey Douglas, she'd momentarily forgotten her lifelong certainty that she would never get involved with a police officer. But that morning he'd reminded her of all the reasons why she'd vowed to steer clear.

"As if I've never heard a shift change briefing," she muttered before realizing she had to get the talking-to-herself thing under control.

Rainey's office manager was seated behind the desk inside the doors to the city offices. Nevaeh's raised eyebrow suggested she'd witnessed the one-sided conversation.

"Morning, Nevaeh, Rainey asked me to come in this morning."

The twentysomething pursed her lips as she studied her monitor. "Looks like you're late. Rainey has you on the calendar at eight. It's almost twenty minutes after." Her stare was assessing, and Lila wondered if she'd ever be as intimidating. Even wearing a Nirvana T-shirt and space buns, Nevaeh had a ruthlessly efficient manner.

Lila was floundering for an appropriate response when Rainey stuck her head out her office door. "Stop terrifying the town's best real estate agent. Save that for journalists and all of my exes. Lila, come in." She motioned her into the office, and Lila whistled at the sky-high heels Rainey was wearing.

"You must have important business to take care of when we're through," Lila said as she settled in the armchair across from Rainey. "No way I rated those shoes all by myself."

"I don't need a reason to look fabulous. They called to me this morning." Rainey turned her monitor around so that Lila could see her screen. "Do you know Monica Denis?"

Lila sighed. The morning was off to a rough start. Lila did know Monica Denis, and she knew why Rainey was asking. "She's the real estate agent from Charleston who just put up the for sale sign on the Lees' house on Duneside." She crossed her legs. "From what I can gather through the grapevine, the Lees are moving to Charleston so that their kids can attend one of the private schools there. She was the agent on the house they bought, so they asked her to get their house here listed and sold."

That didn't thrill Lila, but it made sense for the Lees.

Lila lost an occasional listing or sale to outside agents, but it didn't happen often enough to worry her. She was a Shepard, and that carried a lot of weight in Horizon.

"Anything else?" Rainey asked, her eyes locked on Lila's face.

"She's closer to Bee's age, but we were in the same sorority for half a second," Lila added. She, Bee and TJ had all attended the College of Charleston. Since Bee was the kind of person who collected friends like she breathed, naturally and without thinking about it at all, Lila was certain Rainey could get the inside scoop from her.

Rainey tilted her head to the side. "You in a sorority?" She studied Lila's face as if she was re-evaluating what she knew. "I guess I can see it." Since Rainey had no doubt run her sorority like a mini-state, whether she was elected to a position or not, Lila decided to take that as a compliment. Rainey had a knack for gathering power. It had been on display ever since she'd run a lunch swap in their elementary cafeteria.

Lila rolled her eyes. "You could be the only one. Bee told me not to do it, and then she repeated 'I told you so' for at least six months after I resigned. If you ask her about Monica, I am sure it will come up that she told me I wasn't cut out for sorority life then." Her older sister was a lot of things, but "always right" might be the worst.

The mayor's nod, as if she understood very well, made Lila feel marginally better.

"Why did you call me here to talk about Monica Denis?" Lila asked. Her listing was only a blip in Horizon's real estate market. If Lila wasn't worried, why would Rainey be?

"I was planning to approach her with a business deal, and I never go into these situations without all the information I can gather. I want the strongest negotiating position I can build, so gathering intel beforehand is important." Rainey turned to study the image on the screen. "I can't decide if she's the kind of person who would love or hate lunch at the Sandlapper. What do you think?"

The Sandlapper was a Horizon landmark. The restaurant had been perched on the pier next to

Battery Park for decades. The food was amazing, but the atmosphere was definitely…minimal. Weathered.

It was hard to imagine the Monica Denis she remembered seated at one of the restaurant's beat-up tables, but it was a town landmark. If Monica was "good people," she'd roll with the decor.

"How can you go wrong with those crab cakes?" Lila clasped her fingers together in her lap as she formulated the real question. "What kind of business deal are you hoping to pitch?"

And more importantly, why would she cut Lila out of it? It had to be real estate, right?

"Monica Denis is Albert Denis's daughter." Rainey tapped the screen. "Of the Denis Group." Her tone made it clear that the Denis Group was a big deal.

"Yes, his company is listed on her for sale sign," Lila said.

Working in the family business was a respected South Carolina tradition. She could understand that. Four out of five of the Shepard kids had done the same, even if their chosen law enforcement agencies ranged from Horizon's police department to the United States Coast Guard and Marine Corps.

Lila was the only oddball there.

She had been her whole life. Disentangling herself from police business should be easy. The reminder of the new chief's authoritarian dismissal annoyed her all over again.

Since it sounded like she was about to lose a big chunk of business thanks to Rainey, her irritation levels were approaching the danger zone.

"The Denis Group is one of the oldest housing developers in Charleston. Since the place was Charles Town, the Denis family has been putting up houses and buildings," Rainey said as she clicked a link. The new page showed a subdivision development called Palmetto Estates. The largest image on the site was of a new home with a nod to Charleston's Southern roots. The first level was elevated with a divided set of stairs leading to the front door. A wide porch wrapped around both sides, and the second story featured a beautiful wrought iron balcony and two large dormer windows on either side. The second image was of the lots available for sale.

"Wouldn't it be nice to have a new development in Horizon?" Rainey asked as she scooted her desk chair back. She gazed out of the long gallery of windows that lined her office as if she could see such a thing in the distance, but Lila knew for certain her only view was of Battery Park. She'd just been admiring it from the landing. "That would attract more buyers for the town, even for properties outside of the new subdivision, because the builder would be advertising Horizon as well as the lots and homes for sale. You know

I'm always on the hunt for ways to increase business here to add better jobs that last all year long. We love our tourists, but homeowners mean better schools and more jobs." She focused on Lila again. "If I can make the right pitch to Monica, get her dad signed on to develop, it could be big for the town."

Lila crossed her arms over her chest and tried to ignore the damage to her own pride. What could Monica Denis bring to this that Lila couldn't? Except for connections to the company that could build the actual homes.

Even annoyed, Lila had to admit that was not nothing.

Still, she could put together the land deal. Had she ever done anything like this? No. Had Monica? Maybe, and she did have the family business to fall back on, but Lila knew Horizon in a way that Monica never could.

"Any reason you didn't bring this up to me before Monica Denis arrived in Horizon? We could have worked on this together." Did that sound too confrontational? She hated confrontation. Only slights *to* her family or *from* her family could provoke her to it.

Rainey was more than family. She was Lila's first call for bail money or backup because her loyalty was unshakeable and she was slower with "I told you this was a bad idea" than Bee ever would be.

When Rainey blinked as if she couldn't understand why the thought would have ever occurred to her, Lila inhaled slowly. The irritation levels were rising again.

"Is there anything else you need from me?" She stood. "I've got some research to do on Roberta Hale's house. She's ready to sell. Bee mentioned that the divorce is final now, and she's been talking about downsizing." That was one of the best things about the real estate business in Horizon. The person who paid attention could get out ahead of the game and be ready before the buyer or seller, especially if that person was related to Bee Shepard, who knew everything as it happened because that was who she was. "And at least I'm still getting *that* kind of business, even if it's not a new subdivision development for Horizon."

When she heard the bitter tone in her own voice, Lila lifted her chin. She wasn't going to back down even if it felt wrong to square off against her oldest friend in the world if she excluded her sister.

Rainey dipped her head. "Come on, Lila. I'm not making any comment on your ability. It was a process, seeing her sign sparked the idea. That's all. And her connection to the premier builder in Charleston? You see how the pieces fit together, right?"

Lila bit her lip as she considered how to answer the question. She did understand the logic, but that didn't change the fact that she and Rainey had a lot of history. Rainey's brainstorm should have included Lila if she really believed Lila was good at her job.

"When you and Bee get together later, make sure to pick her brain. She'll have some good info about Monica's college years," Lila said as she waved her hand on the way out the door. There wasn't a good way to answer Rainey, especially since she'd inadvertently hit the nerve that Lila tried to keep buried deep, deep down.

Growing up as the Shepard who didn't fit the mold, that tender spot of wondering if she ever measured up was exposed now and then, and Rainey's stiletto heel had stabbed it.

Lila's only real defense was not to dwell on it. If she ignored the pinch, the pain would eventually recede. She trotted down the stairs, looked resolutely away from the doors leading to the squad room, and hurried to her office a few blocks away in Horizon's historic district bordering Battery Park. The buildings here had been part of the town's original settlement, and she'd always loved her small piece of history.

When she let herself in, her senior Great Dane, Duke, stretched slowly up from his dog bed, which took up more than half the available walking space. "Did you need a walk, buddy?" she asked in the cutesy voice she swore she would never use when she adopted Duke from the Shoreline Animal Shelter. She'd been a last-minute emergency foster during Hurricane Agnes months before. Their relationship was supposed to be short-term, but then she'd discovered that Duke was the perfect dog for her. He taught first-time pet parent Lila everything she needed to know.

Like right now, he stood patiently by the door and waited for her to clip his purple leash to his purple collar.

When they stepped outside, he moved to the edge of the sidewalk and waited for her to check both directions up and down the cobblestoned street before stepping out.

They meandered to the center of Battery Park, where the statue of Captain Emory Shepard, Revolutionary War hero, town founder and her great-great-so-many-greats-grandfather, stood, and Duke veered off the path to investigate slowly and make his mark.

All of this left Lila plenty of time to think about her situation.

If she wanted to be a part of Rainey's deal, she'd need to bring something to the table.

Her mother believed Lila was the best agent in Horizon— which was true because she was the only agent in Horizon—but she often said it was because no one knew Horizon better. If Lila could identify the right piece of land and get the owners on board to sell it for development, Rainey would take her seriously.

If it mattered, Monica Denis would also take her seriously.

"Obviously it matters more than I'd like, Duke," she muttered when the dog came to sit on her yellow sneaker. When he was ready to go back inside, he plunked his not-inconsequential hind end on her foot. His signal was impossible to ignore. "I'm just not sure *why* it matters."

They slowly made their way back to the office, where they both crammed into her tiny kitchen, which was wedged in beside a half bath with the world's smallest sink. Duke got his smelly jerky treat and big gulp of water before he stretched back out on his bed with a happy sigh.

"Living your best life, aren't you, Duke?" Lila asked with a grin as she opened her laptop and pulled up a map of Horizon. She wasn't certain Rainey's big plan included a place for her, but she would never know unless she gave it a shot. After an hour or so, she glanced down at her notebook and tapped her bright purple pen against the list she'd made.

She'd been brainstorming to come up with the requirements for the perfect piece of land.

Her first question: location. She'd decided north of Horizon was key. That would shorten any commute from Charleston.

Any luxury development would need ocean

views, right? Lila had narrowed her search down to focus on proximity to the coast.

Then to make this deal as attractive as possible, she'd listed the infrastructure requirements. Undeveloped land would need roads built, sewer, water...

The investment could be extensive, so taking advantage of existing utilities would be key.

Then she'd studied the Denis Group's other developments to get some idea of average lot size and the types of amenities they'd need space for to calculate how much land would be required. Lila was planning for twenty lots, but if this pitch worked, planning for expansion would be smart.

She ran a finger down her list. Was she doing it? Was she actually building this proposal? What was she missing?

Lila had talked a good game in Rainey's office, but sitting down and working through the questions was building her confidence.

"Maybe you're on the right track," Lila said under her breath. She was placing a lot of faith in her guesstimates of square footage and lot sizes and even how they might be arranged to capitalize on the ocean view. "Tax records. That's the next step."

Lila chewed her thumbnail and took a screenshot of the area she'd decided would be the perfect place for a luxury subdivision such as the Denis Group would build.

A big chunk of the land belonged to the Horizon Shipyard. That land was already accessible by road.

Since the shipyard was owned by the Blackwell family, Rainey would be able to negotiate a sale there if anyone could do it. There would also be some red tape, environmental and security concerns that the town council would be involved in. But as the mayor, Rainey should be able to cut through all of that, too.

That left locating the owners of two or three of the lots adjacent and convincing them to sell. The tax records would tell her who owned what, and then she'd be able to target her approach.

But the pieces were there.

If she could fill in the holes of her plan, she might be able to sell Rainey, who in turn could sell Monica and the Denis Group.

That success would go a long way to covering up her exposed nerve for a bit, too. Measuring up as a Shepard would never be easy, but putting together a big real estate deal would help.

The alarm she'd set before she'd jumped into research went off.

"Time to go get a new listing, Duke." Lila bent down to kiss the dog's head before picking up the folder she'd prepared for her meeting with Roberta Hale. She had a checklist that she always used to determine what repairs should be made before they listed the property, the comparable listings to help her discuss smart pricing and a contract that would give her the exclusive listing.

"You are good at this job, Lila. No one knows Horizon better than you do." She inhaled slowly and then headed out to prove that everything she was telling herself was true.

CHAPTER THREE

AN HOUR LATER, Lila was doing her best to contain her impatience as she smiled at Roberta Hale, the client she'd had such hopes for. Lila had walked Ms. Hale through all the challenges of selling during divorce proceedings, and Ms. Hale was about to tell Lila that she was going with a different listing agent. Reading the signs had gotten much easier after years in the business.

Lila only wished she'd realized this before she'd spent so much time going around the house, inside and out, to discuss repairs that could improve her selling price. Her sneakers were soaked. Her hair was damp.

And it had been a waste of time.

Why? Monica Denis had swooped in this afternoon while Lila was hunting up land to impress Rainey.

The woman was making this Monday a real Monday, and she wasn't even in town.

"I've gotta tell you that Monica Denis didn't have a laundry list of repairs that I have to make in order to get top dollar for this house, Lila," Roberta Hale said firmly before topping off Lila's glass of sweet tea. Since she'd already finished a full glass sweet enough to power a three-day sugar rush, Lila had no intention of drinking any more. "When she was putting out her sign at the Lees', I asked her if she was interested in any other Horizon business. She was, so when I was ready, I called her. She got here first. Her visit didn't take any more than fifteen minutes, and her selling price was higher than yours. Maybe you're used to being Horizon's real estate agent, but she's going to give you some competition around here. She's good at her job." Her matter-of-fact tone suggested she couldn't see any way around it.

"I have no doubt she's good at her job," Lila said, trying not to let the second implication that day that she was not at Monica's level sting, "but she doesn't have the background in Horizon that I do. I know this town. It's my only focus. To compete and get top dollar against the other properties available now, you need to make some repairs. You don't want this house sitting on the market. Then you'll have to reduce your price, or you'll be stuck here a lot longer. I know you want to sell quickly."

Roberta tilted her head to the side. "This divorce has been a real mess, and this is the last piece to tie up." She clutched her hands together. "But I want to make sure I start out the next phase in the best place. For that, I need to get this place sold without putting a lot more into it. You understand?"

Lila nodded. She did understand. Monica was going to let Roberta dictate this listing, and Lila hoped she was wrong about how it would work out.

But there wasn't anything else left to say.

"Thank you for talking to me, Ms. Hale." Lila stood and smoothed her skirt down. She'd chosen the bright pink dress to battle a case of the Mondays, but she suddenly wished for somber colors and sensible heels, two things that were completely out of character for Lila Shepard.

They worked for Monica Denis. Should Lila give them a try?

Roberta shook her head. "I hate to disappoint you, but I have to do what's best. I remember you as a girl, never sitting still if you could run or dance or sing, because here we're all family. Take this as a warning that this Charleston agent is used to swimming in a much bigger pond with more competition. You may need to make some adjustments if people have another choice, Lila. Being a Shepard doesn't automatically mean you're the best choice of real estate agent, does it? Not even in Horizon."

The dig about expecting to win because she was a Shepard hit harder than the implication that Monica Denis would do a better job because she was from Charleston. The urge to respond in a very un-Shepard-like manner had to be mastered.

Lila reminded herself that real estate was a long game, not a short, quick profit. Roberta was not choosing her this time, but that didn't mean she wouldn't need her business in the future.

The desire to explain to Roberta, who was calling herself "family" as she turned Lila down, that she was about to give her business to an agent from out of town, which suggested that Horizon's market was *tighter* than Charleston's also had to be quashed.

Explaining that being a Shepard had zero to do with how well she sold real estate would feel good, but Roberta's comment was uncomfortably close to the doubts she'd been trying to bury way, way down.

"The market has challenges whether you're in Charleston or Horizon, Ms. Hale." Lila opened the door and winced at the loud groan of the hinges. A drop of oil would eliminate that and allow potential buyers to make it all the way inside before they started their list of repairs that would have to be made.

If Lila had been Roberta Hale's listing agent, she would have taken care of that squeaky hinge for her.

It was hard to imagine Monica Denis setting foot back in Horizon after she managed to win the listing.

Unless it was to sell lots in Rainey's newest venture.

"Heard from your daddy today? I guess I never expected the chief to retire. Can't imagine what he's going to do with himself since he practically lived for the job," Roberta said as they stepped out on the front porch. "The whole town is buzzing over this new guy who took TJ's job." She shook her head mournfully. "I heard he was downright standoffish to Leo over at Palmetto State Pizza. You know how friendly Leo is, but the new chief stared at his phone the whole time he waited for his to-go order. Leo didn't learn a single new thing about him in…what would that be? Fifteen or twenty minutes?"

Did she want to join the bandwagon of people talking trash about Trey Douglas? It was tempting, but the fairer side of Lila couldn't fault him for checking his email instead of baring his soul to a stranger in Horizon's pizzeria. It was difficult to imagine Leo taking offense to that, either, so she suspected Roberta was embellishing to improve the story.

"I'm headed over for dinner with my parents right now. I'll tell my dad you asked about him, Ms. Hale," Lila said as she hurried down the steps, eager to escape further conversation about the chief. She should really start using Roberta Hale's first name to signal that she was all grown up.

At this point, Lila wanted to escape, before the

temptation to spill all the gossip she had on Trey Douglas won out.

The whole town was watching closely to see what would happen next with the police department. Telling Roberta that she'd been ordered to leave the squad room would only fan the flames.

Roberta trailed behind her to her car, eager to chat now that the business was over.

"The summer season's wrapping up, so the chief will have time to get his bearings," Lila said as she slid behind the steering wheel. In her head, she could hear her father telling her not to be drawn into the gossip. The right thing to do was support the new chief publicly, even if privately she wanted to tell him to loosen up.

It was good advice when she could remember it, and it made her feel fully evolved to let the opportunity to relay her irritation at Trey's high-handedness pass by. That was nice.

Roberta seemed disappointed as Lila drove away, which felt fair since Lila was absolutely discouraged, but it was hard to concentrate on that while she was so busy worrying about losing another listing to Monica Denis. It was easy to imagine her sitting pretty in a brokerage office on King Street in Charleston.

"I would trust her to sell my house," Lila muttered as passed Monica's for sale sign on Duneside. Her image was polished, and the Denis

Group was well-known statewide. Rainey was correct about that.

Then she turned onto her parents' street. Bee and TJ had taken the closest parking spots, so she was forced to dash through the summer rainstorm to the front door. The fresh rain dampened her mood and her sneakers further.

Before Lila could shove the front door open, her mother held it wide.

"Come in, come in," her mother said before wrapping her arms around Lila in a warm cloud of welcome. "The roast chicken you requested is growing cold, Lila Elaine Shepard. And where is my grand-dog, Duke?"

"The last I saw Duke, he was curled up on his enormous bed, ready for a snooze. He hates rain. You know that." Lila brushed her hands over her messy bun before remembering the messy part was the actual highlight of the style.

Her mother frowned. "Should you be here? If he's afraid, you should take a plate and go."

Lila huffed out a laugh. If her Great Dane was afraid of anything, they had yet to encounter it together. "I will take him some leftovers, and he will be ecstatic." Lila motioned to the dining room with her head. "How is it?"

Her mother had called this particular family dinner for reinforcements. While Lila had been excited to find out what life was like after her father retired from law enforcement, the rest of the family's expectations all included some concern. When he began dropping hints that he was ready to retire, they'd all doubted it would ever happen. His plan to step aside and push TJ into the chief's office had made it easier for her father to consider retirement.

Then TJ had scuttled his plans by refusing to pursue the promotion.

And family dinners had turned awkward as everyone danced around the subject while refusing to directly address it.

It didn't help that there were now whispers in town about Rainey giving the job to an outsider. None of the Shepards had been vocal about TJ's decision to stay where he was while their father was still in the office out of respect for their father's feelings.

"How long have I been asking your father to go through the junk in the garage, to donate whatever we aren't using anymore? Years. I didn't mean for him to do it *today*. All of it, *today*. Started before the sun was fully up." Her mother sighed and bent her head closer. "That's why I was standing at the door, watching for you. I expected your father to be a problem, since getting the man to talk about his feelings, good or bad, is an ordeal. Honestly, if we aren't discussing what happened at the police station or the high school, what will we talk about over the dinner table? Now, I'm guessing Bee and TJ had a bad day at work and..." She gripped Lila's hands. "It's up to you and me to get this situation under control. Poor Summer came in, and whatever happened, she's in the dark, too. If TJ isn't talking to her about it..." Her mother shook her head with a worried frown.

As the youngest, Lila was almost always the last one called in for the big jobs. She already had a lot on her mind, thanks to Monica Denis, but it was nice to have a problem she could tackle to distract her.

If Bee and TJ had had bad days, it had happened after she left, and she wanted to know if the new chief was responsible. If so, he was making an impression right out of the gate.

Being the last Shepard called for support might have bothered her except Lila knew that her skills were unique in the Shepard family. She couldn't interrogate a suspect or rattle off law enforcement codes or statistics on traffic safety like her father or TJ. Bee and her mother had a lock on what was happening in Horizon, legal and in the gray areas, because they absorbed information. The other two Shepard kids, her half sister, Emery, from her father's first marriage and her half brother, Daniel, from her mother's, were scary-good with strategy and planning, so they thought three steps ahead of everyone around them.

Lila's skill was reading people. In the moment, she connected with the person.

And in times like this, around an awkward dinner table, that skill came in handy.

She cracked her knuckles dramatically and laughed when her mother gasped and grabbed her hands. "Lila, don't do that! That sound..." She shuddered.

Since her mother, the principal, spent her days patrolling the high school corridors, Lila imagined the pop of knuckles was pretty common and grating.

"It's quiet in there. Let's fix that," Lila said as she wrapped her hand through her mother's elbow and towed her toward the large kitchen that held a dining table almost big enough for all the Shepards in Horizon.

She could see that her mother had shoehorned Summer Patel in next to TJ's normal spot at the table. If she or Bee ever wanted to bring anyone to the family dinners, they'd have to start eating in shifts or spill outside like they did when all the Shepard kids came home for special occasions.

"Hello, family, I hope you weren't waiting for me," Lila said with a sunny grin as she pulled her chair out. Since their plates were filled and most of the first roast chicken had been picked clean, she picked up the platter and moved to the oven to grab the second platter. Her mother was an excellent cook, and she trusted in the power of leftovers to show how much she cared. No matter how limited the table seating would be, Kay Shepard would never run out of food.

When Lila was settled in her chair, she poked Bee. "Pass the green beans."

Instead of telling her to ask nicely, which would be a very "Bee as the mature older sister" kind of thing for her to do, Bee quietly picked up the bowl and offered it to her. Her eyes were locked on her plate.

Lila glanced across the table and met Summer's stare as the veterinarian took a bite of her chicken. Summer raised her eyebrows.

The loud clink of silverware had to be getting to her mother.

"How was everyone's day?" Lila asked, excruciatingly aware of how perky her tone was. If that didn't generate some push back, she would have to escalate beyond her normal tactics.

"Fine," TJ said promptly before exchanging a meaningful glance with Bee. She nodded in agreement.

Before Lila could force her father to answer, he said, "Busy. Got a lot done around the house. Feels good."

Lila turned to gauge her mother's opinion of that.

Her mother was studiously cutting her chicken into tiny pieces.

Summer cleared her throat. "We got some great news at the shelter today. Did I tell you that Jewel's been working with a volunteer grant writer? Right after the Spring Social, she reached out to Jewel to see if she could help submit grant proposals." She smiled at Lila. "And together they received a five-thousand-dollar grant for adoption events. That's huge."

The reaction around the table erased a bit of the heavy cloud of tension, so Lila decided to pursue the topic. The best way to keep it alive was to ask questions, so that was what Lila did. Jewel, the shelter's manager, had big plans for the shelter Summer had inherited when she'd bought her veterinary practice, so there was plenty to discuss. She and Summer, with occasional help from her mother, carried the dinner conversation until it was time to clear the table.

"Mom, Dad, why don't y'all head out to the swing?" Lila said when her mother stood to help with the dishes. The best way to figure out what was wrong with TJ and Bee was to get their parents out of the picture. The three of them had always conspired well together when they were left alone to do so.

Summer was a wild card in the mix, but it looked like she was destined to be a Shepard sooner or later, so initiating her into the secret plans of the Shepard kids made good sense.

"I like this plan," her father said. He opened the door and held his arm out for Lila's mother.

Her mother shot Lila a glance that she interpreted to mean "Find out the scoop and let me know ASAP."

As soon as they were outside with the door closed, Summer stepped in front of TJ, who had been methodically clearing dishes in a straight-line march, table to sink and back. "Stop. Talk." She tilted her head down to make sure he could read how serious she was.

Amused, Lila bumped Bee's shoulder with hers, and they both rested against the counter to watch.

TJ inhaled slowly. "It was a tough day at work. First day under the new chief and it went…okay." He bent down to press a quick kiss to Summer's lips, and it was impossible for Lila to ignore the flutter in her heart accompanied by a twist of envy.

She was happy TJ was in love.

But she wouldn't mind having her own person, either.

"He was rude to Lila to get the day started off. Explained that he would be enforcing the rule that kept the public out of the squad room to everyone in the room, including her," Bee said and squeezed Lila's shoulder. "You've been to countless morning briefings, and you had banana bread. That right there should mean the doors are wide open."

Lila smiled at her sister because she appreciated the support even if she intended to make sure everyone knew that she wasn't mad. She wouldn't even register his rudeness as far as anyone else could tell because it was so far beneath her. She would tip her nose high in the air whenever she explained that, too.

Had she remembered that embarrassment and fumed off and on throughout the day? Yes, but no one else needed to know that.

"Being rude to Lila is a problem, but it doesn't seem out of the ordinary for the police chief to enforce rules." Summer made the "continue" gesture. "Talk more."

"It's not all mine to tell, but..." TJ shook his head. "He snubbed Lucy."

Lila would have laughed at the way Summer's mouth dropped open in shock, but she was surprised herself at how badly the new chief had managed to step in quicksand. The veterinarian would have taken any insult to an animal personally, but this was Lucy. TJ's partner. The three of them were well on their way to becoming a family unit.

And there was almost nothing else Trey Douglas could have done to cement TJ's bad opinion than to insult his K9 partner. TJ had made career decisions based on that relationship and his desire to improve protections for other K9 officers.

TJ said, "Lucy went to greet him, just like she did with Dad. Front and center. He ignored her, started the meeting without acknowledging her."

He shrugged. "Or any of us, really, for that matter. Straight to business."

Summer met Lila's stare. As the two normies in the room, it made sense that both of them might wonder if Chief Shepard had been that much different. Her father had always been all business when she'd seen him at work. When Hurricane Agnes had come through in the spring, she'd watched him brief his officers on hurricane preparations. It had reminded her that this guy she knew as Dad had a critical role in the town's safety. Her father had always been Lila's hero, but watching him lead that way reminded her that he was also a *hero* hero.

For that matter, Bee and TJ did that same important work, but as their kid sister, it was her job to keep them humble.

Bee caught Summer and Lila's silent communication. "It was different, okay? Dad made sure to speak to Lucy. Every morning. No matter what else was going on. He also insisted that we remember the department's mission before we went to work. None of that happened." She crossed her arms over her chest.

"Could it be...?" Summer paused as if she was trying to maneuver carefully through the dangerous land mines in the conversation. "Were you looking for reasons to dislike the new guy?" When TJ and Bee immediately started shaking their heads, she held up her hands in surrender. "Okay, okay, I believe you."

There was still something missing from the picture here.

If that had been the end of the story, Lila couldn't see any reason why they wouldn't have picked apart the new chief's manner over her mother's delicious dinner. It was a small thing, even if they were united in their harsh judgment of the new chief's faculties.

"But that's not the worst thing that happened," Lila said slowly, "and whatever the other thing is, you don't want to tell Dad about it."

The corners of Bee's mouth quirked up. "Amazing powers of deduction, little sister."

The compliment settled next to Lila's heart softly. All of her older siblings were amazing in their own way, and it could be intimidating if she got too caught up in her thoughts. Hearing the respect in Bee's voice reminded Lila of how lucky she was to be in the Shepard mix.

Bee was the kind of older sister who would tease and torment daily, but she'd never hesitated to make sure Lila knew how proud she was, either.

TJ sighed. "They think we're making too much of this, Bee. You better tell them the rest."

Lila threaded her arm through her sister's. "Yeah, Bee."

Bee hummed out a frustrated noise. "Fine. I was notified that Dispatch does not need to be present for the morning meeting with patrol officers."

Since Lila was of the mind that all meetings were soul-sucking torture sessions only made bearable with good coffee and better pastries, she didn't see the problem at first.

"Like Dispatch is less important than the rest of the squad?" Summer asked TJ.

He shrugged. "That's how I read it. Which is ridiculous. More times than not, Bee's the one who gives us an informal heads-up about things going on around town. She made sure we helped you out when the hurricane was on the way."

After Summer purchased the town's animal clinic, her inexperience with hurricanes had spurred the three of them to assist, and Lila had been impressed with the vet's courage to move so far from home to make her own way. Could she have done the same? Being a Shepard in Horizon was so much of who Lila was, but it was impossible to ignore Summer's success, even if at the time she'd been ready to pack up and head right back to Atlanta. Surviving that first storm had changed so much.

Summer nodded. "Yeah, I can't even imagine how I would have gotten through Hurricane Agnes without the Horizon Police Department and the Shepards." She squeezed Bee's shoulder. "The new guy messed up."

Bee nodded. "Yeah. I just..." She sighed. "His

point was that we get the assignments, so there's no need to attend. That's true." She rubbed her forehead. "I tried to tell myself all day long not to take it personally. He's going to make some changes, and this doesn't impact my ability to run Dispatch." Her shoulders slumped. "I'm used to running Dispatch as I see fit, and that means plugging in to the daily work everywhere we can. We are police officers, but what if this job that I've been so proud of doing has been inflated because my daddy was the boss?"

The worry on Bee's face was the match that lit Lila's fuse.

Trey Douglas had stepped in a mess by calling her out, sure, but it was a minor annoyance.

In one day, he'd managed to alienate TJ and shake Bee's confidence.

That meant he'd lost all of Lila's gracious benefit of the doubt. It was a blessing she hadn't known this before she'd met with Roberta because she wouldn't have been able to resist the opportunity to spread the bad word about the new chief.

Summer broke the silence finally. "Bee, I need you to listen to me." She waited for Bee to turn to her. "I am the only objective observer in this room. Your father is not the man to give out points for attendance. Can you imagine him creating a special role for his baby girl?" She snorted and then cringed. "Sorry. The snort was stronger than I intended."

Lila chuckled and TJ and Bee followed suit. The change felt good.

"What I meant was that your father is the opposite of that." Summer tangled her fingers with TJ's. "He has higher expectations for his kids than others. That was true at work, too. You know it. That's why TJ almost ended up in a job he'd hate. Tom Shepard set big goals, and all of you have hit them."

Since she was losing business left and right that day, Lila wasn't sure that applied to her, but now was not the time to bring it up.

Eventually Bee nodded. "I see your point, Summer, although I'm not sure you're as objective in this as you think you are." She pointed at the way Summer's fingers were woven through TJ's.

"I should have said something, Bee. I'm sorry," TJ said. "Tomorrow I'll explain to the new chief that he's made a mistake. Two mistakes." He shook his head. "Three mistakes, counting Lila. I've been stewing on this all day, telling him what I thought in my head. I should have gone back before my shift was up and set him straight."

Bee shook her head. "Not for me. I have to do it myself."

"Or for me. I'm happy to stay out of the Horizon Police Department and away from Trey Douglas," Lila said. "Police business has nothing to do with me now."

Lila could tell that TJ wanted to argue, but

Summer squeezed his hand. "Fine. I'll wait until you tell me to set him straight." He frowned at Summer. "But it's really hard."

Her teasing smile lit up her face. "We call that growth, Officer Shepard. You're learning."

TJ grumbled as he moved to turn on the hot water. They worked together to load the dishwasher and put away the leftovers. After TJ and Summer stepped out on the deck to tell their parents good night, Lila pressed her head against Bee's shoulder and squeezed her tightly. "We've eliminated retribution by TJ, but I am still a loaded weapon, Bee. My revenge can be as swift or slow as you like."

Bee wrinkled her nose. "My little sister, you might be the scariest of all of us."

"Scarier than Emery?" Lila asked skeptically. Their half sister, the oldest of the five of them, was the kind of supercop that jumped from helicopters and took down smugglers in rough seas for the Coast Guard.

Bee tilted her head to the side. "Well, maybe not as far as mortal weapons, but when it comes to plotting revenge, I would put you very close to the top."

Lila sniffed. "Flattery isn't necessary. I will destroy him for the family honor. You won't even owe me a favor at the end."

Bee's chuckle improved Lila's mood.

Bee threw an arm over her shoulder and squeezed her close. "This goes without saying, but…"

"We don't tell Dad about any of this police business," Lila answered and Bee echoed it.

"Or Mom," Bee added.

"Or Rainey." Lila knew it would be difficult to keep this separate from the group discussion when she, Bee and Rainey had their coffee breaks at the diner.

Was it time to put some distance between herself and Rainey anyway?

Especially if she managed to put together her own pitch and Rainey decided to go with Monica Denis.

"Right." Bee nodded. "You and me, possibly TJ, who will no doubt tell Summer, but that's it. We don't spread gossip."

Lila met her stare and nodded while doing her best to display complete innocence.

Bee was a good person, and her instincts would always lead her in the right direction.

But given the opportunity, there was nothing to stop Lila from making it clear to Trey Douglas that insulting her sister had been a big mistake. If the right opportunity arose, she'd be ready.

CHAPTER FOUR

On Monday night, another loud burst of laughter from right outside Trey's door at the Needlegrass Motor Lodge made him flop over on his side and yank his pillow over his head. The digital display on the ancient alarm clock read 2:57 a.m., and every one of the college kids gathered around the pool should be in bed.

The Needlegrass Motor Lodge had been built when air-conditioning was a luxury and the rooms there reflected bygone fashions, including an abundance of knotty pine on the walls and orange shag carpet that couldn't be original because…

Thinking about what might be infesting the original carpet after all this time wouldn't help anyone. The place was remarkably clean, just out of date. When Rainey had called it "budget friendly" and "vintage," what she meant was run-down and old but in a classy way.

"Complaining to the night manager would be a pathetic version of an old man yelling 'Get off my lawn,'" Trey muttered before throwing the thin blanket off to sit up on the side of the bed. It wasn't like they were waking him from a deep, restorative sleep. Instead, they were interrupting his staring at the ceiling by making him angrily toss and turn.

After the first night this had happened, Trey had made sure to check the signs around the pool. It closed at ten o'clock, or so they said. The nightly party around the pool wrapped up earlier sometimes, but it was never before midnight.

He'd stopped into the office the next day to discuss the issue with the manager on duty, a crusty old guy who had been less interested in Trey's complaint than the game show blaring from his TV.

Honestly, what was the point of having rules, much less posting them, if no one was going to enforce them?

Trey ran his hands through his hair as he considered his options.

"One, you can continue to stew and glare at the ceiling all night." He stood and moved to stand next to the door. The full-length mirror on the back showed a man in a rumpled T-shirt and shorts with a dark frown on his face. "Two, you can step outside and tell those kids to go to bed immediately." He wondered how successful that order would be and what he was prepared to do if they ignored the angry guy in room eighteen. "Three, you can march down to the motel office, bang on the door until whoever should be doing this answers and throw your weight around to make them handle the problem." He had his hand on the doorknob when another choice occurred to him. "Four, you can put your uniform and badge on, find the ringleader of this group and arrest them for disturbing the peace."

That last one was tempting, but he had a feeling his boss, the mayor, would loudly disapprove.

Trey understood how important guests staying at the motel would be to Horizon. The small town depended on tourism all year long, and every bit of revenue now would help the Needlegrass keep the doors open in January.

But if he spontaneously combusted and burned the place down, would that be worse than a few disgruntled kids? It would be worse.

Of all his options, number three seemed the best course of action, so he slipped on running shoes and stepped out onto the walkway that led to the office. He made sure to glare over his shoulder toward the pool, but the hoots and conversation never died down, so he was sure they'd missed his exit and his displeasure.

The glow of light from the motel's office gave him a tiny spark of optimism. Maybe this was a matter of a brief conversation. He'd outline his expectations, and whoever ran the desk at night would be alerted to the issue.

The rules made perfect sense. They were posted plainly. Enforcing them would be simple enough.

He bent to peer in the window and saw an empty desk but refused to give up hope as he stepped inside. The jangle of bells over the door was loud during the day. At night, the noise triggered his fight-or-flight response. Since he was already swinging heavily toward "fight," this didn't help his mood.

"Hello?" he said as he leaned against the counter. The door behind the desk was closed, so by process of elimination, it was easy to identify where the night manager was. Trey banged on the bell on the desk, even as he wondered how much good it would do. Anyone who missed the clang of the bells on the door would have no problem ignoring the tinny clank from the one on the desk. Repeatedly smacking it with his hand made him feel marginally better, though, so Trey kept it up until someone opened the door a crack.

"What is all this ruckus? I was having a snooze in my recliner," Joe Morgan said as he peered up at Trey. "Oh, it's you again." The older man's gray hair made a fuzzy fringe around his head as he yanked hard on the belt of his robe.

"The snooze explains why you were missing the ruckus going on around the swimming pool, but I'm having a harder time sleeping through the noise than you are." Trey braced his hands on the counter as he reminded himself that he had no other place to go, so maintaining a cordial relationship with the motel's manager was important. Rainey had told him the first week he was in town that finding a place for him to stay had taken some finagling. Until the summer season ended, empty hotel rooms were sparse in Horizon.

"They're kids." Joe waved a hand. "And no one else has come to complain, Mr. Douglas."

Trey rolled his head on his shoulders and reminded himself he needed to choose his battles carefully. He'd heard enough people singing the praises of Tom Shepard to know that they had all called him "Chief." He had expected the same treatment, but apparently he hadn't earned their respect yet.

He wasn't sure forcing Joe Morgan to do his job would improve that, but he was certain he couldn't back down now.

"Would the motel's owners be interested to know that there is a party around the pool at this hour of the morning?" Trey asked. Escalating to "let me speak to your manager" didn't feel great, but he was in a mood to get this handled.

The older man stepped forward with his chin jutting out. "You're looking at the owner. What do you think?"

Trey *thought* he'd like to rewind the tape and not threaten to go over his head, since it wasn't going to accomplish anything, but it was too late to do that.

"Please clear out the pool area. They are breaking your posted rules," Trey said in what he thought was a reasonable voice.

Joe Morgan crossed his arms over his chest. "Or I could tell you that you'll need to check out in the morning. The mayor pulled all her strings to get you in here at off-season rates. I could have your room booked and be earning twenty percent more revenue by tomorrow afternoon."

"I understand." Trey inhaled slowly. His words had the ring of truth. That didn't mean Trey had to accept defeat. "And if I put on my uniform right now, I can enforce those posted rules by making some arrests, loading the back seat of my patrol vehicle and booking them down at the station. You don't want that. I don't want it, and neither will the mayor," Trey said firmly.

"Interfering with a man's business is a mistake." With a huff, Joe moved around the front desk. "Fine, but you can believe I'll be talking to Rainey about this first thing. And if your tenure in Horizon goes as smoothly as your stay here has gone, the next mayor will be hunting for your replacement. Rainey's choices aren't looking too good to me. Gonna make her next election tricky. For both our sakes, you need to be finding permanent lodging elsewhere ASAP." He hit the door with a stiff arm and stepped outside.

After he disappeared, Trey questioned whether Joe Morgan had threatened not only his job but Rainey's, too. That was concerning. He hadn't been sure about bringing his problems to her doorstep, but she'd insisted. The last thing he wanted was to cause her trouble in her own career because she'd given him this shot.

But there wasn't much to be done at that hour of the night. He'd warn her about this disgruntled voter after the sun came up.

Trey returned to his room without detouring to observe how the motel's owner handled shutting down the party. When he was back inside his room, he kicked his shoes off and watched with some satisfaction as they went soaring across the room to thud on the orange shag carpet.

The noise outside immediately disappeared.

"What a relief." Trey smoothed out the sheet and blanket that he'd twisted into a rope with his tossing and turning and climbed back into bed with a sigh. He closed his eyes and waited for sleep.

After a few minutes, he opened his eyes again to stare up at the ceiling.

His inability wasn't helped by the party around the pool, but it had started before he'd made the move to Horizon. Late at night, it was hard to stop the replay of all the events that had led him here.

Discovering his partner had been taking bribes. Reporting that as required. Losing his friends and the respect of his team and leadership who couldn't believe he would have missed the clues for so long.

Struggling to convince the man he looked up to of his innocence.

Making the move to Horizon and the Needlegrass Motor Lodge.

And now he could add confronting the motel's owner and starting the clock on his impending eviction.

He had a sinking feeling that tomorrow night, he'd be able to add a scene where Rainey handed him his head for messing up his lodging.

"I should be proactive, head the problem off at the pass," he muttered as he picked up his phone. Finding a place to rent needed to move to the top of his priority list, so he went to the website he always used and entered "Horizon, SC" in the search bar.

Lila Shepard's smiling face appeared in an ad along the side of the screen with the search results, and Trey forgot his task for a moment. It was the same headshot from the billboard in town, but at this resolution, he could see her eyes better. They were green. They weren't sparkling with irritation in the photo, and it didn't do her justice. Now that he had seen her in vibrant pink, he knew the gray business suit was a mismatch for her personality, too.

Without looking too hard at his motivation, Trey clicked the link, which took him to her business website. It included all the standard items: address, phone number, information on her current listings. A calendar showed her events, which included the back-to-school night and an open house on Saturday. Lila's About Me page loaded slowly and featured a vibrant photo of her and an old Great Dane front and center. They were both wearing a deep purple, and Lila's eyes were impossible to forget.

"Business degree, Horizon native," Trey read and stopped on that. Everyone would know that, wouldn't they? She was a Shepard. Then he realized that fact was for people looking to move to Horizon. Smart. "More than ten years of real estate experience in Horizon."

When Trey realized how long he'd spent staring at her photo for no discernible reason except that he couldn't look away, he forced himself back to the rental search page.

The search pulled up only two places available for long-term rentals. "And one of the two listings is the Needlegrass Motor Lodge. Wonderful." The other place was…fine, a boxy apartment with zero personality, but he didn't expect much. "I'll call in the morning. By the time Rainey gets wind of this little dustup, I'll have a plan in motion."

This time, he closed his eyes and refused to give in to the memories or more scrolling. Lila's face popped into his mind, the casual shot that he'd have a hard time forgetting, but he finally managed to fall asleep. When the alarm went off, he felt like he'd barely closed his eyes, but the sun was creeping in through the split in the curtains over the window.

His phone dinged to alert him to a new text so he picked it up.

The investigation should be wrapping up this week. Won't be too much longer until the trial clears this whole mess up. How soon can you get back to Columbia?

DEA Special Agent Dennis Browning had been the first guy to tap Trey to work on federal drug investigations and the first to cast doubt on Trey's version of events—asking how he'd cooperated with the bribery scheme. It seemed he was ready to move on, to let bygones be bygones now that Trey was about to be formally exonerated.

All without admitting his mistake in believing the worst, much less apologizing for it.

Rainey had believed him instantly, but she'd also understood how hard it was to sit in the middle of the whispers and suspicion. When she had been hunting for Tom Shepard's replacement, she'd approached him because they had worked together when she'd been in Columbia. She'd offered him an escape route.

He owed Rainey, no matter how tempting it was to go back to the work he knew and loved. Trey wasn't certain he'd chosen correctly, especially since his neighbors surveilled him whenever he stepped out in public, but he was here now.

His answer was short and to the point.

I've got work to do in Horizon.

Browning answered seconds later.

The trial will stir up this story in your small town. You may be looking for new work soon anyway.

Browning's point about the story hitting Horizon raised the specter of facing down a new group of cops who didn't trust him and dragging Rainey into the mess.

"She knew the risks," he muttered to himself and tried to have faith that it was true.

Besides that, Trey knew any investigation would clear him. Though the suspicion might always linger in some minds. Cops were generally a suspicious group, after all.

There was no way to answer Browning's text, so Trey finished putting on his uniform.

Then he headed into the station early. It was a relief to make it to his squad car without running into Joe Morgan or any of the kids he'd had run off.

"They are still sleeping, obviously," he muttered to himself as he pulled into his designated parking spot in front of Town Hall. Rainey's parking spot was still empty. That was good. He made it into his office with only a crisp "good morning" from the officer on the front desk and Officer Rodriguez.

He had another chance at nailing the morning briefing, but he wasn't sure what he'd do differently. One quick turn by the communal coffeepot turned up a cup of terrible coffee and the second-to-last slice of banana bread. When he made it back to his office, the mayor was blocking his doorway.

"Wild night at Horizon's fine Needlegrass Motor Lodge? Joe Morgan called bright and early to tell me that you threatened to take matters into your own hands last night, rousted him out of his comfy recliner. These kids are tourists, Trey. They party. It's expected. The season is almost over. We need every visitor we can get right now," Rainey said as if she was repeating verbatim things Joe had complained about. Trey realized he needed to rethink the speed of how information moved through Horizon. He'd thought he'd have until that afternoon, which would give him time to implement a solution.

"He was taking pages from my campaign speeches, trying to out-mayor me. I did warn you. At the end of the season like this, every room in Horizon is booked with kids looking for the last gasp of summer fun at the beach. This is a tourist town. So we welcome them, we make sure they have a good visit and when they go home, we relax," Rainey said as she paced in a tight line in front of his doorway.

Trey had understood that at one level. After midnight, when he was trying to sleep, was a different level.

"Your power can't get me into one of the places in town? One with older tourists who sleep at night?" Trey wasn't sure it would make any difference to how he slept, but it was worth a try, especially if renting another place would be as much of a challenge as it appeared. He maneuvered around her and urged her inside his office. He didn't want an audience for this conversation.

Rainey plopped a take-out coffee cup on the spotless desk in front of him. "Don't drink the stuff from the squad room. It can remove paint, and that can't be good for your stomach lining."

Trey sipped and sighed with relief. "Where did you get this?"

"Daybreak Diner. It's on the pier in the Battery. Best breakfast in town." Rainey crossed her arms over her chest. "Terrorizing tourists, Trey? You can't do that here."

He shook his head. "I didn't." He'd only threatened to arrest them. That was different.

The pinch of his conscience at the half-truth faded as he swallowed the last bite of banana bread. It was delicious. Kay Shepard was by far his favorite Shepard.

Lila's photo instantly popped into his brain,

and he realized that baked goods could have stiff competition from green eyes.

"Joe Morgan says you'll be moving out by the end of the week. Did you know that you're moving out by the end of the week?" she asked.

Trey hadn't picked up on the deadline, but it made sense so he nodded. "It's time."

When she didn't immediately answer, he glanced up.

"You aren't thinking about running, are you?" Her shrewd stare as she sipped her own coffee reflected not a single worry.

"Even if I was, how do I already know that you have a plan in place to stop me?" Trey responded.

"I guess my reputation for ruthlessly pursuing my own ends through political power plays precedes me." Rainey shrugged. "Or it could be that you know me too well from all the time we spent working together to curb South Carolina's drug imports through one of the government's many task forces… Definitely one of those things."

Rainey had been a senator while he'd headed up one of those task forces. Their working relationship had a rocky start, as Trey had no time for politics or the people who spent their lives campaigning for public approval. Rainey hadn't exactly changed his mind about politicians, either. But he had learned that her mission was to take care of the people who voted for her. She happened to be skilled at pulling strings to make that happen, whether it impacted the entire state or her small hometown.

They'd been friends for long enough now that he trusted her to use her powers for good instead of evil.

Since she was not only his best friend in Horizon but also maybe in the world at this point, he had to trust her.

"Or," Trey said slowly, "it could be that you were the only one ignoring all the whispers about me to offer me a job, so my escape route is seriously curtailed at this point. Where would I run to?" He rubbed his forehead and wished for a few more hours of sleep. "Even if we should have asked ourselves if I was going to make it in a town the size of Horizon."

"Nowhere else to go, huh? Not sure that observation is complimentary to my position of great power. Do I make bad decisions, Trey?" Rainey asked before running her fingers through her hair.

They both knew the answer to that question.

"Nope." Trey shook his head. "Or at least, you don't *normally* make bad decisions."

She narrowed her eyes at him. "I will allow that the tiniest sliver of possibility exists that I make a mistake now and then, but how many times did I approach you with this job?"

Trey slumped back in his chair. "Three phone calls. One extremely awkward appearance at a bar where I was trying to drown my sorrows."

"And we agreed, no more drowning. If you had vomited on my date's Hermès loafers, you would have ruined my night completely. He was already judging you for your taste in bars and me for my taste in friends." Rainey waited for him to agree again. It was easy to nod because he never wanted to see the inside of a bar again. "Taking over the Horizon PD from Tom Shepard is a big job. It will take some time to feel comfortable with the role, but it's all possible. Just don't commit unforced errors like harassing tourists to make this any tougher, Trey. Making enemies of your neighbors? That's going to be a setback. Joe Morgan will tell everyone he meets about your late-night demands."

Trey nodded. Joe Morgan could spread the story through the entire town by lunchtime, based on how fast he'd gotten to Rainey.

That would take some getting used to.

"It's a lot harder to repair relationships than it is to just…not mess them up in the first place in my experience." Rainey tapped the neat stack of folders he'd built. Some of them contained Tom Shepard's monthly summaries, and the rest held printouts of the source data files he'd requested. "The Needlegrass was only supposed to be temporary, Chief." Rainey rolled her eyes. "Get busy finding a place to live. Really live. Once you have a signed lease, I will stop watching you for signs of flight. Even better, think mortgage." She spread her hands out as if the word was emblazoned on a marquee in lights.

Trey nodded even as he considered how to break it to Rainey that he wasn't in Horizon for a thirty-year term. He'd be here long enough to do good work while the whispers died down in Columbia or until an opportunity in Charleston or Savannah opened up.

"Trey, this is another time I'm right. You're going to love it here. Stop wasting time and call Lila Shepard," Rainey said. "It would be better for you to work with a local than some outside agent."

The way she paused and tilted her head caught his attention.

Then she huffed out an angry breath. "Which is exactly what Lila told me yesterday."

Before he could ask about the part of the conversation going on in her head, the side he couldn't hear, she stepped closer to the desk. "Listen, forget about what you left in Columbia. You're going to like this place." There was not a bit of doubt in her voice. "You are a good cop. You know it. I know it. In about..." She pursed her lips as she calculated. "Six months. Yeah, in about six months, everyone in Horizon will also know this. You can change Joe Morgan's mind. Those officers outside know Horizon and the job. Once you're up to speed on this town, you will be the leader they respect, too."

That was the closest thing to sympathy that he could expect from no-nonsense Rainey.

Under most circumstances, he appreciated that in his friends.

Having a boss who understood him this way might take some adjustment, but at least she wasn't trying to puff him up with fake positivity. He mistrusted cheerful people on principle. The mayor called it plainly, so Trey knew where he stood. He respected that.

"Running away from Columbia..." Trey shook his head. "It makes me look guilty of everything they're saying. When someone out there in the squad room gets a whiff of all the gossip, you and I both know we'll have trouble on our hands." He met Rainey's stare. "I hope this isn't one of your rare bad decisions."

"Me, too, but I don't think it is. Go out there and prove yourself today. Then do it again tomorrow." Rainey checked her watch.

"Yes, boss." Trey stood slowly, wondering if there was any chance the last piece of banana bread remained.

"I like that," Rainey said slowly. "Boss. Tom Shepard would have run naked around the Battery before he called me boss." She pointed at him. "Forget the past. No more rookie mistakes, Chief. Be great."

Trey waved as she marched out the door and studied his desk. He had the clipboard, the overnight reports, the day's assignments and another chance to do a good job for Horizon. Sooner or later, another story would take center stage and people would forget about this blip at the Needlegrass. He had to stay the course until that happened and build a strong base that would withstand the storm when the bigger story hit town.

He owed that to Rainey, but he had to do it for himself first.

CHAPTER FIVE

ON WEDNESDAY MORNING, Lila was doing her best to catalog important details as she drove down the two-lane road toward one of the back gates to Horizon Shipyard. She had no idea what it would take to widen the narrow road, but it would work for construction. The gate was no longer used, but the road was still in decent shape. All of that was good.

She turned down the music she'd been singing along with as she approached the boundary of the shipyard, which was marked by some pretty serious fencing. Some kind of landscaping would be required to sell homes in a luxury subdivision there because the shipyard's current "secure military installation next door" vibe could impact the general atmosphere.

Lila glanced in her rearview mirror, half expecting to see the police chief's SUV behind her. It felt as if her father was summoned every time she edged closer to somewhere she shouldn't be.

If Trey Douglas had somehow inherited that instinct, she would absolutely have to leave Horizon.

He'd been popping up in her mind at unexpected moments since their encounter on Monday. The frequency was wholly unacceptable, as was the way she had memorized the details of his handsome face.

What was it about a man in a police uniform? She should be immune due to close proximity to her brothers, the pests, but it was impossible to deny that Trey Douglas wore his well.

"You're doing it again, Lila," she muttered to herself. Being distracted by Trey was silly. He didn't appear to like her much, and that should be the cherry on top of why she wanted to have nothing to do with him. "Concentrate on the job."

The shipyard wasn't strictly a military installation, but its owners took on projects for the navy so it was secured against all manner of threats, foreign and domestic. This area outside the boundaries of the shipyard was deserted. She didn't pass another car, there were no houses visible from the road and she might question if she was the only person on earth except her phone rang as she pulled off the road onto what had been a driveway at one point.

"What are you doing at the shipyard?" Bee asked before Lila had a chance to say hello.

Lila stared hard at the phone display on her car's dashboard before shaking her head. "Do you have a tracker on my car? Have you bugged me somehow?" Was she discovering how her father had done it for all these years at last?

In this singular case, she immediately felt better about not being lost in the wild as she eased down the bumpy dirt path that she really hoped led to the house she could see on the satellite map she was using to plot this subdivision venture.

"No, but I should. The shipyard has some pretty extensive security measures. There are cameras all around that gate out on Landing Road, and any traffic triggers them. The shipyard's security team gets images as soon as someone passes, and they send anything suspicious to us. I guess John McEntire thought you were suspicious. Were you singing 'Stronger'?" Bee asked.

Lila slid out of the SUV to hunt for cameras. All she saw were trees. So many old trees, live oaks and towering pines, that the area around her car was shadowy. When the land was developed, how many of them would be left standing? Lila frowned at the thought.

"How did you know what I was singing?" she asked to push the troubling question away.

"I recognized your Kelly Clarkson power ballad face. I've seen it so many times," Bee said dryly. "What are you doing all the way out there?"

"Research." Lila studied the aerial photo she'd printed out and tried to gauge the distance she was about to walk. She wanted to verify the number of structures and their state before she approached the owners to discuss selling. The only way to do that was to walk. "Rainey has an idea for a subdivision. This could be the perfect place for it."

"So she sent you out there alone?" From the tone of her voice, Bee didn't like that at all. "Why didn't you wait until I could come with you? I know this is Horizon, but you should be more careful, Lila."

The cool shade did surprise a shiver from Lila, but she wasn't going to let Bee know that a little company out here would have been nice. She'd never hear the end of it.

"Rainey doesn't know I'm here. Her plan is to work with an agent from Charleston, but I'm going to change her mind," Lila said confidently. If she could convince Bee, she stood a chance of selling Rainey on the idea. "Once I have a tentative agreement with the owners, I know I can make this happen."

Bee was quiet for too long before she said, "Why would Rainey even think of using any other real estate agent but you?"

Relief made it easier for Lila to dip and dodge through the brush and overgrown trees. Someday, she would be confident enough in her career and abilities to ignore what her older sister thought, but until that day came, it was nice to know Bee believed in her.

"Well, this agent has a connection to one of the biggest residential developers in the state, so I can see the logic, but it's not very Horizon of her, is it?" Lila stopped as she entered the clearing at the end of the driveway. "Blue Vista." There was a sign over the gate that blocked the overgrown sidewalk leading up to the front door. "Know anything about it? The tax records say it's owned by a Mike Wilkins of Tampa, Florida."

"Do not go in that house alone, Lila Shepard," Bee said firmly. "If I hear the creak of a door, I am sending the full contingent of the Horizon PD and you can't stop me."

Before Lila could defend her decisions and her intention to never step inside old abandoned houses, Bee cleared her throat. "Yes, sir. Four o'clock works. I'll add it to my calendar."

The chief must have made an appearance. That explained the tension.

Trey's face popped immediately into her head again, so now Lila was tense, too.

"You have to go, so go," Lila said when Bee took a deep breath.

"The chief has requested that I meet with him this afternoon," she said. "I'm not sure how I'm supposed to work here feeling like this, but what else can I do? Leave?"

Lila tripped over a root but managed to catch herself before she hit the ground. "Ever think about it? Leaving?"

Bee sighed. "Never. Or at least not before now."

Since Lila had occasionally daydreamed about

leaving ever since her father had grounded her at sixteen for an offense that literally no other father in Horizon would have even known about, she wasn't sure how that was true. But she also knew how hard it was to leave Horizon.

"Besides, who would keep you from walking into a creepy old houses if I leave?" Bee asked.

Lila groaned. "I'm not going in. It looks like it's at least a hundred years old, but it's…amazing. Unique." She took a picture of the front and sent it to Bee.

"Oh, is that a round tower?" Bee asked loudly before she hushed herself. "I love that it's all… wonky."

Lila smiled. "Asymmetrical. It was a style choice, not a mistake. I'm no expert, but I think it's a variation on the Queen Anne style, like some of the bungalows you see in Charleston." But she knew what Bee meant. Around Horizon, the historic buildings were all classically symmetrical. Blue Vista had round edges and off-center dormers.

She stepped carefully around the side of the house to peer in the windows. The kitchen was frozen in time. The year was 1989 inside, according to the calendar hanging on the fridge.

Lila kept walking around the side of the house, edging the dilapidated fencing that had probably been painted white at one time, toward the ocean view she knew had to be there somewhere.

Bee said, "Never heard of Blue Vista, but I'm pretty sure Mike Wilkins is part of the branch of the Shepard family tree that belongs to Dad's great-uncle William. Is that right?" A pause filled the air as Bee thought. "He moved away, but I think I'm right. You'd need to confirm with Dad before you lean on the family connection to make the sale, of course."

Lila laughed. "Who is the real estate agent here?"

"You can't fool me. If you don't use every tool you have, you aren't my little sister Lila." Bee huffed out a breath.

"I can't believe I have to go to a meeting now. 'Don't attend the one in the morning, but now, let's have one in the afternoon,'" Bee muttered.

"Something will change," Lila said softly. "Either the chief will get his head screwed on straight and realize he's made a terrible mistake, or he'll be run out of town like a cattle thief. This won't last forever."

Bee chuckled, which made it easier for Lila to concentrate on where she was walking. "Those are the only two options? Nothing in between?"

"Those are my top choices, but I suppose there could be others," Lila answered as she brushed a spiderweb from her hair.

Bee said, "Text me when you're back in Horizon. The clock is ticking. I will send the police force with sirens, Lila."

"Fine. Tell me what the chief says. I'll prepare my revenge accordingly," Lila answered. She was relieved that Bee was laughing as she hung up.

Lila walked slowly to the gap in the trees, and there it was, the blue vista. The Atlantic Ocean stretched out in a wide-open expanse, water meeting the horizon in the distance. To the north, Lila could see the coastal development of the communities that rolled up into the Charleston metro area. To the south, Battery Park jutted out into the ocean.

And she knew she'd found the key to winning over Rainey, Monica Denis, Albert Denis and whoever else it would take to get this deal done.

Her next step was convincing Mike Wilkins he wanted to sell.

TREY GRIPPED THE steering wheel tightly as he studied the GPS display and made the final turn on Landing Road. He hadn't intended to investigate the closed gate of the shipyard that afternoon, but he'd paused outside of Dispatch when he'd overheard Lila's name.

Then, instead of doing the right thing and walking away, he'd hung around long enough to hear Bee's concern that Lila was in danger and the location.

But he'd also stepped too close to the doorway and been spotted so he'd had to scramble to come up with a cover as to why he was lurking like some kind of weirdo. As soon as he made it back to his office, he was going to have to find some plausible explanation as to why he needed to meet with Bee Shepard.

Finding a good excuse to take her out of Dispatch when he'd just made a big deal of not doing that for the morning shift change was going to be a tricky exercise. He hoped he could do it, but first he needed an even better reason for him to be here, checking up on her sister.

"She's an adult. A professional. She knows what to watch for in old buildings, you fool," Trey muttered as he slowed on approach to the gate.

Then he realized that the shipyard security might decide to send the report of his visit back to Bee in Dispatch as his SUV was technically more unusual traffic near their perimeter.

"And that is going to be awkward." Trey stopped opposite an overgrown driveway, wondered briefly he had any chance of preventing that embarrassment and spotted a blue SUV parked off to the side.

Since there was no way to avoid whatever came next, he pulled in behind what had to be Lila's vehicle and parked.

As he slid out, he was hyperaware of how quiet the heavily forested area was. It was easy to imagine he was the only person in the world at that moment. When he closed the door, it seemed twice as loud as usual.

"Hello?" Trey called as he walked down the winding driveway. "It's Chief Douglas." He didn't want to frighten Lila, approaching quietly from behind, but he was aware that warning her he was nearby meant he had lost any advantage, too. Her bright green eyes were probably going to be filled with hot irritation by the time they met.

"I'm over here," she yelled.

He wouldn't call the tone "friendly" by any stretch, but she also wasn't in any distress. That was a relief.

She had her hands propped on her hips when he rounded the corner of the old house.

"Did Bee send you?" she asked.

Trey shook his head. "No, I heard the shipyard's report about unexpected traffic." He stopped next to her and had to catch his breath at the stunning view of the Atlantic Ocean. "Wow."

Lila nodded. "It is pretty impressive, isn't it?"

Water rose and fell, and the ocean spread out as far as he could see in every direction.

"I guess it's not every day you get to sell a property like this, is it?" he asked.

She shook her head. "No, it isn't. This will be a first." She shrugged. "If I can manage it."

Trey studied her face as she stared out at the view. Her expression wasn't confident, but there was a determined tilt to her head. As if she'd give it everything she had.

"I'm not going inside. I'm also not breaking

any laws by being here." Lila crossed her arms over her chest. "There's nothing posted, no no-trespassing signs. I'm not sure what you're doing here… Chief."

Was it hard to use the title because it had belonged to her father or because she wanted to inflict some type of punishment for his excluding her from the squad room?

He wasn't certain, but the set of her shoulders convinced him they had a ways to go until they were cordial again.

"I haven't had a chance to survey the shipyard's setup yet." Trey spoke slowly, mainly because he was figuring his answer out as he went. "I saw the SUV parked and decided to investigate."

"Investigate." Lila didn't roll her eyes, but he could read the urge to do so all over her face.

Why did that strike him as cute instead of disrespectful? Maybe it was actually both.

"A drive-by…on foot. To keep an eye on things." He rubbed his ear and wished for a better answer. Flimsy was all he could come up with on the fly. "If you're planning to inspect the building, I can wait for you." Something cracked in the shadowy trees behind them.

Lila shook her head, and he decided the timing of whatever forest creature had caused the noise was in his favor.

"No, I have the pictures I need." She turned

away and walked quickly back around the house to the path leading back to their cars.

Lila stalked silently.

Trey followed easily behind until they reached the clearing where their cars were parked.

"Don't make a habit of this, Chief," Lila said firmly as she opened her car door. "Showing up where I am unexpectedly. I'm really not a fan."

The urge to argue with her had to be quashed. This was the first time he'd done it, right? Otherwise, she'd been in his space unexpectedly.

"Have a good afternoon," Trey said and got in his SUV and backed out of the driveway. He led the way out but stopped at the stop sign and waited until he saw her pull out of the driveway. It was hard to make the turn to head back to town, leaving her out alone on the deserted road. But she was an adult, the former police chief's daughter, knew Horizon and had her sister in police dispatch on speed dial.

Lila Shepard could take care of herself. She'd just told him so.

None of that had much effect on his urge to make sure she was safe, but he'd already set himself up for major embarrassment in about a dozen different ways. Returning to his safe desk in the almost comfortable police station made perfect sense.

CHAPTER SIX

LILA TEXTED BEE that she was leaving Blue Vista. When Trey finally made the turn to head back to town, she dropped her phone on the passenger seat and tried to calm her nerves. His ability to ruffle them was unexpected and unwelcome.

If the two of them were going to coexist in Horizon, she needed to find a way to prevent that fast. Especially if he was going to continue popping up out of the blue when she least expected or wanted him to like the former chief had.

"So what if you don't want to be caught up in police business. Apparently, police business is determined to be caught up in you," she muttered. She stretched her arms to release some of the tension that had snapped her shoulders tight when she'd heard his voice.

At least she'd been almost prepared to see him again by the time he'd joined her in front of that amazing ocean view.

There were a dozen questions she should have demanded answers to.

At least three of them, delivered in varying tones of exasperation, were, "Why are you here?"

She was uncomfortable with that because it reminded her of a dozen other times she'd asked her overprotective father the same thing.

Lila studied the road ahead of her and tried to figure out what to do next. Trey Douglas's arrival had scattered her thoughts. Gathering them took more effort than she liked.

"Irritating." Lila considered her options.

Rainey was the queen of pulling strings to create an intricately woven plot. "What would Rainey do?"

Obviously, she would gather all the intel she could before reaching out to the current owners. Whether or not Lila convinced Rainey to take a chance on her proposal, she was learning a lot from the process. The source of critical intelligence on Mike Wilkins was easy enough to determine.

She picked up her phone again, hit her father's number and waited for the call to connect.

"Are you okay?" he answered. Lila smiled. When the Shepard kids were growing up, their father had always answered their calls immediately, but the chief had no time to waste. Whatever they needed, he would make it happen, but then he had to get back to work.

Three days of retirement hadn't changed that attitude.

"Hi, Dad, how is all this free time working out for you?" she asked. Could he learn to chitchat now that he had unlimited minutes?

He grunted. "Your mother told me to leave the house and not come back for at least four hours. It has only been two at this point."

Lila shook her head as she studied the stop sign. Left would take her back to Horizon and her parents' house, but he wasn't there if he'd been kicked out for the day. "Where are you now? I was hoping to come by for a chat. I need some help."

"But you're okay," he said. It was easy enough to picture him poised to spring into action.

"Yeah, fine, it's information I need," Lila said.

There was a pause on the line, and she realized she could ask him what she wanted to know, no need to track him down.

But now that he had time for her, she wanted to do it this way.

"Well, okay, I'm out at the Admiral's. We're down on the dock, trying to catch red drum," her father said.

Then she heard her grandfather say something in the background. He'd retired from the navy as a rear admiral, but most everyone in town called him "Admiral" the way they called her father "Chief." It had been a job, but the nickname stuck long after the job was over.

"It's Lila, Dad. Nobody is invading your privacy," her father said. Lila grinned as she turned right. She hadn't intended to take a jaunt out to the Admiral's house, but it was amusing to watch her dad transform into an annoyed son when his father was around. It reminded her of at least a hundred different interactions she'd had with her father, but where she was the long-suffering party, and he was the one who was being unreasonable.

"How long 'til you get here?" her father asked. "I'll be watching for you."

Phrases like that would have irritated her as a kid.

Now she thought it was mostly part of her father's attempt to keep her safe.

That helped her let go of the urge to tell him she was smart and independent and all the other things she'd explained to him over the years. She also knew he was never going to change.

For questions like this, she'd learned to overestimate her travel time. Otherwise, if she was wrong, her father would be ready to climb into the car and come looking. "Give me thirty. See you then."

"Drive safe," her father responded before ending the call.

At the abrupt end, Lila shook her head. "Love you, too, Dad." Then she turned up Kelly Clarkson again and put her foot on the gas.

Twenty minutes later, she parked in front of her grandfather's weathered house. It had started life as a fishing camp. When the Admiral retired after a long career of distinguished service, a widower with no other plans but rest and relaxation, he'd bought the remote place, dropped his stuff and headed out with a fishing pole. He came into Horizon for family events, holidays, and to restock groceries.

Lila had loved his place on the river from the moment she'd seen it.

Not because of the house, obviously. It gave the impression that spiders were the original owners, and the Admiral was only renting a room, but the interior was much nicer than the outside would suggest. She had a feeling the Admiral preferred it that way.

It was behind the house where everything changed. The land gave way to salt marsh that stretched out as far as she could see. One of the tiny creeks that fed into the Ashepoo wended through the marshes, and a long wooden walkway cut across the marsh. At the end, a tiny little gazebo provided some shelter against the sun.

Lila shaded her eyes with one hand.

She could see two smallish specks. Her father and the Admiral were perched on the end there, facing opposite directions. "Bet they haven't spoken more than fifty words altogether and wouldn't have it any other way."

When Lila was at about the halfway point of the walkway—which did not appear to be longer than the Great Wall of China when she started but somehow grew every time she made the journey—her father raised his hand to wave, so she picked up her pace.

She was still catching her breath when she stepped under the shade of the gazebo. Her father immediately stood and wrapped her in a hug that made the trek worthwhile. Lila inhaled slowly and realized that she would have missed this if she'd gone with the efficient phone conversation instead of the detour.

She made a mental note to be more aware in the future that efficiency might not always be the top priority with her father. His life had changed, so her part in it could, too.

Then her father stepped back and her grandfather took his place. His hug was strong, and he rocked her side to side the same as he had when she was small.

"Fishing for red drum, caught an actual prize," the Admiral said as he squeezed her harder and stepped back. "Little Lila. Brighter than the sunshine today."

Her grandfather appeared as untamed as his house at the moment. Shipwreck survivors were better put together. He was wearing a ratty gray bucket hat with some indeterminate splotches that matched the stains on his long-sleeved work shirt, and his white beard obscured his smile. She hoped he cleaned up before his next visit into Horizon or her mother would decide he needed an intervention.

Lila smiled at his familiar welcome. Retired Admiral Thomas Shepard had the stern expression of a military man, but he'd always had a soft spot for his family. He might not show that gooey side for his son. They were both the strong, silent type.

They were both also defenseless against the Shepard kids.

"Are the fish biting?" Lila asked as she waved off the Admiral's offer of his seat. "I can't stay long. The back-to-school event is tonight, and I have to set up my face-painting booth."

"The chief here managed to catch the first one, but I've got the biggest one," the Admiral said as he cast his line again.

Lila smiled at the way her father raised his eyebrow at her.

She'd seen TJ make the same face about him.

"I need to get in contact with Mike Wilkins. Can either of you connect me?" Lila asked as she moved to rest against the railing and stare out over the marsh. There was only a low breeze, but the grass waved softly over the top of the black water that flowed toward Edisto Island and Saint Helena Sound. She could understand why the Admiral was insistent on keeping the guest list small. This place was beautiful and undisturbed.

"Cousin Mike. I haven't talked to him in an

age," the Admiral said as he pulled out his cell phone and scrolled through the numbers. "Haven't gotten any funeral notices, either, so let's see if he answers."

Lila chuckled at his leisurely tone. Nothing much ruffled his feathers.

"Well, Mike Wilkins, you're still alive and kicking," the Admiral drawled, so Lila assumed that the phone number still worked. "How have you been? You ever get out of Tampa and up this way anymore?"

Even only getting half of the conversation, Lila understood that Mike was still living in Tampa, and he had seven grandchildren scattered throughout Florida and Georgia. She thought at least one of them was in medical school, but she wouldn't swear to it based on the Admiral's question about whether podiatry was the "one for feet or brains."

She and her father both rolled their eyes at that. The Admiral was doing his best country-boy persona. It was easy to imagine Mike Wilkins doing his version on the other end of the line. He was entertaining the Admiral who was laughing loud enough to disturb a flock of birds.

"Well, I've got this granddaughter. Three of them, actually, if you can believe it, every single one prettier than a speckled pup. Two grandsons who take after their father, but we don't hold it against them." The Admiral paused. "Yep, law enforcement, the Marines, Coast Guard. All of them. Very proud."

Lila pulled her arms in tighter because she knew she wasn't in that select group.

"But this granddaughter I called to tell you about today, she's Horizon's best real estate agent..." The Admiral paused and nodded. "I know. I'm a lucky man. Anyway, she asked to talk to you. Do you have a minute?"

Mike Wilkins must have had the time because the Admiral offered her his phone and then picked up his fishing rod, satisfied that his job was done.

"Hi, Mr. Wilkins—"

"Call me Cousin Mike, please," he interrupted. "We're family even across state lines, Lisa."

Lila smiled. "All right. And it's Lila. I wanted to ask if you've ever thought of selling Blue Vista."

The pause on the other end of the line tightened an anxious knot in Lila's stomach. Before, when it had been an abstract spot on a map, she might have easily moved on if it didn't work out. Now that she'd seen that view, it seemed like it was the only place that fit her requirements.

"Well," Mike said slowly, "I have, Lila. I surely have. It's been years since we made it up to South Carolina to visit, and I have to believe it would fetch a solid price. A man gets to this age and he starts to consider what he's leaving his kids. That land is my biggest asset but figuring exactly what to do about it for the next generation is a question mark. Selling it and splitting the money is a nice, clean solution, ain't it?"

Lila clutched the phone tightly. Was this going to work?

"On the other hand, it belongs to the family. Our family, yours and mine. It'd be a shame to let that go too easily," Mike said with a sigh. "Not that I know much about it. Last time I saw the house there, it wasn't livable. Do you have a buyer?"

Lila bit her lip as she formulated an answer. "Not yet, but I have a developer who is looking for the right spot. If I do the research to come up with a fair price and get a commitment from him, would you be interested in reviewing the offer?"

She watched her father and grandfather exchange a look, but neither one of them spoke up.

"Of course I would. That's the piece missing here. Hard to say what I could give up without knowing what the exchange would be. You call me when you have that, and we'll talk again."

It wasn't an enthusiastic yes, but it also wasn't a firm no.

For now, Lila would take it.

"Yes, sir, I will absolutely do that." Lila nodded as if he could see her.

"And tell your grandfather not to be such a stranger," Mike Wilkins added before he ended the call.

Lila handed her grandfather the phone back and

slumped against the railing, relieved and anxious in a new way.

"A developer? For what?" the Admiral asked as he slipped the phone back into his shirt pocket. "Not a hotel or a shopping mall or some such thing."

Lila realized both men were frowning at her.

"Houses. A subdivision, for commuters from Charleston." She crossed her arms over her chest and watched both men turn to stare in opposite directions over the marshes. "Rainey's planning to work with an agent and one of the biggest luxury subdivision developers in the state. I decided to build a proposal to get some of the business myself." Saying that aloud felt good. She was proactively building her business here.

Her grandfather and father were facing away from each other, so they couldn't see the nearly identical slow shakes of their heads, but she could. It would have been funny if the implied disapproval wasn't there.

"Once you open that door, it'll be hard to close it again. One subdivision will spawn another," the Admiral said, his frown growing. Since he guarded his undisturbed spot of South Carolina jealously, it shouldn't be surprising that he'd be against spawning more neighbors.

"And Horizon's growth has been slow and steady, adding good neighbors without overwhelming us," her father said. "The last big project in town, Bay View Tower, has taken years to sell out—apart from that final unit—but every new person it brought in fit. A subdivision like that, one with 'luxury' in the name…" He finished the thought with another slow shake of his head.

As if he couldn't put into words how bad that could be.

Everything he said was true. Lila had experience selling that "big" project herself. It had taken more than two years to sell eleven of the twelve units, but each of the new residents was a welcome addition to Horizon.

"Expansion is Rainey's goal. She ran on adding jobs for Horizon. Shouldn't I pursue the business that she will bring in?" There was no doubt in Lila's mind that Rainey would be successful. She didn't fail. The timing was the only real question about this subdivision.

Because Lila knew where it needed to go.

Both men were quiet for so long that Lila wondered if the conversation was over.

Eventually, her father cast his line back out. "You know how much Horizon means to this family. Generations of service and family centered right here in the town. You'll make the right choice, so I certainly don't want any other agent making this deal. Rainey's good at her job. Her ambition is admirable, as long as it's tempered with service to the people who already live here. You can ensure that happens."

Lila shifted her weight from one foot to the other as she listened to him speak.

When he settled easily in his chair, she decided he had said his piece. It wasn't approval. It also wasn't disapproval.

What her father had done was hand her a whole chunk of responsibility. He was the police department's motto in physical form. We Serve might as well have been tattooed on his forehead.

Her comfort here was that he was including her in the "we." Not being part of the family business of law enforcement meant she hadn't had service to Horizon reaffirmed at every daily shift change, but her father had been instilling the idea in his kids around the dinner table forever.

"You build your plan. Growing your business is a worthy goal," the Admiral added and held his arm out. Lila moved to hug his neck. "And when it comes down to the final decision, you weigh the costs against the return, and you do the right thing for Horizon."

Lila stepped back. She almost asked how she would know what that would be.

The way time was getting away from her convinced her not to ask questions that she suspected had no easy answers. "Thank you for your help, Grandad." Then she hugged her father. "I'm glad you finally made it out here to fish, Daddy." He'd been saying he wanted to do so for as long as she could remember.

"Next time, I'll bring another pole for you," he said as he squeezed her tightly.

Lila held the warmth that bloomed in her chest at his promise close and stepped back.

"Will I see either of you at the back-to-school night?" Lila asked as she stared down the long walkway that led back to her car. It would take a minute to prepare herself for the return trek.

The Admiral immediately shook his head no. His certainty made her laugh.

"Your mother says I have a job." Her father's face conveyed his doubts about the whole thing. "But she's not giving me any details."

Lila grinned as she patted his shoulder. "On the bright side, you have the time now."

He squeezed her hand, and Lila decided to get on with her own work for the evening.

"Come back tomorrow, Lila," her grandfather called, and she waved. That had been his way of saying goodbye forever. When she surveyed his sunny spot of South Carolina salt marsh, it was hard to understand why she wouldn't be back the next day and the one after that.

But at that moment, she had a lot of business to tackle, all of it back in Horizon.

It might not be police business, but her father had reminded her that her business was as much a part of the Shepard family commitment to their hometown as the Horizon Police Department.

Shepards served Horizon, and deciding how best to do that was her next step.

CHAPTER SEVEN

After he drove back into town, Trey settled behind his desk and pulled the stack of old reports closer to dig through them again. It was tempting to replay and dissect his short conversation with Lila Shepard, but he wanted a distraction.

Since he had called that spontaneous meeting with Bee Shepard to save himself from his earlier preoccupation with Lila, he'd get that distraction soon enough.

He knew he was in for an awkward conversation. But on the drive from the shipyard, he'd come up with a decent justification.

These reports were the key.

He hadn't spoken directly to Bee since the first morning except to set up this discussion. He'd decided to stay the course, keeping shift changes short and efficient to get his officers out on patrol quickly. The awkward tension in the room would improve once everyone adjusted to the new normal. Working while people skirted around him was uncomfortable.

The fact that he could always feel eyes watching him but never spot anyone doing so directly was annoying,

He was used to being the best surveillance around, but his new neighbors were giving him a run for his money.

Since he needed background on the town, the types and volume of calls his officers answered, Trey had turned to the former chief's files. Tom Shepard's files were sparse, but Trey had been pleased to learn that there were extensive weekly summaries with statistics compiled on calls, investigations and citations issued.

All of them had been prepared and filed by Dispatch Supervisor Bee Shepard before she shared them via email to the area's cooperating law enforcement agencies.

He'd read a month or so of reports and a tiny seed of an idea had been planted in his brain.

Now he had the perfect opportunity to water that seed to see if it grew. His panic might have turned into inspiration and the perfect way to open up conversation with Bee Shepard again.

Before he could decide between "good afternoon" and "thank you for meeting with me" as the correct small talk icebreaker, Bee stuck her head in the doorway. "You wanted to see me, Chief?" She didn't step inside.

Her eyes also didn't meet his.

Should he insist she sit? Would that make this better or worse?

"Do you have a minute to sit, Shepard?" he asked. He'd freed her up from the shift change meetings to avoid shortchanging Dispatch. So it didn't make sense to keep her away from her desk if it was a bad time, even if he had the feeling that asking for her help could restore some of the peace in the squad room.

The question about whether Lila had called her sister to discuss his arrival at Blue Vista popped into his brain, but he tried to shove that worry aside. It was inevitable. Lila didn't hesitate to make her opinion of him clear to his face, so he could imagine what took place in the Shepard family's group chat.

But none of that showed on Bee's face. She was clearly reluctant to enter, but straightened her shoulders and stepped inside to perch on the edge of the chair across from him. "Is this about taking personal calls on duty?"

Trey frowned, thrown off course by the question, just as his phone dinged to indicate that he'd gotten a text. Without a second thought, Trey picked it up to read.

Your first official community event tonight. You can't miss it. The Boss.

Trey rolled his eyes before slipping his phone in his pocket. It had definitely been a mistake to call Rainey that. She would run it into the ground.

Then he realized Bee Shepard was watching him and waiting to hear his policy about personal calls on the job.

And that there was no way she'd missed his response. Better not let her know it was Rainey or he'd have another unflattering tale sweeping through town.

"The call… I was following up on an alert from the shipyard. Their security cameras caught some unusual traffic, and we're copied on those findings," Bee said as she clenched her hands together in her lap. "I didn't feel it was necessary to send a patrol out since I recognized the car."

"No threat, then," Trey said as he made a note that he needed to contact the head of security at the shipyard. He'd had no idea this was part of their protocol. As the town's biggest employer and a site with national security concerns, it made sense that the local police department was looped in.

"My sister was scouting out some land for a real estate deal," Bee said. "But that won't be the only phone call you see between me and my sister. Whatever her feelings about police business, all of us take Shepard business seriously, but it never comes ahead of the job. Not for me or TJ here, but Lila's focused on the success of her own business, too."

Trey realized he was on the verge of looking like both a hypocrite and a jerk, a tricky spot he felt like he'd been tap-dancing around pretty often since he'd arrived in Horizon.

He liked to hear Bee's confidence in her sister. It also brought Lila's face to his mind. Since it had been less than three minutes since the last time it happened, he understood he might have a problem. Driving all the way out to the shipyard to check on her when she was in zero danger… Well, that was just serving a member of the public.

"Personal calls are part of the job, since we are people first and officers second," Trey said as he realized he needed to determine his workplace policies. Tom Shepard's were sound, no doubt, but he wasn't certain what they were.

No civilians in the squad room, obviously, but what else?

This might be the first time in his life human resources were up to him, but it didn't change his mind about his answer. They were people who had a job to do. The occasional call wouldn't interfere with that.

He thought Bee's shoulders relaxed a fraction, and he wondered how much of the tension in the air was because his officers were on guard about how he'd judge their performance.

For some reason, the memory of Dennis Browning's suspicious frown popped into his head. Leaving Columbia had been the only way to keep working in law enforcement. Once that image was in his head, he'd started second-guessing all his decisions, past and present. He didn't need his officers in Horizon struggling under that. Everything he'd seen supported Rainey's claim that the police department provided exemplary service.

Bee's uncertainty was his fault. He should correct it.

Trey motioned at the stack of files on his desk. "I've been going through the chief's files. I see your name all over them. This is good information, Shepard."

Bee blinked slowly. "Thank you. When I first started them, the chief wasn't sure they were required. Horizon's crime stats are pretty constant, across the different time periods, but we have a pattern now. It helps when we're planning for the year, considering personnel."

Trey nodded. "You didn't have that before you started measuring, and now you can see if there are any changes. It's very useful, especially for new officers or agencies who respond to calls for help but don't patrol the town regularly."

Bee frowned for a second before agreeing. The ice was still there, but was there any thaw happening?

Trey decided to get on with his request. "What I was hoping for was an overlay on a city map with pins marking each call. That will help me, since I don't know the streets or neighborhoods the way I want to. Do you have anything like that to go with the reports?"

He watched the way her eyes lit up at the idea, and he realized he had found a kindred spirit in Bee Shepard. Data was good. Visual displays were exciting.

Excusing her from the morning briefing was a hasty decision he was already regretting.

"I don't have it yet, but I can," she said slowly.

"If you need software, send me a requisition, and we'll get it through. This will help outside agencies, and it's worth the investment." Trey picked up his pen and tried to find a smooth way to tell her to report for morning briefings again. He knew it would look like he'd backed down.

And he had, mainly because he hadn't known the full story and that had caused him to make a mistake. He heard Rainey say "rookie mistake" in his head again.

"I did some research last year on software that could plug in our stats and create an interactive map that would show the details of the calls from the police report, even feed them out to the officers on patrol. I was hoping to convince my da... The previous chief didn't see the need, but I've still got the information I pulled together," Bee said as she stood. She was halfway to the door before she realized he hadn't excused her. "Was there anything else you needed?"

Pleased at how well his seed had sprouted, mainly because he'd discovered a hidden data nerd like himself in Bee, Trey said, "I'm hoping you can have a preliminary map by the end of next week?"

Bee blinked. "I was aiming for Friday afternoon. Not final, but something you can look at."

The way her feet shifted as she stood there convinced him she was in a hurry to get the project started, too.

"Even better." Trey almost let her leave without addressing the briefings, but he'd made a mistake that had to be corrected. It was much better to do that sooner rather than later.

"When you have the time to leave Dispatch, please attend the morning briefing. I will understand when you can't, but this information you're collecting is necessary." Trey inhaled slowly as he watched Bee process that. Eventually she nodded, so he added, "Let me know what you need for this project."

"Yes, sir," Bee said and inched a step closer to the door.

Trey nodded and she took that as permission to leave.

He slumped against his seat and tried not to replay the conversation in his head to look for flaws. Then he checked the time and logged out of his computer. He'd made an appointment to go and see the apartment available for rent, since his clock was ticking at the Needlegrass Motor Lodge. If he left now, he'd be early, but that would give him a chance to drive around the neighborhood surrounding Island Manor—a grand name for a small complex that had been built before Trey could drive if he had to guess. It was small, fourteen units in total, no pool or even landscaping to label as such. Two stories, brick facade, no elevator, a long open gallery across the front with identical doors, all painted beige. The architecture was uninspiring, but he knew that much from the photo online. Houses surrounded the complex, and it was at the foot of a bridge.

Since he was still ten minutes early, he drove over the bridge to survey the Horizon Animal Hospital and Shoreline Animal Shelter. He cruised along the streets that ranged off the two-lane until it dead-ended. Trey returned to Island Manor and parked in front of number four, the unit Sam Pulaski had told him was available. As he slid out of his SUV, a tiny woman wearing a purple top that flowed behind her as she marched down the sidewalk appeared. He waited for her to make the full journey.

"Mr. Douglas," she said firmly, "I'm Sam." Was she reserving the use of his title for some later date? Trey wondered how long it would take.

Sam waved her key ring. "I'll show you the apartment." She turned with military precision to unlock the door before opening it briskly and stepping inside.

"Two bedrooms. One bath." She motioned as she spoke and then stopped in the middle of the living room. Trey could see a small kitchen in the corner. "Before you sign any lease, you should know that TJ Shepard will be your neighbor on this side." She pointed sharply. "His good friend, Wade, is on the other." Then she raised her eyebrows, but Trey couldn't decipher what that meant.

"And I'm assuming there's also someone in the unit above this one?" he asked as he walked through.

Her eyes narrowed. "Nevaeh is intimidating, but I wasn't aware you had a problem with her."

Since he'd never met Nevaeh, Trey wasn't aware of a problem, either, but from that comment, he inferred that he did have one with TJ and his good friend, Wade.

"I thought warning would help you make your decision. Living next door to the guy everyone expected to have the job you rolled into town to take," Sam said with a dubious shrug, "could get uncomfortable. TJ Shepard would have made a great chief of police, too. He and Lucy have been outstanding tenants for years now."

Trey did his best not to show any reaction, but this was the first time anyone had come right out and said TJ should have had the chief's office. And it was clear whose side Sam would come down on in the event of a disagreement.

Since he'd yet to hear one bad word about

charming TJ Shepard, it made sense that he would lose the battle every time.

"We all get along very well here," Sam added. "No need to make arrests in the middle of the night if someone gets loud."

Trey swallowed a sigh as he realized Joe Morgan and Sam Pulaski had conferred about what sort of tenant he would be, and they hadn't reached a positive conclusion.

"Understood. Is the apartment available for lease now?" Trey asked as he stuck his head in the small bathroom. Shower. Toilet. Island Manor had the basics covered but not much else.

She pursed her lips. "It is." Trey could read "against my better judgment" all over her face. "But you would be happier renting a house. More space. Fewer neighbors to disturb your peace."

Trey agreed with her there. "I didn't see any houses for rent."

Sam nodded. "Nothing for rent stays available for too long around here. Not a lot of inventory, but Lila Shepard could help you with that. She will know of someone ready to sell or thinking of selling who would be interested in some income instead."

Yeah, that fit his life at the moment.

The one person in town who could help him get what he wanted was the one he'd probably annoyed most on his first day as chief.

And the one who kept popping back into his head even though he needed to stay far, far away.

Sam moved to the open door and waited. Trey took that as a sign that his tour was over and headed back to his SUV. "I'll give you a call tomorrow and let you know if I want to sign a lease."

Sam sniffed. "We can do a short-term lease, too. Since I know you have to check out of the Needlegrass soon. To get you to whenever you can move into your permanent spot."

Which she hoped would not be her apartment complex.

By the time he started up his SUV, Sam was already sailing back around the end of Island Manor. She moved quickly.

As Trey followed the turns to head out to the football stadium, he had to admire how clearly Sam communicated. She wouldn't leave him homeless, but she would be counting the days until he moved out if he decided to go with the apartment.

Learning more about the full extent to which he was unwelcome in Horizon didn't fill Trey with confidence as he turned into the large, chaotic parking lot. The woman motioning cars into parking spots along the perimeter of the lot scowled at him before waving him through a barricade next to the police booth.

"Just call me Mr. Popularity," he murmured as he parked.

Obviously, no one was ready to call him Chief yet.

When he had a minute to corner Rainey, he needed more information on TJ Shepard's career path at the Horizon Police Department, but before that he had to survive his first community event as chief.

CHAPTER EIGHT

THE SIZE OF THE CROWD at the back-to-school event caught Trey off guard. It appeared the whole community turned out, not just the families with students in Horizon schools. The crowd for the animal shelter's Spring Social had been a similar size. His reception there had been much more welcoming.

Maybe everyone in Horizon showed up for every event in town.

A delicious aroma from one of the food trucks floated in the air. Trey's stomach rumbled in response. Here and there, groups were gathered around tables and tents. The fire department had an engine with the lights turning, and firefighters stood next to the truck to answer questions.

There were so many kids—screaming kids, laughing kids, running kids.

An overwhelming number of them had painted faces as well. Whoever was responsible enjoyed loud colors, had questionable drawing skills and seemed to love pirates.

The multitude of painted eye patches and

swoopy moustaches confused him until he caught sight of the high school mascot—a pirate—who was waving pom-poms alongside the cheerleaders.

The Horizon High School Pirates meant a lot of wannabe pirate face paint.

He stopped next to the pop-up tent where Rodriguez was accepting school supplies.

Trey felt the weight of a stare and turned slowly to see a couple of women watching him from a spot near the police booth. They had their heads together and their frowns conveyed disapproval.

"Ladies," he said politely, wondering if he'd caught them staring because they wanted him to.

In a synchronized move that they had to have practiced, they turned on a heel and marched over to TJ.

"TJ, you look thirsty. Have some lemonade," the older woman said and motioned for the younger woman to give him the cup she was carrying. "You remember my daughter? Her divorce is final already."

Trey crossed his arms over his chest as TJ sipped the lemonade. Watching matchmakers could be entertaining when he wasn't the star of the show.

"Now, Mrs. Lamb, you know you broke my heart in first grade, and I've never gotten over it." TJ sighed heavily. "Besides, I'm not quite as single myself as I used to be, thanks to a veterinarian around here somewhere." Then he grinned. "But the chief here is unattached." Then he motioned Trey closer. "Let me introduce you all."

Whatever amusement that had been bubbling up in Trey's chest evaporated immediately. "Ladies." He was repeating himself, but he had no clue what else to say.

"Mrs. Lamb works over at Horizon Elementary. She got me through first grade with nary a scratch. And this is her daughter, Trina." *Whose divorce is final.* TJ didn't add that part, but Trey thought he could read it in the gleam in his eyes.

Instead of making further awkward conversation, both women nodded. Before they left, Mrs. Lamb said, "Hope things are good over at the police station, TJ." Then she met Trey's stare, tipped her nose up in the air and led her daughter away.

"I don't know that I've ever seen Mrs. Lamb do the cold shoulder," TJ murmured as they stood there watching them leave. "Have you been fighting with Mrs. Lamb as well as Joe Morgan and Belinda at the Daybreak Diner, sir?"

Trey sighed. News of his misdeeds was spreading rapidly.

He hadn't even been inside the Daybreak Diner yet and had no idea who Belinda was, but he had no doubt his reputation had preceded him.

Before he could answer, Rodriguez motioned them to stand in the center of the booth in front of the We Serve banner with Lucy as the star. "Smile for the socials, please."

Trey realized it was the first time anyone had ever said anything like that to him. Social media was so far off his radar that it was in another universe, but in his role in Horizon, he had a feeling he was going to learn a lot about photo opportunities.

After Rodriguez took the photo, Trey retreated quickly from the center of the action.

A little girl skipped up with her parents following behind. She knelt down in front of Lucy, both hands under her knees as TJ talked to her.

Trey couldn't hear what she asked, but TJ nodded, and she offered her hand to Lucy.

"Having them here is always a big hit," Rodriguez said as he took a photo of them.

"Not too many drug investigations around here, I guess. Shepard and Lucy have the time." Trey crossed his arms over his chest as he watched. He'd checked Shepard's stats, but everything appeared normal as far as searches he and Lucy had completed and calls they'd answered.

"Chief." Rodriguez braced his hands on his duty belt and waited for Trey to acknowledge him. Since Trey didn't hear his title as often as he expected, he appreciated it. He turned from scanning the crowd, evaluating any threats with special attention to the group of teenage boys gathered next to a pickup truck near the fringes of the parking lot, to see Rodriguez frowning at him.

"Permission to speak freely, sir," Rodriguez said. In Trey's experience, the phrase was most often intended to be a question, but he didn't read any uncertainty in the officer's face.

"Proceed," Trey said slowly.

"You're doing it again," Rodriguez said.

Trey raised an eyebrow as he wondered if he and Rodriguez were acquainted well enough for this kind of conversation.

Then he realized Rodriguez was the only person interested in getting acquainted, so he better lean into it. "Doing what again?"

"You're making judgment calls based on insufficient information, sir." Rodriguez pointed at Shepard and Lucy with his chin while Trey rocked back on his heels. The statement was firm and unexpected. Since it was an echo of what he'd thought about his mistake excluding Dispatch from the morning meeting, he was off balance.

"TJ and Lucy do good work—traffic stops, searches at the shipyard, assisting the Coast Guard and state police. They perform crowd control and everyday police work, same as any other officers." Rodriguez pointed at where TJ was still talking with the girl. "They also volunteer their time to work in schools and at community events like this. Right now, TJ is teaching Abby how to address a K9. At the same time, she's learning not to be afraid of the police."

They both watched the little girl grin as her parents took a photo.

And Trey realized this was not the kind of work he understood.

"You'll get it, Chief," Rodriguez said, his hand frozen in the air between them as if he'd planned to thump Trey on the shoulder but thought better of it. Instead, he pivoted to pat the banner hanging from the table. The familiar bright blue letters spelling We Serve rippled. "This is the important piece."

TJ asked the little girl, "Want to sit in the police car? I'll show you how the lights and the siren work." He was good with the public. His manner was easy and charming. The little girl and her parents both nodded. Were the adults as excited about the chance as the kid?

Then he realized the little girl was pointing at his SUV instead of TJ's squad car.

"I want to see the big one!" she said before sprinting to stand next to Trey's SUV.

TJ held up both hands. "Wait a second, Abby. That's the chief's vehicle. You'll need him to show you around it."

Then everyone turned to stare at Trey.

Perfectly hemmed in, Trey smiled. "Of course." Trey was painfully conscious of all the attention focused on him as he opened the driver's side door. "Jump in." Since he was fully out of his depth in this conversation, his only choice was to channel TJ Shepard. "Mom, Dad, do you want to get in the back seat?"

Abby's parents shared a glance before nodding. Some of the enthusiasm had evaporated. Sitting in the back of a police car was less about pushing fun buttons and more about places they never wanted to see.

Since no one there wanted to disappoint Abby, Trey opened the door to the back and the couple slid inside. Trey decided to leave the door open, in case they wanted to make the tour brief. Then he walked around to the passenger side and sat next to Abby.

When he pushed the start button, the dashboard lit up to Abby's delight.

Trey cleared his throat as he evaluated the proper way to illustrate all the equipment. "Well, let's go left to right. You see the spotlight." He pointed as he moved across. "A pretty standard electronic instrument cluster, including the speedometer, odometer, gas gauges. If they're too bright, we can choose a dark mode, make it easier for stakeouts, things like that." He leaned back. "Laptop, of course. And here in the center, the radio stack which lets us talk to Dispatch. And then the light and siren controls. Pretty simple."

When he faced Abby again, he had the feeling he had not nailed the presentation.

That was mainly due to all the silence.

TJ bent down and met his stare across the front seat. Before Trey could fumble his way through another attempt, TJ tapped the spotlight. "Hit this switch, Abby."

She flipped the toggle on, and the bright white light lit up.

That made her smile again.

"Wrap your hand around this and turn it," TJ said as he helped Abby follow his instructions. "See how the light turns. Then you can lift and lower it like this." Abby's grin as she watched the spotlight turn was positive feedback.

"I want to turn on the siren," Abby said.

TJ pursed his lips. "Of course you do. Chief?"

TJ stared at him. His face was marginally friendlier than Abby's. She had given up any hope of getting good information from Trey after his early flop.

But nobody liked a quitter, so Trey said, "See that right there? Move that lever all the way to the right side. Put your finger on it and push it over." When the light bar lit up, twirling red, white and blue silently, Abby clapped her hands, and Trey sat a little taller in the seat.

"And now..." He waited to build up the suspense. "The siren?"

Abby nodded enthusiastically.

Trey pointed at the red knobs in the center control. "We have different settings, but this is the one you want. Turn the knob to Wail. The center one. See it?"

Abby immediately twisted and then clapped her hands over her ears at the noise.

Trey realized he was wearing a big grin when he turned the siren off. Abby was happy. Her parents were smiling.

All it had taken was pushing a button.

And some help from TJ Shepard.

It also didn't last long. Once she'd seen all there was to see and pushed the buttons, Abby was ready to move on. "I want to get my face painted next."

She hopped out of the driver's seat, and Trey turned off the dashboard before joining TJ in front of the police table to watch her tug her parents across the parking lot.

Since Abby walked right over to the face-painting booth, Trey spotted Lila with a paintbrush in her hand. She was the source of all the bad moustaches in the crowd, and even from this distance, he could see the sparkle of joy in her broad smile. She was having a blast, and he wanted to move closer to her.

Then he realized that TJ Shepard was standing next to him, watching Trey stare at his sister. The awkward silence between them spun out.

Making amends with Officer Lucy was the easiest item on his list, so he knelt down on a knee and held out his fist for her to sniff. “Officer, you are doing a good job out here.”

Lucy’s eyes were trained on TJ. After he nodded, she sniffed and eventually shoved her chin against Trey’s hand in the universal dog language. Trey scratched the yellow Lab’s ears and did his best to make up for being a too-serious stick-in-the-mud.

And because dogs are perfect, she let him.

When he stood, he decided TJ’s body language had relaxed a bit.

“I don’t know much about dogs in general. Never had one of my own and the K9 officers I’ve worked with…” Trey shook his head. “They didn’t have a normal dog mode, I don’t think. Not sure they were safe candidates for community socializing like this.” He’d seen one German shepherd take down a massive skinhead after a brutally short race across open ground. It was almost impossible to imagine Lucy doing the same.

TJ’s lips firmed and Trey realized he’d taken two steps backward again.

“Lucy is every bit as serious about work. She can detect a wide range of contraband and follows orders flawlessly, but she’s not a weapon,” TJ said firmly. Then he spotted someone in the crowd. Trey thought it was the veterinarian he’d met at the Spring Social. She was walking toward Lila’s booth.

Whatever TJ saw convinced him to restart. He

rolled his shoulders as if he was trying to relax some of the tension there.

"But I know the kind of officers you mean. Some don't give their K9 partners much chance to be dogs. I'm working with the state association responsible for K9s' welfare, and I'd like to change that," TJ added.

There was no mistaking how important his K9 partner and the work he wanted to do was to TJ. That was admirable.

"You and Lucy are a big hit." Trey fought the urge to shift nervously from side to side. "Thank you for helping out with Abby."

TJ nodded once. "Not a big fan of community outreach events, I'm guessing."

"All my time has been spent on public safety so that other officers could make friends," Trey answered.

TJ's chin tipped up, and Trey realized he'd insulted the man who had been doing exactly that so well that he'd envied it.

This was not the way to earn TJ Shepard's good opinion.

In Rodriguez's words, he was "doing it again" *again*.

"And I realize now how important that is to what we do, our mission," Trey answered honestly as he tapped the table banner, copying Rodriguez's earlier gesture without shame. "My day-to-day in Columbia was a lot less wholesome than photo ops and face painting, but I can learn."

TJ nodded. "Learning new things is hard but it can be good." He met Trey's gaze. "Chief."

Trey knew TJ was offering him the olive branch, but neither one of them was sure peace would be possible yet.

And TJ didn't even know they might be neighbors soon.

His point was good. "Yeah, plenty of ways to expand my experience here."

TJ propped his hands on his duty belt. "You know, the former chief wasn't big on these events, either. 'Optics' were never his thing."

Trey nodded. It was easy to believe that was true. Tom Shepard struck him a man who kept his eyes on the business at hand. He admired that.

"But…" TJ paused and Trey wondered if he should brace himself. "He surrounded himself with people with a lot of different skills."

"Smart," Trey said as he met TJ's stare. "That's what a good leader does."

TJ nodded. "Almost everyone would call him a good leader. I would. For a brief minute, I had to think about what kind of leader I'd be in your shoes, and I wasn't sure I'd measure up."

If TJ had his heart set on taking over as chief, Trey had never gotten a whiff of injury before his problematic morning briefing. If anyone was spreading discontent about TJ losing the chief's spot, Trey didn't believe it was TJ.

"If I had stepped up to take over as chief," TJ added, "I would have had to choose Horizon over Lucy and improving police dog protections in South Carolina, so I didn't. I learned about service and police work from one of the best in the business. One of those lessons was hard to learn, but it might help you here."

Trey raised his eyebrow.

"When the former chief made a mistake, he corrected it." TJ pointed at Lucy. "For example, he wasn't much interested in all the hoops I jumped through to get Horizon's first K9 officer, but I bet if you ask him now, he understands Lucy's value."

Trey wasn't certain if this comment was related to his missed greeting at the morning briefing or if he'd been making his opinion of TJ and Lucy's contribution more obvious than he intended, but he understood TJ's meaning.

His most recent conversation with Bee Shepard had been an excellent introduction to the theme for this evening. Correcting rookie mistakes.

Any doubt remaining that TJ Shepard was spreading discontent in town over being passed over for a promotion had been erased. TJ had his own goals, and he was passionate about them. What was less clear was how the news that he'd turned down the opportunity instead of being passed over had remained under wraps in this town where information traveled so quickly and easily.

It didn't matter much why Horizon still believed TJ should be chief. Trey was going to have to accept that a lot of his current situation with the Joe Morgans, Sam Pulaskis and Belindas he'd never met was self-inflicted.

Rodriguez was right. He'd assumed he knew the situation and had made bad decisions based on it. He knew better.

He knew how it felt to be judged unfairly.

Before Trey could figure out how to address that, two little boys came barreling up to the table, fully focused on Lucy. TJ asked, "You want to take this one, Chief? For the practice?"

Trey shook his head. "Don't like the numbers, Shepard. We need a pro here."

TJ paused until he accepted that Trey had been making a joke. He didn't laugh, but some of the stony indifference left his face. After TJ walked away, Trey watched the people milling around in the crowd as he evaluated his options. He could continue standing around like a weird statue in a uniform while people watched him out of the corner of their eye, or he could strike out into the crowd of people he didn't know.

"No good choices here," he muttered before moving toward the food trucks. It was in the same general direction as the kids around the pickup truck. He could swing by, break up their fun and find dinner. It was an efficient plan. It also kept him from hanging around the police booth awkwardly.

When all else failed, fried food would be there for him.

CHAPTER NINE

LILA DABBED A dot of black paint near the corner of Summer's eye to finish off the paw prints she'd painted across her cheek. Since her mother was hovering somewhere off to the left, she and Summer were doing most of their communicating in silent stares. Summer had learned quickly what it had taken the Shepard kids some time to grasp: even when their mother was occupied with something else, she was always listening.

Tonight she was handing out the magnets and pens that Lila used for these events and chatting with all the students and parents who passed Lila's booth. Lila had managed to avoid being cornered by her mother for details from their family dinner this long. Anything she or Summer let slip would be snapped up like a fish on a fly, but Lila wanted to see if there had been any new developments in the police department.

If she could get her mother out of earshot, she and Summer could chat without interruption. The last time Lila had seen her father, he'd been running a dart game that required him to keep small children from poking each other with sharp objects. He was good at it, but his expression made her wonder if he wished he was back on duty in the police booth.

TJ was there. He and Lucy were drawing in the kids, as expected.

Bee was absent. That had Lila worried. Normally, she wished her sister would take on fewer volunteer duties because she was on track to let her job consume her life just like it had their father's.

All of them had lived the law enforcement life, rearranging their schedules and dinner conversations based on what happened in the Horizon PD. Lila had carved out some distance and was better for it. She wanted the same for every other Shepard now that her father had officially retired.

TJ worked as many hours as Bee did, but he also had his mission to serve on the statewide association for K9 officers.

And now, he had Summer to help him clock out. Lila was less worried about TJ giving everything to the Horizon PD at this point.

If Bee had found a hobby, great, but it wasn't like her not to show up for something like this.

Summer was her best available source of information.

"Hey, Mom, could you do me a favor?" Lila asked before turning to face her mother. "Could you grab me a glass of lemonade?"

Her mother immediately set everything she was holding down on the table. "Absolutely. I saw the new chief headed that direction." She hurried away as if she had important business to carry out and had been waiting to seize her opening.

Lila was suspicious that the business was getting Trey and bringing him back to her table. She swung around to face Summer. "We don't have long before she returns with company."

Summer raised an eyebrow. The movement made the paw prints shift as well, and Lila was impressed with her own skill. It was a pleasure to paint something other than a droopy pirate moustache.

"Why? Is she trying to put you and the chief *together* together?" Summer's grimace made her opinion of that clear. "I haven't heard a single positive word about him from anyone."

Lila sighed as she wiped off her paintbrush. "Honestly, I'm not sure that would deter my mother. New in town. Handsome. Single. She'll be predisposed to be optimistic about his character. What's TJ saying about work?"

"Not much. I did see him talking to the chief before I came over. I wouldn't say the body language was friendly, but it wasn't overtly hostile, either." Summer stood from the folding chair and took the mirror Lila handed her to check her reflection. "This is really cute, Lila. You should take a page from the police department and put some photos up on your social media. Community outreach, you know."

Lila considered that for half a second before pulling out her phone. "TJ really did something by winning you over." She pulled Summer closer and snapped a selfie. Summer's grin sparkled along with the paw prints. Lila's new website made it easier to post photos, but so far, she'd focused on Horizon's attractions. Adding some people made so much sense. They were the best part of the town.

"Where is Bee tonight?" Summer asked, a worry line wrinkling her brow.

Lila shook her head. "I'm not sure. I texted her to let her know I made it back to town after visiting the Admiral this afternoon. Her response was a thumbs-up emoji." She pulled out her phone and checked for a missed call or text. When the chief had rolled up and Bee was still absent from the police booth, she'd called but Bee hadn't answered.

"My mother will be hunting details about how things are going at the police department, whether or not she manages to tow the chief back. You should go find TJ. See if he has any info." Giving Summer the chance to escape was the right thing to do, even if she wouldn't mind the company. She spotted her mother leading Trey through the crowd. They were headed right at her.

"What if I take your mother with me?" Summer

offered. She could clearly see the collision course as well. "If we're going to be grilled for information, TJ should have to be present as well, right?"

Lila pursed her lips as she studied the woman who would eventually be her sister-in-law, just as soon as Summer and TJ came to terms with the idea. She'd been prepared to sacrifice herself, but Summer's suggestion made much better sense. "I like this plan a lot, Summer. Let's see if we can pull it off."

They shook hands as her mother stopped in front of the table. "Look who I found!" Her mother's eyes were locked on their hands, so Lila and Summer hastily broke apart. "Trey, you remember Lila? She's my youngest. When you're ready, she can help you find a house to make into a home."

Her tone seemed to imply that Lila would help in some way other than negotiating a purchase price. Like picking out paint colors and hanging framed wedding photos on the wall.

Then her mother handed Trey one of the magnets, and Lila had to fight the urge to take it back.

Imagining her mother's reaction to such a move made it easy to bite her tongue.

"Kay, Officer Rodriguez was right here looking for you," Summer said before reaching out to take Lila's mother's hand. "They want a photo of the principal with all the school supplies they've collected tonight."

"Oh, but surely the elementary school prin..."

Her mother's words trailed off as Summer tugged her toward the police department booth. Lila wasn't sure how successful Summer's plan would be when Officer Rodriguez had no clue what she was talking about, but she'd been impressed more than once at how Summer worked things out.

"You didn't tell your mother about me tracking you down out at Blue Vista?" Trey asked as he studied her magnet closely.

Lila wanted to pick up a magnet to examine what he might be observing that she never intended to give away but managed to keep her hands busy putting the caps on her paints. "No, why would I?" She did plan to register her outrage with Bee, but her older sister had delayed that satisfaction by not showing up.

Trey glanced up and caught her watching the magnet he held. "I talked with Sam Pulaski today about renting the place next door to TJ. She wasn't excited about the prospect."

"I'm sure I can't imagine what kinds of stories have made it back to Sam to make her reluctant to add you as a neighbor." Lila swiped her hair behind one ear, mainly to have something to do with her own hands. "I guess she would like to avoid more involvement with *police business*, too." She straightened her brushes and wished for an overexcited kid to plop into her chair. Even a jaded teenage boy would get her out of this conversation. She'd happily paint another pirate moustache to make that happen.

"Asking you to leave the squad room is one tale of my bad behavior that I haven't heard repeated back to me yet. People have made it clear that I've insulted TJ somehow, but nothing about my treatment of you and how I rudely enforced entirely appropriate workplace guidelines," Trey murmured. "Does that mean you haven't added to my bad press in Horizon?"

Lila bit her lip as she considered arguing the point about the appropriateness of the rules as she would have with her father, but she remembered something more important. "Where is Bee? When I talked to her earlier today, she was fine. Normal. 'Normal' Bee would be here working this event, but she is conspicuously absent. I know you clouded up her sunny day somehow, and let me tell you, that is a mistake, Mr. Douglas."

His chin tipped up as if she'd landed a jab right there.

"Kick me out, that's fine, but you better stop making my sister doubt how good she is at her job." Lila realized she was millimeters from landing a jabby pointer finger right in the center of his chest and forced herself to take a step back.

Trey held up his hands in surrender. "We met. I wanted to discuss how good her reporting has been and ask for some help with a project. She seemed excited about it, so maybe she stayed behind to get a jump on it, but I did not ask her to do that. I swear I'm not Scrooge forcing Bee to work on Christmas Eve."

Confused, Lila asked, "Scrooge? Christmas Eve?" It was a weird analogy for South Carolina in August.

"I don't know. It seemed to fit, maybe because I have this feeling that, long after I'm gone, my name will become synonymous with bad behavior like his." He shrugged. "'Okay, kids, don't be a Mr. Douglas,' and it'll mean 'bossy jerk' or something. 'What happened to your new boyfriend, Sally?' 'Oh, he turned into a real Mr. Douglas.'"

The way he mimicked the conversation he imagined amused Lila. It was almost like he had real personality behind the badge.

"I don't even know who Belinda at the Daybreak Diner is," Trey continued, "but I have heard she is not a fan of mine."

Lila bit back a smile at his bewildered expression. "She is TJ's biggest fan. Anyone who threatens TJ better not run into Belinda in a dark alley."

Trey frowned. "Since I somehow threatened him without even knowing how, I'm much more powerful than I knew."

Her urge to reassure him was a surprise.

Blasting him for his bad behavior was one thing.

Disliking him for taking a job he had been offered and was fully qualified for did seem unfair.

Then he added, "Whether Bee is working on this new project or not tonight seems like police business. You don't get involved in *police business*." His tone seemed to imply that he didn't believe her.

If she was being fair, she might see his point. Since they'd met, she'd been buried in police business, but the overlap between the Horizon PD and her sister meant she was *involved*.

Lila leaned forward in her best effort to look mean and intimidate him. Since her nose reached the center of his chest, she wasn't certain it was effective. "When the business involves my sister, I will be the first in line to take care of it. Bee's good at her job. The Horizon Police Department would be lost without her. I will find you five different officers who will say the same thing."

The volume of her voice registered about the same time she noticed people staring.

She crossed her arms over her chest.

"I'm going to be hearing how I made Lila Shepard shout tomorrow, aren't I?" Trey asked, his lips curling slightly.

Embarrassed and reminded that she wasn't supposed to be arguing Bee's case anyway, Lila sniffed. "I'm sorry."

Instead of graciously accepting her grudging apology, he pointed. "You've got a…"

When he reached for her face, she froze. Trey cupped her chin with one hand and then traced his thumb over her cheekbone. The sensation of his skin sliding against hers made it hard to breathe.

In the very best way.

Eventually he eased back and held up his hand to show her gold paint on his thumb. “You had a smudge.”

Lila wrapped an arm around her abdomen to quell the butterflies. “Thank you.” She wanted to tell him he should have let her get the paint herself—then she wouldn’t know what his touch did to her—but the words caught in her throat.

Trey inhaled as if he was coming up for air. “I get defending your family. As an only child, it’s not something I’ve ever experienced, but I have envied it from the outside looking in. Closest thing I have is my team. Right now, that’s the Horizon PD, including your sister and your brother. Getting this job done well is my first priority. Bee has the skill to help me with a project, so I asked for her help. If she’s staying late to work on it, it’s because she’s dedicated to the job. I appreciate that. I understand it, too.”

Lila wasn’t sure what to do with his words. It was easier to be irritated with his high-handed ways when he wasn’t being so sensible about how awesome her sister was.

Trey cleared his throat. “Sam thought you could suggest a better rental option, a house with more space and fewer TJs to upset.” He dropped her magnet into the shirt pocket of his uniform and took a bite of the walking taco he was carrying. For some reason, she expected him to be dissatisfied with his food, but his happy sigh told her she was wrong. Since Mae and Jesse Gibson had the most popular food truck in town, she knew everything they served was good. The fact that Trey enjoyed it didn't serve as much of a character witness. Then he sipped his lemonade and his gusty exhalation of bliss almost made her smile.

"I can't help you." Lila needed to end this conversation before the ground under her feet got any slipperier. "I don't know of any houses for rent."

"So look at houses for sale," Rainey said as she marched up next to him. "The whole town would prefer a chief who was putting down roots here, Trey. What you need is a mortgage." She shook her head. "And considering how many complaints I've heard about you, you need all the help you can get making friends here. You and I could both use an upturn in your popularity."

Lila would have backed out of the conversation slowly, but she had no escape. She was hemmed in by Rainey on one side and her table on the other. What she needed was a face to paint, but her chair remained empty.

"Lila will help you," Rainey said and nodded her head firmly to get Lila to nod along.

Instead, Lila darted a glance at him to see that he was watching her closely.

"I'm sure the chief doesn't want me interfering with his business. If Island Manor doesn't work, try a place over in Seabrook." Lila knew she'd made an error as soon as the name of the next town over—and Horizon's biggest rival in sports, business and general reputation—slipped past her lips.

"Chief, you can go. Call Lila tomorrow. She'll have some houses to show you." Rainey patted his shoulder, and to his credit, Trey hesitated, but Lila heard her mother call him over to the police booth. He did glance back at her, his eyebrows raised, as if he was offering to stay to rescue her.

Since she had some business to discuss with Rainey herself, she decided this was working out perfectly. She still took a minute to watch Trey walk away. Seeing him join the rest of the officers working the police booth felt like something clicking in place. He fit in perfectly with them from this distance. It was easy to imagine him working other community events, shaking hands, talking with kids, even if Lila could tell he wasn't fully comfortable doing so.

Trey would work at it, do whatever it took to be good at the job. Somehow she knew that already.

Holding on to her dislike and general commitment to avenging her sister was harder than she expected.

Lila had to brace herself when Rainey stepped in front of her. "What's your deal? That was completely un-Lila-like. You aren't buying into all this gossip, are you? He asked Joe to empty the pool area at the Needlegrass, but it was after midnight. That is the only bit of gossip I've been able to confirm. You know he didn't take any job from TJ. I can't believe you aren't helping someone who has just moved to town, Lila."

Her judgment was unexpected. Hurt bloomed in the center of Lila's chest. "Maybe ask the chief why I would be disinclined to offer my help, Rainey."

Her eyes sharpened and locked on Lila's face. "Oh, he did something. What did he do?"

Lila waved a hand. "Doesn't matter. It's police business and I'm not involved."

And Rainey knew her. As one of her oldest friends in the world, Rainey should have asked herself if there was something else happening between Trey and Lila before she'd lectured Lila about acceptable behavior.

Rainey bit her lip. "So, whatever he did was work related." She huffed out a breath. "Okay, but as a personal favor to me, can't you help him get settled here? You know Horizon better than anyone else, and it's important to me that Trey finds his place. He's a good cop, Lila. He could be so good for Horizon. And then there's the fact that the half of the town who isn't whispering about him is eyeing me with suspicion, waiting to see if I've made a tragic error in bringing him here. Having your help—Horizon's top real estate agent and one of the Shepards— could help him and me, and get you a nice commission check if you can find the house he can't live without."

Her tone was the same one she used to campaign. Persuasive. Firm. Hard to argue with.

But her attempt to cut Lila out of one of the biggest pieces of real estate business the town could attract was too fresh in Lila's mind to make it that easy.

"*Now* I know Horizon better than anyone else..." Lila shook her head. "Either you didn't agree with that on Monday or you did but would choose to work with someone else anyway."

Rainey's eyebrows shot up. She had to be shocked. They had been friends as long as they'd been alive, the way cousins have no other choice but to be the best of friends and occasional enemies.

Lila didn't normally stand up for herself like this, but this opportunity was too important to let pass by.

"Is this about the Denis Group?" Rainey asked as she bent her head closer. "I explained that to you. That's business. This is a personal request from me to you."

Something about that reminded Lila of her conversation with Roberta Hale about being family. Family and friends who couldn't separate Horizon's best real estate agent, Lila, from the singing, dancing Shepard were a problem.

Rainey would only respect someone who negotiated the way she did. Her style wasn't a natural fit for Lila, but she would give it her best shot.

Lila matched her loud whisper. "I have a plan Monica Denis won't be able to match. Tell me right now that you'll only go ahead with me, and I'll offer to help Trey find a house to rent if he asks me." If her offer was lackluster enough, he could still be persuaded to try Seabrook.

Rainey narrowed her eyes. "Can you find the house that convinces Trey to settle down in Horizon?"

"If anyone can, it's me," Lila said. Whether it was possible or not, she knew the right answer. Then she offered Rainey her hand.

"Fine," Rainey said as she gripped her hand hard, "get him on board to *buy* here in Horizon, and I'll listen to your pitch." Lila tried to disentangle her hand because this wasn't much of a win. Rainey held on firmly. "Then together we'll figure out the best way to move forward on this deal."

Lila shook but held Rainey's hand. "My way will be to demand the exclusive listing for any lots or houses built in this new subdivision, Rainey. I don't care who builds it, but I'm not giving up the listing to any other agent." Not even Monica Denis of the Denis Group.

Rainey's eyes narrowed. "I heard Roberta decided to go with Monica Denis to list her house."

"Encouraging Monica Denis to spend more

time selling anything in Horizon would not be in my best interest." Lila smiled slowly. "Just like losing the new chief because he couldn't find a comfortable place to stay in town would not be in yours."

"This new ruthless side to you..." Rainey squeezed her hand before stepping back. "I like it."

Lila laughed as the rescue she'd been hoping for finally arrived. Four-year-old Luke Middleton scrambled up to sit next to her table. He was chanting something. She hoped he was saying "truck."

Before she settled down across from Luke, she turned to check on the police booth. TJ and Summer were tangled together while Lucy stretched out at their feet—the image of a perfect little family in front of the police department's We Serve banner. Officer Rodriguez was stacking up school supplies in the large bins next to the table while he laughed with her mother.

And Trey Douglas was watching her. When their eyes met, he raised his eyebrows. Lila interpreted that to mean "Everything okay?"

She nodded once. She had made a deal with Rainey, and it was a strong incentive to help the new chief.

Following the letter of the law in defiance had been one of her most successful maneuvers against her father's oversight. She could meet

Rainey's terms scrupulously while also keeping an eye on Trey Douglas. She would make sure he understood that Bee and TJ deserved respect and show him some houses around town. A couple of listings came to mind as she painted the outline of a dump truck on Luke's cheek.

She would check in with Bee to make sure that no revenge was required first, but in the course of their latest encounter, Lila had gotten the sneaking suspicion that Trey Douglas might actually be likable. That made him dangerous. If she liked him, this attraction would be impossible to fight. Losing that battle would only lead to more police business, more Horizon PD in every minute of her day. She'd spent a lifetime pushing back against the demands of her father's career, wedging herself in to get his time while struggling to get independence from the family business for herself. Volunteering to do more of that for the new police chief would be silly.

Wrapping up their business as quickly as possible was the only way to go.

CHAPTER TEN

THURSDAY AFTERNOON, Trey was wrapping up his initial meeting with the head of Horizon Shipyard's security team when his radio crackled to life. Since the three people showing him the security room—a dark space lined with monitors displaying camera feeds covering the sprawling complex—were all wearing similar radios, everyone reached for them at the same time.

"Chief, this is Dispatch. Over." Bee Shepard's professional voice was easy to place.

"Go ahead, Dispatch." Trey had told Bee to put any emergencies through on the radio, but he pulled his cell phone out to check for any missed calls.

And as expected, he'd missed a call from Rainey.

"The mayor would like you to answer her phone call at your earliest convenience. Over." It was easy to imagine a deadpan expression on Bee's face.

"Copy. Thank you for relaying the message, Dispatch. I will make it clear that the mayor should not waste department resources to make such a request. Over." Trey watched John McEntire, the man leading the shipyard's security team, stifle a smile and realized everyone in the room knew he was fighting a losing battle.

"Good luck with that, Chief. Over and out." He thought he could hear a smile in Bee's voice and amended the number of people who knew he had almost no chance of influencing Rainey's behavior to everyone in this room and most likely the entire police force, who would be listening to their conversation over the radio.

With police scanners, the audience could be even bigger than that.

Before he could apologize for the interruption, his phone rang. Trey inhaled slowly before he said, "One minute, please."

John McEntire waved a hand as if it was absolutely no problem.

"Hey, Rainey, is this an emergency? Can I call you back?" Trey asked.

"It's not an emergency. It wasn't when I called you this morning and you sent me to voicemail. Or around lunchtime when I tried again. Yes, you can call me back, but you better be prepared to tell me whatever is going on in the police department. By the time I tried to corner you in your office twenty minutes ago to demand information on this issue, you had gone out to the shipyard." Every word out of her mouth was clipped, as if her patience had been exhausted. Rainey never had a deep well of patience to begin with, so he knew he was pushing his luck.

Trey turned away from the security officers observing his conversation as he formulated an answer to Rainey's angry words.

"Okay," he drawled, "but I'm going to need more information on this 'issue' you're referring to. As far as I know, everything is business as usual."

"TJ. Bee. The frosty shoulder Lila was giving you yesterday. Ring any bells?" she fired back. "And why I had to negotiate a complete business deal to get her to agree to help you find a place in Horizon."

As he realized what this call was about, Trey rubbed his forehead. "Fine. I'll talk to you about it later." By that point, he would have a better defense in place to explain how he hadn't made any errors. He knew Rainey would not agree, so it better be a good one. "Right now, I am being briefed on the shipyard protocols."

There was a long pause.

"Fine. That is important. You aren't dodging me, as I expected, or you *were* but you won't be anymore. Lila is going to reach out to you today. Answer her phone call, Trey," Rainey said firmly. "At least go look at houses that are for sale, or I will hound you for answers regarding whatever is happening at the police station. You have my word on that."

Since Trey had zero doubts she meant what she said, he accepted that he was about to go house hunting with Lila Shepard.

And the instant lift to his spirits worried him. When he'd reluctantly abandoned her to Rainey's clutches the evening before, he was concerned that the slight improvement they'd managed in their brief encounter would be lost. What he could observe of Rainey's conversation with Lila had seemed tense, but they'd shaken hands at the end. It didn't surprise him that Rainey had gotten Lila's agreement before it was over. No one prevailed against Rainey forever.

"I will answer. Gotta go, Rainey." He ended the call and turned back to face the audience that was not even pretending not to have been eavesdropping. "Sorry about that."

John McEntire looked up from the phone he'd been studying. "No apology necessary. Rainey is a force known far and wide. When I retired from the Coast Guard, I had three different Blackwells show up at my door to recruit me for this position. Not exactly sure how she does it, but the mayor has a scary ability to make things happen."

Trey nodded, followed McEntire out to a crew-sized tactical UTV and slid into the passenger seat. He listened as McEntire pointed out the main areas of the shipyard, including three expansive buildings that housed a variety of shops for hull, machinery, paint and finishing. Three massive overhead cranes caught Trey's attention as they toured. McEntire outlined the security requirements in place due to the shipyard's repair contract with the US Navy. They were extensive, but McEntire rattled them off as if they were standard operating procedures, another boring day at the office.

His delivery convinced Trey that the security at the shipyard was solid.

This was another area of his job where Trey was out of his depth, but it was easy to see that the Horizon Shipyard security team was on top of the operation.

Of course they were. Rainey wouldn't have it any other way.

When they made it back to the administration building, Trey asked, "What's Rainey's actual involvement here at the shipyard?" It seemed helpful to know more about the politics of Horizon since he was knee deep in them now.

John McEntire shrugged. "She's a Blackwell, but I'm not sure how she connects to the Blackwells on the board. The shipyard was established about the same time as the town, but I don't know how the family branches." He motioned over his shoulder. "There's a plaque. Behind the reception desk. Want to read all about it?"

From that, Trey understood that John wasn't too interested in continuing his history lesson.

"No, that's enough to be getting on with," Trey said as he shook hands around the small circle. "Thank you for the brief. I didn't know my department was involved until I heard Dispatch discussing your video feed and unexpected traffic yesterday."

John propped his hands on his hips. "We don't shirk protocol, even though we know Lila Shepard is not a security threat. Seeing her drive by was a bright spot in an otherwise mundane shift, but it was a good exercise, a test that the system is working." John followed him to his SUV. "Horizon has a citywide disaster preparedness and safety meeting in January. You will hear some mumbling about it, but it's handy to have a chance to review our systems, make sure they're up-to-date. If you have suggestions before then on ways to improve our coordination, please let me know. Officially or when you run into me at the Sandlapper. I'm usually there on Saturday nights."

"Who coordinates this security review?" Trey was almost certain he knew the answer. It was something else that had been omitted from his list of duties.

McEntire paused in opening the office's front door. "Chief Shepard has led it for as long as I've been here. Guess that means you're up, Chief."

Trey nodded and made a mental note to add

this exciting development to his next conversation with Rainey.

"I wasn't too sure what to expect, stepping into an operation like this in a small place like Horizon," McEntire said, studying Trey closely. Trey understood that he was as much under observation as the shipyard's security in that moment. "Turns out, Tom Shepard built a strong security network. You can't throw a rock without hitting a law enforcement officer who knows and respects him, whether you're in Columbia or Charleston or points in between."

Trey wasn't certain how to respond to what he was reading as a warning.

"The easiest thing I had to learn when I moved into town was how to look out for my neighbors." McEntire crossed his arms over his chest.

Immediately, Trey understood that his reputation had arrived before his SUV that morning, but he wasn't sure which bit of gossip to defend himself against, so he slid into the driver's seat and slammed his door. As he started the engine, he lifted his hand through the open window and said, "Thank you for the tour."

McEntire nodded once. It wasn't warm or friendly but was assessing. "We'll have to work together." He didn't seem particularly pleased about it, either.

As Trey drove back down the long road to the shipyard's main gate, he wondered how many other things about his job he would learn along the way. Rainey hadn't covered how the shipyard tied into the town's police work. There were probably other holes.

Which meant there might be other people like John McEntire from whom he needed cooperation.

Trey wondered if the previous chief would be interested in filling in the holes Rainey had missed.

Since he was on such shaky ground with almost every Shepard he'd met, he decided to put the idea on the backburner. He was approaching peace with three of Tom Shepard's kids after his rookie mistake, but it wasn't going smoothly yet. He had no doubt that getting on the wrong side of the former chief would be a fatal error.

To further his attempts to map Horizon in his mind, Trey drove the roads that branched off from the main entrance to the shipyard. He discovered houses dotted here and there, but he imagined there was little activity for the Horizon PD except any calls coming from the shipyard itself. Having that in the neighborhood kept a lid on sketchy activity.

As he drove into Horizon, he hit his radio. "Chief to Dispatch."

Instead of Bee Shepard, her second-in-command, Helen Wheeler, answered, "Go ahead, Chief." Then he noticed he'd missed the afternoon shift change already. It was past quitting time.

"I'm signing out for the day, Dispatch. If anything urgent comes up, reach out. Over." He had always had trouble walking away from his desk at the end of the day, but something about the way this afternoon light hit made it seem simple enough to quit at quitting time.

"Copy, Chief. Over and out," Wheeler said.

Instead of pulling into his reserved spot in front of Town Hall, Trey continued down to the two-lane highway that meandered along the coast. Peekaboo views of the ocean made the drive to the Needlegrass Motor Lodge pleasant. It had been easy to get used to the way some of his worries floated out the window every day after his shift ended. Giving up this proximity to the water to move closer into town would be hard, even if it made sense.

Trey preferred to be close to work. He always had. It probably had a lot to do with how hard it was to clock out when the job remained unfinished. The task forces had been a mix of high-adrenaline action and tedious paperwork, and neither had been easy for him to ignore for any other reason than required rest.

Would Horizon give him the opportunity to find balance? He hadn't expected that or even desired it when Rainey approached him. Time to gaze at his belly button and listen to the waves crash didn't do much to keep Horizon safer, but he wondered if clearing his mind and unwinding could make him a better chief.

Why was this the first time he'd ever considered how he wanted his life outside of work to look?

When he moved closer to town, he'd have to enforce whatever new boundaries he wanted to put in place if he planned to have any time free from the Horizon police department.

Could he do that? Trey wasn't sure.

The image of Lila Shepard informing him she was happy to avoid police business flashed in his mind. He had a feeling her firm stance had been shaped by the countless times people had ignored the previous chief's work-life boundaries.

If Tom Shepard had even tried to draw the line.

Trey had made such a splash already in Horizon that he thought he might have what it took to protect his leisure time. The people of Horizon wouldn't like it, there would be gossip and he might never be able to get a complete order in any restaurant in town, but he could convince people not to call him when he was off the clock.

He parked his SUV in his usual spot next to the fenced area around the pool. It was only after dark, when the crowds returned from the beach, that the Needlegrass Motor Lodge became much less pleasant. In the late afternoon, the place had a hazy golden glow.

Then he saw Lila Shepard seated at one of the metal tables near the pool.

The way his adrenaline spiked in that instant was new. His heart rate kicked up, and everything in the background faded so that Lila was his focus. He would be able to describe all the details forever: her watchful eyes, the tentative smile, the way the collar of her bright green shirt settled across her collarbones and how her long white skirt fluttered in the breeze.

If she was here to discuss working with him, at least she wasn't dressed in the stiff suit from her professional head shot.

That set some of Trey's nerves at ease. This was the real Lila. He wasn't sure how he knew it from a wardrobe change, but he could feel the warmth that broke through when she had given the kids in her face-painting booth a genuine smile and the snapping irritation in her eyes reserved for him.

For some reason, it was important to him that he saw the real Lila. There, glowing in the warm afternoon sunshine, she was magnetic.

"I brought a peace offering," Lila said as she held up a cup, "and a contract. I want to be your real estate agent."

Her tone was pure business. Horizon's best real estate agent had arrived.

Trey moved to take the seat across from her. It didn't escape his notice that she'd chosen the same table and chairs he always did because they were situated with the best view of Needlegrass's private beach access. Tall grass framed the sandy path that led down to the beach. The water was out of view on the other side of the dune, but he could hear the waves and the birds.

He picked up the plastic cup and ice rattled inside. He cautiously took a sip to find it was more of the lemonade that had changed his ranking of favorite drinks forever at the back-to-school night. "Okay, where did you get this?"

Lila laughed. "Are you sure you can handle that information, Mr. Police Chief? Once you know where, you will be fighting the battle every day not to have more."

Trey sipped again as he considered her question. He hadn't paid much attention to the food truck at the back-to-school drive. There were too many eyes on him, and blending in with the crowd had been his priority. He'd made his choice because the line in front of that particular truck was long, and after he'd taken a sip, nothing else mattered.

"Good point. Keep it a secret, please." As he put the cup back down, a true test of his willpower, he said, "When I want more, I'll have to track you down. Seems like a win-win solution."

Her eyebrows shot up at that.

Trey understood. He was just as surprised as she was that he was flirting with her.

But it felt good.

"Did Rainey come after you today?" Trey asked to get them back on track.

Lila licked her lips. "We had a conversation last night where we negotiated terms favorable to both sides."

His curiosity raised its head. He wanted to know what terms Lila had managed to wrest from Rainey in exchange for agreeing to help him. The fact that Lila was too stunning for words in that warm sunshine probably damaged his ability to reason, but hearing her say she'd stood up against Rainey and come out with concessions was impressive. Finding anyone who could win favorable terms with Rainey was remarkable.

"I am the best one to help you find the perfect place in Horizon, and I am happy to do so, as long as you'll consider buying. That's what Rainey expects, and I know we can find a place you will love." Lila bent down to pull out a folder from her bag. The tote was long and flat with a riotous bouquet of multicolored tulips on the side. The folder featured the same headshot from the for sale signs and the billboard on the front. "I've got a standard contract that says I will be your exclusive agent for sixty days. After that, if we're still house hunting, we can decide whether to continue together or not. This lists my commission rate and how to end the contract earlier if you decide. But the most important piece is notifying you that, because of the size of Horizon's real estate market, I often act as a dual agent, meaning I represent the buyer and the seller." She shrugged as if it was just the way things were.

"How do you proceed in that situation? The seller wants the highest price, and the buyer wants the lowest." Trey scanned the first page of the contract before flipping to the last page to sign. Her bright pink pen wrote smoothly with bold, black ink.

"You didn't read the whole thing? That seems…" Lila tilted her head to the side as she chose her words. "Incautious."

Trey smiled. "Incautious? Good way to say foolish. Silly. A bad idea."

Lila immediately nodded. "I wouldn't think I'd need to tell a law enforcement officer about bad actors who might take advantage of a decision like that."

"I guess there's a first time for everything, but I trust my gut. It's telling me that you're trustworthy." And if his gut didn't offer its opinion, Trey could ask anyone in town about Lila's character and receive glowing reviews. She was a Shepard, after all.

She leaned back in her chair. "Well, I appreciate you asking how I handle the potential conflict of representing the buyer and the seller on a sale. A lot of people accuse me of always choosing the seller, the higher price, and my commission. You're right about the problem, but there is always a good compromise."

Trey understood what it felt like to be instantly judged guilty of something that went contrary to his character. Lila's example was different from his experience with DEA Special Agent Dennis Browning, but he imagined she faced it over and over.

"There's always a *good* compromise?" Trey asked uncertainly. He didn't know real estate at all, but he'd been in some places where every compromise was a bad outcome. Sometimes, the least bad was the only winner.

She nodded firmly. "Always. For my business, fairness makes a difference. Doing the right thing will mean I'm building my career the right way." She shook her head. "I swear, if you didn't hear those words in my father's voice, it's only because you haven't been around Horizon long enough. Even though he meant police work, I have it embedded in my brain."

Warmth spread in his chest at how rueful and exasperated and still appreciative of her father Lila was. That was the kind of family the Shepards were: they might cause each other problems from time to time but no one could doubt they cared for each other.

The values Tom Shepard encouraged in his police officers ran deep in his kids.

He didn't realize he was smiling at her until she

added, “It’s okay to laugh. Being the odd Shepard out comes with some baggage. I wish I was business savvy enough to always choose myself and my commission first, but the fact that I’m not, that I’m still trying to do the right thing for everyone…” Lila seemed to realize she was gesturing broadly with her hands and dropped them to her lap. “Well, I’m not sure it’s good for maintaining my spot as the leading real estate agent in Horizon, but as a Shepard, it’s my only choice.”

Trey wasn’t sure which of the multiple crumbs she’d dropped he wanted to pick up first.

Then she huffed out a breath. “That was a lot, wasn’t it? You probably wish you’d hesitated a few minutes before signing.”

“No way. You’re the best agent in town. Rainey is always right in a way that’s annoying, but I trust her opinion. I prefer to work with the best, but I like it even better when they say things that I understand.” Trey ignored the alarm bells sounding in his head at being so open about how he viewed her. Holding his cards close to his chest had always been his preferred position with new places and people, but something about how honest she had been made him want to try something new. “I agree. Doing the right thing means you’re building your career the right way. That strikes me as very business savvy.”

Their eyes caught and held long enough that the silence became awkward.

"Even if the tale of enforcing the curfew and rules around the pool after midnight or at the morning shift change doesn't earn me friends in my new town, I have to do the right thing," he murmured.

Because he was watching so closely, he could see the minute Lila fought the urge to roll her eyes. Amusement bubbled inside but he managed to maintain a serious expression.

"You do love a rule, don't you?" she asked, but her lips were twitching so he counted that a win.

"Not when it puts me at odds with my officers," Trey said slowly. Was he really going to say this? "Or the most beautiful woman I've met in a long time."

Yeah, he said it.

Her audible gulp would have made him laugh if he hadn't been contemplating making a run for the sea at that moment.

He rubbed his forehead. "Sorry. I just signed a contract. Flirting with my agent is probably against the rules, right?"

Lila slowly shook her head. "I might have misjudged you. I thought you were a bossy autocrat on a power trip Monday morning."

Trey rubbed the center of his chest. "Ow. That stings." He shrugged. "But I can see how that happened. Bossy is fair."

"But power trip isn't." She sighed. "Yeah. Sometimes his commitment to the police department's mission looked the same way on my father. I should have known better."

Their eyes caught and everything else in the world faded for Trey.

He understood Lila. She'd made her judgment based on a lifetime of other moments of *police business*, the rules, the sacrifices officers made to serve and how they impacted their time outside of the job.

And why she wanted a whole lot less of that now.

"Okay, the first rule I have for our agreement is for you to tell me, your agent, what kind of house you're looking for. Number of bedrooms. Bocce ball court in the backyard. Whatever it is that you have your heart set on." Lila picked up her bright pink pen and flipped open her notebook.

"Not the budget? Seems that's the easy question." Practical concerns should guide his decisions, right? He needed to consider his investment and the resale value more than what his heart wanted.

Lila pursed her lips. "Well, cost is a factor, sure, but I've always thought that a price range can be filled with a million different possibilities. Seems to me that if you know what you want, what will make you happy, we start there and find it in your price range."

Trey traced the circle of condensation left from his lemonade. "Interesting philosophy. You think everyone can find their dream home?" She wanted him to lead with his heart and trust that everything would fall into place. He couldn't imagine anything scarier.

Lila twiddled with her pen for a second. "I want to believe that, so that's where I start." She met his stare. "Does that make any sense to you?"

She didn't glance away as he turned her words over in his head. "I think so. Whether it's true or not, that's how you want things to be, so that's how you're going to live your life."

She winced as if she wished it was different.

It seemed pretty risky to him, putting the dream out front that way instead of protecting it, but it fit Lila.

She was brave. Could he ever be that brave?

He leaned forward to brace his elbows on his knees, closing the distance between them but not nearly enough. "I like it. Whether you're right or you're wrong isn't in your control, but if you don't go after the dream, you'll never reach it."

She blinked as if just realizing how long their gazes had been locked. "Tell me about your dream home."

When the spell was broken, Trey sat up straight. Something about her made him want to give it a try, this dream thing, but he didn't know where to start. "I've lived on army bases all over. I've chosen apartments as an adult based on proximity to work. This time..." He sighed. "I don't know the style or the number of rooms, but I want it to feel like home."

He knew it wasn't much to go on, but Lila nodded as if she completely understood him.

There was something about her that made him think she might.

"I know that it's less about how it looks than how it feels anyway. We can find you the basics, the number of bedrooms and bathrooms, a garage, a chef's kitchen, whatever, but you won't be happy until it fits you. Why don't we start with a few houses, different areas of town, and see what works and what doesn't. I'm not sure you will know what you want without seeing some of what you don't," Lila said as she pulled out her phone. "Are you free anytime this weekend? I'm not sure what your schedule is like, but I can work around it."

Trey pulled his own phone out. "You have an open house on Saturday. Should we try for Friday after my shift is over instead?"

Her mouth dropped open and he realized he had confessed to stalking her web page without intending to. "After Joe Morgan invited me to leave the motel at my earliest convenience, I decided to do a web search for a new place to rent. Your ad popped up so I visited your website." He coughed to clear the knot of nerves choking him. "I guess your calendar stuck with me."

A small vertical line wrinkled Lila's brow. "And?"

Trey could think of a collection of different responses to the question. Many of them led to danger. "And what?"

"What did you think of my website?" Lila asked as she brushed her hair over one shoulder. "I don't often have an opportunity to get feedback from new visitors."

No alarm bells sounded, but they had to be imminent. Trey stared in the direction of the waves for a minute. "It's good. Informative."

Lila nodded.

"The photo there? Of you and your dog?" Trey should have stopped. He'd been in the safe zone, but he'd gone one step further. "I like it. It's more you than the one on your billboard." He tapped the folder on the table between them.

"More me." She sighed. "Less business is more me." Her shoulders slumped, and he realized he'd said something he hadn't intended or Lila thought he had. "Okay, Friday is better. The sooner we start, the sooner you'll be moving into the perfect place."

"Absolutely. You know Rainey will be hounding us until we get started," Trey said.

"Put my number in your phone," Lila said as she took the card out of the folder she'd given him, "and then text me so I have yours. I can send you links tonight, and I'll arrange appointments."

Trey stifled a smile as he followed her orders. There was a hint of her father that came through when she knew the way forward, and it was easy enough to fall in behind her.

Filling Chief Tom Shepard's shoes felt like such a big job because the man inspired confidence and respect. Lila was doing the same thing in her own way.

Clearly satisfied that she'd handled all the business on the agenda, Lila stood and waved at the view from the pool area. "It may be hard to leave this behind."

Hearing her echo his thoughts as he drove in removed any doubt that Lila was the right person to help him find his first house. Spending more time alone with her was going to be tricky, though. He was drawn to her, but every time he talked to her, she made it clear that she was planted deeply here and that police business had run its course for her life.

His roots were only going to be deep enough to get his life on track.

And the job was as much a part of him as it was Tom Shepard.

Trey had the feeling that if the suspicions about his involvement with the bribery scheme in Columbia made it to Horizon, every bad opinion currently circulating through town would be confirmed. Lila had her own reasons for keeping him at a distance at this point. If she bought into the gossip from Columbia…

Yeah, it would be safer to maintain some distance. Absorbing more unfair judgment from Lila on top of everything he'd lost already might be the final straw.

He might need to examine why her good opinion was so important.

But not right now.

"If you can keep an eye out for a solid investment property, that would be a good place to start," Trey said slowly, finding his way carefully as he went. "A property that may need cosmetic improvement that I can do over time and turn a profit when I sell. That seems smart."

"So this isn't your dream home, but an investment." Lila frowned. "We better not tell Rainey that part."

He couldn't read her opinion of that, but she didn't press him for more details.

As she slung a bag over her shoulder, Lila said, "I promised I would stay out of whatever is going on at the police department…"

Trey braced himself. "You promised who?" She'd firmly stated her opinion of police business often enough, but this sounded different. Like she'd offered to wade into police business on behalf of someone else.

He remembered her suspicions that he'd saddled Bee with extra work the night before.

Lila ignored his question. "As long as Bee and TJ are okay, we're okay." She straightened her shoulders. Then she added, "Chief."

He nodded. "You will go to battle for them because they're family. I'll do the same because they're my responsibility, my team." He shrugged. "Sometimes that means enforcing what seem like unimportant rules in order to get my officers out on patrol ASAP."

Trey fought the urge to fidget as Lila considered that. "Fine. No hard feelings. I guess we're on the same team now?"

That was a generous interpretation, but he liked it.

Lila's small smile matched his as she turned away, the sea breeze stirring her hair and long skirt as she marched to her car. Trey watched her back out of the parking spot closest to the pool area and drive away.

He was not surprised to see that Lila's speed and use of the turn signal were all correct. Tom Shepard had been a strict but fair driving instructor, no doubt.

Then she rolled through the stop sign onto the deserted two-lane road with a jaunty beep of her horn to tell him she knew he was watching her and drove away.

Trey shook his head as he sat back down in the chair to watch the sun set.

Lila knew the rules and thought about when

she wanted to break them. He could imagine her doing so a thousand different times to tweak her father for his oversight. She might be trouble, but she would never be boring.

He'd have to fight this attraction or end up hurting them both. He was only in Horizon temporarily, while Lila's roots ran deep. As much as he needed to keep his distance because of that, she had taken some of the afternoon glow with her when she left.

But if his days at the Needlegrass were coming to a close, he would soak up as much of the peace as he could while he considered Lila's parting words.

He'd been focused on establishing his command that first morning, and he'd overshot the mark. Add to that his missteps with Joe Morgan and Sam Pulaski and whatever he'd done to upset Belinda at the Daybreak Diner, and he'd created a real tangle that needed to be straightened out.

He stretched his legs out and crossed them at the ankles as he mentally listed ways to get started. It wasn't going to be easy, but he knew his new real estate agent would have an opinion on what came first.

Getting her advice and looking at houses to appease Rainey would be good. Anything more would be a problem.

CHAPTER ELEVEN

On Friday morning, Lila was chair dancing to her favorite playlist as she finished entering the details on the offer the Powells were making on the last available two-bedroom condo in Bay View Tower. Being able to present an offer on the final unit felt good. It wasn't technically an over-fifty-five community, but the amenities had won the Powells over, and now Lila wished there were ten more units to sell because she'd found a winning angle.

She'd reached out to the couple after their daughter had mentioned to Bee that they were moving to South Carolina to be closer to her family. Thanks to Horizon's information network, every branch of which ran through Bee at one point or another, Lila had helped them find a better solution than the retirement community they were considering in Charleston.

"The price is much better than they would have gotten in Charleston," Lila muttered. She hadn't known anything about retirement communities before she'd approached the Powells, but she could easily imagine networking through their friends and pursuing the same advertising opportunities the places in Charleston used. Finding new ways to reach clients was exciting.

Now that Bay View Tower was fully sold, she was going to have to scramble to find a new way to bring in business, unless Rainey's development took shape.

Especially since Monica Denis appeared to be targeting Horizon for her own expansion.

It was time to move to the next step of the plan.

"Trey is signed on to look at houses, so it's time to tackle Rainey." Lila picked up her phone to text.

Are we on for coffee this afternoon?

Lila clicked through Horizon's listings as she waited for Rainey's response. When she realized she was trying to imagine Trey making himself at home in each one, with too much concentration on how his handsome face would reflect his happiness, she sighed.

Lila was uncomfortable with how often he was on her mind.

At least the boring suit she'd chosen for the day would help set the right tone with Trey. Their house-hunting process would be efficient, professional and leave very little room for any emotional development.

If she could think of him less frequently after it was over, that would be great.

Rainey's answering text dinged.

Of course we are.

It was easy to imagine Rainey's confused frown along with her answer. Why would Lila be asking? They had coffee breaks every day.

I have a pitch for you to review. Any time available after?

Lila hit Send and then straightened the papers on her desk.

Rainey's answer was immediate.

Before is better. Your office at 1:00.

Lila responded with a thumbs-up and felt a surge of anticipation. "Duke, this is my day. The sun is out. I added one to my win column," Lila said to the elderly Great Dane stretched out on the plushest dog bed she could find in size Enormous. It was velvet and bright purple and perfectly fit her aesthetic and his, so the fact that it cost more than any other piece of furniture she owned didn't matter much. That dog bed made them both happy, and Lila was committed to always choosing happiness.

Everything in her small office fit her perfectly. The inexpensive knockoffs of expensive reproduction chairs were a nod to the history of the building, but the lion heads carved in the arms of each were pure Lila.

Duke stood to begin a lazy stretch as her mother breezed through the door. She bent to speak to Duke, dropped a small white paper bag in front of Lila and then picked up three different items on Lila's desk and rearranged them to her satisfaction.

"Hi, Mom, make yourself at home." Lila wasn't certain why her mother had dropped by, but it was likely related to the fact that no one had given her any details about what was happening with TJ and Bee at the police station.

Summer's maneuver the evening before had been a complete success.

So far, Bee and TJ had held firm.

It was critical that Lila avoid being the weakest link.

"I went into the diner to get your father a slice of coconut pie, and Belinda insisted I take some cookies to go. I have bags for TJ and Bee in the car." Her mother peered out the window at the street, but the sidewalk was almost empty.

Lila snatched the bag and yanked it open to find one of the chocolate chunk cookies that the diner always had on hand inside. Her beautiful day kept getting better.

When Lila finished the first bite, her mother was rearranging items on the bookshelf again and humming happily to herself.

Distracted by her sweet treat, Lila couldn't tell exactly what her mother had done, but the shelves made more sense after she was finished.

Her decorating style was "what I like." She made purchases and then she put them in places. That was all.

Her mother liked "vignettes" and would rearrange all of Lila's decorative bits and bobs every time she visited. It was hard to argue with success. Her mother finally settled in a chair and clasped her hands together demurely, so Lila was immediately on alert.

"Been a minute since it was just the two of us," her mother said brightly.

The menace in the air grew. Her mother was getting ready to pounce.

"Other than the time you spent helping me in my booth on Wednesday night?" Lila asked as she stretched contentedly back in her chair. "It was the two of us then *before* you towed the new police chief over."

"Summer was there, too." Her mother ignored the rest of Lila's point. She'd gotten really good at skipping over pieces of the conversation she had no need of. "Want to tell me what's going on with TJ and Bee yet?" Her mother's eyes were sharp. She was prepared to pick up all the clues, verbal and nonverbal.

Lila tipped her head back to stare at the ceiling,

aware that she had no one to blame but herself for being in this vulnerable spot.

"In this life, I have learned that if I am patient, the right opportunity comes along. Besides, it was nice to see you and Summer conspiring together. She's the perfect fit for all of us," her mother said airily. "At least ninety percent of working with teenagers for years has boiled down to patience. My stores are not infinite, but they had plenty of opportunity for growth as the wife of this town's police chief."

Since Lila had had a front-row seat to all the demands made on Chief Tom Shepard's wife, she understood what her mother meant.

Lila took that as a gentle warning that no one was going to defeat her mother here.

"TJ and Bee are having trouble with the new chief, but these are the bumps that come along with the changeover. That's all." Lila thought that was a reasonable answer.

And after her conversation with Trey on Wednesday night, she had started to believe he was catching on to his mistake. Bee had finally texted her as she was packing up her face paints to say that she'd gotten involved in a project and lost track of time. There had been some words about a map and data points—words Lila was familiar with, but she had no idea what they meant when strung together in that particular order.

Not that it was important.

Bee had sounded like herself again. Losing herself in a project was normal, and doing so at work suggested that some of her fears about how much she deserved her position had faded.

If Trey could straighten out his thinking regarding Bee and TJ, that would remove one of the barriers that Lila had retreated behind in her head. What were they barriers to? That question, she refused to look at too closely.

He was still chief of police, and so he was still not the guy for Lila, even if his handsome face was hard to ignore. Her mother had made life as the chief's wife work, but choosing that, knowing what it entailed, made no sense to Lila.

Her mother narrowed her eyes. "No reason we couldn't discuss work issues over dinner. Your father would have stern but encouraging words about working with new leaders."

It was impossible to argue with that, so Lila shrugged.

Which made her mother raise an eyebrow. She didn't normally accept wordless answers.

Then she crossed her legs slowly and Lila knew the conversation was not over.

"I did hear a most interesting tidbit at the diner when I was in there to pick up the pie. Belinda told me she heard that the new chief isn't high on TJ or Lucy. I couldn't see how that would be true." She shook her head. "Doubting TJ is a big mistake as far as Belinda is concerned, so the chief is not making any friends in town with behavior like that. Belinda said that she deliberately 'forgot' to put ketchup in for his fries." Her mother pursed her lips. "But your father wasn't so big on K9 officers to start with, either, so why keep that conversation away from him?"

She was right about that, but explaining Trey's misstep with Bee would be harder for her mother to brush off.

If Trey was going to turn things around, there was no reason to give her mother the story.

Today, Lila wanted to give him the chance to do so.

"Whatever Belinda's hearing sounds like police business," Lila said as she raised her hands. "I stay out of police business. You know that."

Her mother snorted. "Right. I remember a shouting match with your father where you informed him that if the police couldn't stay out of your personal life, you'd make sure none of your personal life involved the police."

Lila closed her eyes. "How did that work out for me?" The threat had been weak while she'd been at college, but when she'd moved back to Horizon, it had been nearly impossible to keep.

Her mother sighed. "It was a lot, wasn't it? Growing up a Shepard?"

"It really was," Lila agreed. His retirement was the chance they all deserved to get to know him outside of the job. It was also an opportunity to redefine being a Shepard in Horizon, even if she was the only Shepard interested in changing that definition. There was a new chief to shoulder all the headaches.

She didn't have any obligation to worry about police station problems anymore.

"You were quiet at dinner. You were quiet at the back-to-school night, which I thought was a success for the kids and for your face-painting booth. You were quiet with the new police chief who just moved in, a potential client for the town's best real estate agent. You should have been pitching your services. It's only the two of us here today, so there's no need to be quiet." Her mother narrowed her eyes. "How is business?"

Lila shook her head. "How do you do that?" The Shepard kids had never stood a chance of keeping a secret. Ever.

Her mother's smug grin made Lila laugh. "I am your mother. Besides that, the process of elimination helps. Other than whatever it is that Bee and TJ have going on at work, your family is all good. Duke here is happy and healthy. You could be sad about your single status but only if you'd had a complete personality change, so it better not be that." She held up her hands. "That leaves business. Plus, I saw the for sale sign on Roberta Hale's house last night on the way home, and it isn't yours."

Lila closed her laptop and tried to decide if she was happy for the change of topic.

"That suit is beautiful," her mother added, "but it's not you. Too..." Her mother paused to evaluate the right word. "Dull. It's too dull."

Lila winced, but it was hard to argue with the description. The heels she'd paired with it were worse. They were sensible, but they also pinched. And the jacket was too tight across her arms, so she removed it and slung it across the back of her chair.

How could she explain her concerns over her business without making the issue bigger than it needed to be for her mother? She didn't want her mother trying to solve the problem.

Lila needed to find her own solution. Having a different Shepard rush in to save the day would confirm her own fears about how well she did her job.

"I can't expect to win every single listing I go after," Lila said slowly. "That doesn't mean I like to lose." That part was easy to express.

Her mother settled back in her chair.

As if she was saying she had all day, so if it took another few rounds to get to the truth, she could wait.

This was how both of her parents had gotten to Lila. Persistence and patience.

"I gave Roberta good advice, but she decided to go with an agent who told her what she wanted to hear." Lila rubbed her forehead. "An agent from out of town, who she didn't know at all—especially not well enough to talk about how the agent used to sing and dance as a little girl."

Her mother nodded.

Which wasn't exactly a satisfying response.

"And it doesn't help that you know this agent already, I bet," her mother added.

Surprised, Lila raised her eyebrows. How did her mother know that part?

"I got curious, so I looked her up. Her bio on the brokerage firm website listed the University of Charleston as her alma mater. You had to have been there at the same time," her mother said as if it was only reasonable. She had always been good with internet searches. "I tried to verify the year she graduated, but I couldn't do it, so this was a guess. Educated but not certain."

Lila shrugged again. It was a testament to her mother's concern and interest in keeping the conversation alive that she didn't immediately tell Lila to use words instead of her shoulders in her best principal's voice.

Her mother leaned forward. "You know Horizon, Lila. Roberta chose the wrong agent. That's all."

"Well," Lila said slowly, "Rainey has some doubts about that. She was ready to approach Monica Denis to put together a huge development deal because of her connection to the Denis

Group. She wanted to gather information on Monica from me, but it never occurred to her that I could be the real estate agent she needed."

Her mother blinked as if that had caught her off guard.

Getting all of it off her chest was a relief, even if she'd never intended to do it. Her parents were both good at being in the right place whenever she decided to come clean with whatever was bothering her.

"So." Lila braced her hands on her desk. "I took a page from your book and did some research. I found the perfect land for development and talked to the current owner, who happens to be some kind of Shepard cousin, and today I'm going to show Rainey how this works best for Horizon." She waved a hand at her suit. "I may not be as fabulous as Rainey, but I'm hoping that speaking her language and wearing her uniform will convince her to see me as real estate Lila, not singing, dancing Lila."

Then she pointed at the clock. "She'll be showing up any minute."

"Fine. You need to work. I hear you." Her mother stood reluctantly. "I am not satisfied with this conversation, Lila Elaine. I haven't forgotten that three of my children are trying to keep something from their parents regarding all the gossip about the new police chief and his inability to get along with anyone. This conversation is to be continued. How about that?"

Lila stood to hug her mother and open the door for her.

"How about that?" was always her mother's way of saying that she knew there was more going on than one of her kids wanted to admit but she would wait patiently for an undetermined time before returning to the issue with renewed energy.

Because she would have the answer, sooner or later.

"Love you, Mom, but you're going to have to go home now and see what Dad has torn up today," Lila said as she squeezed her mother tightly. Even if it might have been nice to keep a few secrets, it was hard to argue how much her mother meant.

There was never any doubt about her support.

"Wednesday was so nice. That fishing field trip made us both happier. Your father was out of the house, and I had some quiet time. I'm thinking of instituting an hour-long recess where he has to leave the house every day," her mother muttered. "On Tuesday, he decided to reorganize the pantry." The way she held Lila's stare communicated exactly how much she had enjoyed it. "I may never find my paprika again."

Lila stifled her smile as she patted her mother's shoulder. "School is starting soon. You'll be back in your office next week. I will buy you new paprika and bring it over."

Her mother nodded slowly. "And Monica Denis is just an agent. You are creative, good at your job and part of this town. I put all my money on you in this horse race. Rainey nearly made a mistake, but you'll save her from it."

Having her mother's confidence had never been one of Lila's worries, but it was nice to hear her say it aloud.

"I absolutely will," Lila said confidently.

"We didn't even get to your thoughts on the new single police chief himself. I was reminded again of how handsome he is. Did the two of you talk at all and what about?" Her mother clutched her hands together under her chin. "That's what I need to know."

Lila crossed her arms over her chest. "You and I are the only Shepards speaking to him this week, Mom. Based on your gossip about Belinda, Trey Douglas may be having problems with most of Horizon, too. No way do I need a headache like that, never mind that he's also a police officer and I am not suited for life as a chief's wife."

Her mother's sly grin would have made Lila laugh if it had been aimed at anyone else. "Wife, you say?" Her tone made Lila shake her head. "I was thinking you could go to dinner or something. That's it."

Lila rolled her eyes. "Right."

With a quick glance at her watch, her mother said, "Leaving just when things get interesting.

When I left the house, your father was up on the roof—" she raised her hands to make air quotes "—checking the shingles."

Lila swallowed the smile that bubbled up at her mother's dry tone.

"What is he going to do about whatever he finds?" she asked.

Her mother shook her head. "I have no idea. People ask how I managed as the chief's wife for all these years, but I'll tell you, every bit of that depended on the man. He was worth waiting up for, worth fighting with people who didn't agree with his decisions and worth running interference with his children…who often belonged in that same group. He deserves to enjoy every minute now, even if that means he's up on the roof, I guess."

Her glum resignation was ruined by the sparkle in her eyes. The old chief's retirement might be as bumpy as the new chief's first few days, but they would work it out.

With a final hug and a kiss for Duke, her mother left, and Lila settled back at her desk to run through the papers she'd printed for her pitch. She was considering putting the gray straitjacket back on when Rainey marched into her office.

She was in mid-conversation, her cell held close to her mouth as she closed the door. "Listen, Joe, I know he ruffled your feathers, and you have every right to determine who stays at the Needlegrass, but I am asking for a favor here." Her eyes met Lila's as she said, "The chief is house hunting, so if you could give him some time—"

"How much time have I got left in this season, Rainey? And exactly what am I going to do with another favor from you? You already owe me for getting him in here," Joe Morgan interrupted. "The atmosphere around my establishment has taken a turn with your chief in residence."

Lila stepped over closer to the phone. "Hey, Joe, it's Lila. How are you doing?"

"Oh, can't complain," he said, even though he had just been complaining loudly. "How are you? How is your daddy doing with retirement? I hear things have been a little topsy-turvy over at Town Hall… What does he think about the chief's changes?"

Rainey frowned, so Lila hurried up to say, "Dad's doing good. He and the Admiral got some fishing in, and you know that will raise a man's spirits."

"Yessir, it will," Joe said, "not that I know about that kind of freedom. I have a business to run out here, you know." She and Rainey both nodded. "Don't suppose he'd consider running for office in Horizon in his free time?"

Lila and Rainey exchanged puzzled glances. There was really only one important office for Horizon and Rainey was already filling the role.

"He's having too much fun right now for a new

job, Joe. Listen, I'm helping the chief. We'll find the place he's looking for this weekend, but it will take some time to go through all the closing and everything. It would be a favor to Rainey and to *me* and to the chief if he didn't have to move twice." Lila paused. "Can you help us all out?"

His gusty sigh would have stirred the curtains if he'd been standing in Lila's office. "How can I say no? You two have put me in a real bad spot. It's lucky I like *you* so much, Lila. Fine. I won't pack his bags and leave them in the parking lot today. But don't you be surprised if I check in on how that house hunt is going."

Rainey smiled. "Thanks, Joe. I won't forget this."

"Thank Lila, Mayor." He was still muttering when she ended the call.

Lila returned to her seat, and Rainey greeted Duke next because he loved her with a single-minded adoration reflected in the pounding of his tail against Lila's desk. "Duke, my handsome boy." Rainey knelt down next to Duke's plush bed with a stream of silly chatter that thrilled Duke's soul.

All three of them were grinning when Rainey finally plopped down in a chair.

"That suit is…" Rainey wrinkled her nose. "Not you. You should give it to me."

Lila wanted to be offended, but the comment

was so typical of Rainey and their friendship that she let it go. It steadied her nerves, too.

Rainey pointed a finger. "You have Trey on board? He's house hunting?"

Lila should have expected that whatever plan she'd outlined in her head would be immediately hijacked by Rainey. Instead of stressing over that, Lila slid a stack of papers across her desk. "A copy of our signed contract is on top. We have plans to tour the first two houses tonight when the chief's shift ends."

Rainey nodded but didn't pick up the papers. "Good. It's important to me that he falls in love with Horizon, but it's more important to him, even if he doesn't know it. He needs this place. After a lifetime of moving, no ties except the job, he needs more, Lila. When he left Columbia, he was in a bad spot. Help me make sure he has a chance at something really good here."

"A bad spot? Why did he leave?" Lila asked before she could stop herself. It wasn't important, but she wanted to know.

"That's his story to tell," Rainey said slowly, "but the reason I wanted him here is because I know what kind of officer he is. Your dad is a hard man to replace, but Trey has the same commitment to the job and his officers. All we need to do is convince him to commit to Horizon."

Lila wanted to ask ten different questions, but Rainey's serious expression convinced her to nod her agreement. She was right anyway. Trey's history was his to share as little or as much of as he liked.

Besides that, she needed fewer reasons to think about him, not more.

"Okay, the next item on my agenda is..." Rainey huffed out a slow breath. "An apology. Even if Monica Denis's sign triggered the idea to develop a land deal with the Denis Group, I should have gone one step further to make sure this had as many ties to Horizon as possible. My goal is always to help my family, friends and neighbors, and you are all of the above. This was not any kind of judgment on your ability, Lila. Just me moving too quickly to get all the pieces in order."

Lila leaned back in her seat. This wasn't expected. Rainey didn't admit mistakes. She didn't have much practice at it because she was usually right on track.

"Well," Lila said slowly, "I appreciate that. I..." She shook her head. "It's provided some good experience. I had to get mad to get motivated, but this is something we can do, Rainey. I have the perfect spot, and I've already talked to the owners."

Rainey scooted forward in her seat. "Show me."

The surge of adrenaline was back. Following each loose thread to find the information she needed to build this pitch had been exciting, a rare new chapter for her life in Horizon.

Rainey and her neighbors would view her differently when this deal was successful, and Lila would be ready to take the next step in her career, whatever it was.

Helping Trey Douglas to find the perfect home in Horizon was a small price to pay for this exhilarating new direction.

Now all she had to do was remind herself not to get too distracted unraveling his secrets.

CHAPTER TWELVE

TREY CHECKED THE time on his laptop as Bee Shepard finished writing her notes about the changes they'd discussed on the mapped zones of Horizon. She'd made amazing progress over two days, and her first attempt was already a step ahead of what he'd imagined.

He'd almost made a colossal error by excluding her from the squad room briefings.

If he hadn't been eavesdropping on her conversation with Lila and needed a quick cover, how long would that error have continued? All signs pointed to forever. That was a sobering thought and made him wonder how many other errors he'd made that he'd never corrected.

"Do you have somewhere to be, Chief?" Bee asked as she closed her notebook.

Was that the first time she'd called him "Chief" and if so, what did it mean? Trey mentally replayed several different "sir" addresses and several more instances where she didn't address him at all.

Then he realized he was staring off into space

again. This distraction was new, and it was not a quality he wanted to encourage. Getting distracted on the job could have fatal consequences.

Unless he was safe behind his desk at the Horizon PD while one of his officers watched him struggle to get his head in the game.

Then it was just embarrassing.

"I made an appointment to look at some houses with Lila. I didn't want to keep her waiting, but I was locked in on your presentation, Shepard. Sorry if I appeared to be multitasking," Trey said. "You've made so much progress. Working after hours on this?"

Bee fiddled with her printouts. "I like the data. It's a fun project, but these are minor adjustments. Keeping it up going forward won't take a significant investment of work hours."

Trey realized she was bracing for criticism again. She'd expected a discussion about taking personal calls on work time when he'd handed her this task. Now she waited for him to tell her to either work less on the project or work more efficiently.

While he was sitting on the other side of the desk, quietly impressed with everything she'd already accomplished.

That was what his error at the first morning shift change had caused.

It was also a sign his leadership skills needed improvement.

"Thank you for the extra time and the hard work. You've accomplished something truly impressive in a short time," Trey said. "This map will help me."

Bee nodded but the frown wrinkling her brow suggested she wasn't sure what to make of his turn from bad boss to better boss.

She seemed uncertain as she stood. "I will return to the briefings next week, Chief. I used that time on this project, but we'll be back to business as usual on Monday." Her eyes met his and he hoped she intended it as a promise.

He wanted things at the police department to operate smoothly, so his officers had only service to Horizon to focus on.

Having her assistance drove home Rodriguez's point that he'd formed a habit of making bad decisions based on incomplete information.

Trey rubbed his forehead as the thought that he'd done the same thing in Columbia with nearly disastrous results popped up. There, he'd missed clues because he didn't want to see them. Here, he'd hunted for clues to support his hypothesis, a mistake every cop had to learn to avoid.

Bee Shepard was central to the operations of the Horizon Police Department, and she played her important part from Dispatch. Her ability to gather information, arrange it into full stories and disseminate it added up to so much more than he could see on the surface.

He had the suspicion that he'd learn the same thing about charming TJ Shepard.

And that raised the question of what he'd discover about Lila Shepard.

The anticipation that tingled across his skin at the reminder that she was on her way worried him.

Then he realized Bee's concern had transitioned to amusement because he was lost in his thoughts again.

"Enjoy your weekend, Shepard," Trey said as he stood to follow her out of his office.

"Good luck on the house hunt, Chief. Lila might have annoyed me daily by bursting into unexpected loud song for most of my teenage years, but you won't find anyone who understands matching buyers to their dream homes better than she does. She helped me find a fixer-upper with a slice of beach access, which I would have said was impossible on my salary." Bee must have realized who she was speaking to about her paltry salary and cleared her throat. "Have a good weekend, sir."

He hadn't seen much of Bee's smile since Monday morning, but she gave him one over her shoulder as she left.

And it was finally time to meet with Lila.

Trey waved at the officers on duty for the overnight shift and hurried through the lobby to look out the front doors' glass panes. He realized he was watching anxiously for Lila's arrival when Officer Rodriguez stepped up to join him. From their vantage point at the top of the stairs leading up from the sidewalk, they could see both directions of the street and across it into the Battery.

He wanted to be sure he saw Lila when she arrived. He'd offered to meet her at the first house, but she'd explained that touring the neighborhood to point out the selling points was part of her process.

And he was unreasonably excited to be spending time with her, so he was ready to embrace her process.

"What are we looking for, Chief?" Rodriguez asked. "Isn't it quitting time? Big plans for Friday night? If you're looking for entertainment tomorrow night, you should stop by the Sandlapper."

That reminded him of John McEntire mentioning the same thing. Maybe he should drop in. It sounded like another opportunity to get to know his neighbors, and live music and good food would ease some of the friction.

Rodriguez added, "Charlene has an outdoor stage, and a local band plays there every Saturday. There will be college kids, but they'll be easier to take when you aren't trying to sleep." His grin suggested that Rodriguez was getting more comfortable around Trey.

Trey wasn't sure that was a good thing. "Tonight I'm heading out to look at houses to please the mayor. Lila Shepard is picking me up."

Rodriguez almost clapped him on the shoulder but hesitated again and propped his hands on his duty belt. "Good! That's good. Lila helped my wife and me find the house we're in now."

He pulled out his phone and scrolled through photos until he offered it to Trey. Rodriguez, a pretty brunette who must be his wife and what Trey estimated to be a newborn baby girl wrapped in a pink blanket were posed in front of a ranch-style house with white siding and black shutters. It had some seventies flair, but someone had done some work to update it. Massive trees loomed behind the single-story house.

"We thought we wanted new construction. Low maintenance, you know? With a baby on the way, my wife was firm about having no renovations," Rodriguez said before shaking his head. "So Lila showed us a few of those and listened to our nitpicking before asking us to trust her. Then she showed us this house, built in 1973, which I would have said was one of the worst years for architecture. The list of things wrong with it was extensive, and we were horrified by her choice when we parked in front."

Trey crossed his arms over his chest to wait for the rest of the story because he was certain Lila's wrong had turned out to be very right in the end.

First, Rodriguez was still obviously positive on Lila as a real estate agent.

But there was also something about Lila that convinced Trey that she was right more often than she was wrong about these things.

All the Shepards he knew were giving him that impression, which reminded him of Rodriguez's advice about them.

"Then we stepped out into the backyard," Rodriguez said with a sigh, "and found this absolutely amazing tree house." He glanced at Trey. "It was like something out of a storybook, weathered but built by someone who made things to last. There's a door, a window with a flower box." He shook his head. "I had to climb inside immediately. Imagining my kids playing there was easy. Instant. I could see backyard grilling, and something about that yard brought everything into focus."

Trey studied Rodriguez's face as he spoke. Lila had managed to find what Officer Rodriguez and his wife had needed before they knew it themselves. She had a talent.

"And has all that come true?" Trey asked. He wasn't sure what kind of daydreams he'd ever have about a house, but he needed to know if reality matched the dream.

Rodriguez wagged his hand to show it was so-so. "Well, my daughter just turned four, so we have some time on the tree house yet, but I've had my dad come in to make sure everything is safe.

We have had barbecues back there, with nieces and nephews climbing in and out, and it's sweet to have that attraction, the thing they all look forward to exploring. I know those family gatherings are only going to get better."

That was a pretty powerful statement.

They were only going to get better.

It must be amazing to feel that way about a home.

How much sweeter would it be to feel that way about the life they would build in it?

"What about the house itself?" Trey asked as he watched Lila Shepard stop next to his SUV.

Since she wasn't in an actual parking spot, he had to reassess his estimation of how well Tom Shepard had enforced traffic laws with his kids again.

Rodriguez groaned. "A work in progress and about twice as expensive as you expect, but there's satisfaction in working slowly to transform something old into something better, a place that fits you perfectly. Going into it, we wanted simple. This has not been simple at all, but every day when I come home, I see the progress. My wife is happy. My daughter is happy. If I have to figure out how to remove textured ceilings and wood paneling as I go, it's worth it."

Trey's phone dinged. He pulled it out to read the text.

Parked out front. Hurry before the cops write me a ticket.

He raised his eyebrows before deciding she was poking fun at him. Teasing him, maybe.

"Are you handy, Chief? Got any carpentry skills I can put to good use?" Rodriguez grinned.

"None. Not much DIY experience at all. I've never had a house to experiment on and moved on so often it never occurred to me to get one. For this first one, I better find someplace ready to go," Trey said as he started to open the door.

"Or you could rope a friend in who has those skills." Rodriguez tilted his head to the side, and Trey wondered if that was an offer to help him when the time came. It was hard to call to mind any other friend or acquaintance who would assist with home repairs. "Electrical is the big one I've been putting off, but everything else I've attempted has resulted in only minor injuries and one panicked call to Boogie Howard for his expertise. I have learned it is never too late to start," Rodriguez said.

Trey absorbed that as he opened the door. He had no idea who Boogie Howard was, but it sounded like he was into home repairs. That was good information if he went through with this purchase.

But Rodriguez's assertion that it wasn't too late to start felt important.

He could find a place to make a home here in Horizon. It wasn't too late to figure out how to do that.

Why did that feel so big?

Lila beeped her horn, reminding him she was waiting.

Trey waved a hand and then trotted down the steps to Lila's SUV.

When he opened the door and slid inside, she said, "It was only a friendly honk, Officer. Please don't issue me two tickets, one for parking and the other for violating the noise ordinance."

Trey smiled as he buckled his seat belt. "You are fine on the noise at this hour of the day, but it is pretty bold to park on the yellow curb in front of the police station."

Lila held up one finger, as if she had an important point to make. "I never parked. I never left the vehicle, and I only stopped for loading and unloading passengers."

Trey turned to study her. Today Lila was wearing a gray business suit. It was very…presentable. Polished.

But it was like the change of clothes dulled some of her spark.

He really enjoyed her spark.

"Spend a lot of time finding loopholes growing up as the police chief's daughter?" he asked.

Lila's light laugh floated between them as she pulled away from the curb. "You have no idea,

Chief. Whenever you're raising your own kids, be prepared to argue the ins and outs of the law as if you were standing in front of a judge. When I was in college, I had a whole running conversation with my dad about surveillance and how it should not be allowed near college dorms."

Trey was distracted at the suggestion he'd have a family of his own and face the same problems Tom Shepard had someday. He'd never spent much time considering that, but he couldn't immediately dismiss it, either.

"Were you running a stolen goods ring or something?" Trey asked. "Surveillance is usually frowned on unless there's suspected illegal activity. Too expensive and crosses the line to harassment." Implementing it to keep watch on kids would be a serious overreach of authority. He wouldn't have believed that of Tom Shepard.

She shot him a glance as she came to a complete stop at an intersection, and he realized he had taken her too seriously. "It was unofficial surveillance. No illegal activity and no assigned officers, but his informants included almost every kid from Horizon who also attended the College of Charleston. They would tell their parents something, and it would always trickle back to the chief, usually faster than I could have confessed even if I'd wanted to."

Lila made the turn. "Not that there was all that much to confess. I was a model student." She squeezed his arm and waited for him to nod his understanding. Her teasing eyes invited him to join her joke. Apparently Lila Shepard had *not* been a model student.

Trey realized he needed to know more of her story.

"I should have gone to school farther from home. But Bee was there, and it..." She shrugged as she pulled into a short driveway. "I guess small-town Lila wasn't quite ready to make the leap to a bigger pond all alone. Bee could have given me a warning about how quickly the town grapevine works, but she was also doing all these Shepard-like things, volunteering for student action groups and earning academic honors. Meanwhile, I was pledging a sorority and then dropping out of it almost as soon as I paid the first dues."

Trey frowned. He hadn't fully considered the downsides to being the daughter of the town's revered police chief. TJ and Bee had made him think of all the advantages of being a Shepard in Horizon. Some of the respect and admiration their neighbors had for their father transferred to them without any effort, setting them one step ahead before they even started.

But it sounded like Lila had battled the flip side of that coin.

She had wanted freedom to be herself while the whole town watched her, wanting her to be like the other Shepards. Moving as often as he had growing up had given him the opportunity to reinvent himself over and over, to try new things at each place without a whole lot of people expecting him to be someone else.

"What made you drop out? I thought it was an achievement to get into a sorority?" he asked as he studied her face. He'd enlisted, and college might as well have been another world, but he enjoyed imagining a young Lila taking over her college campus.

He waited for her to answer while she removed sensible heels to slip on yellow sneakers. They did nothing for her professional outfit, but he liked seeing a touch of the bright Lila.

She shook her head. "Now, I almost wish I'd stuck it out. The advantages to my career would have been significant. That's what they told us anyway. But being pressured on every side to dress a certain way and socialize with a particular group of people and having demands on my time when I only wanted to be free to do what I wanted away from Horizon… It wasn't right for me then."

She had tried something new and then left it behind when it didn't fit her. He admired that. Moving to Horizon might be the first time he'd taken such a gamble on something new.

Before she opened the car door, Trey said, "It sounds like you made the right decision."

Lila slumped back against her seat. "You know,

I didn't understand what it would mean to hear someone else say that. Bee gave me some of the 'I told you so' after I dropped out because she was against my joining the sorority from the start. Since she's never had a day of trouble gathering people to her, she never saw the potential."

Trey smiled as Lila grimaced. Being an only child had some benefits. He didn't have any siblings who were always right to deal with.

"It makes sense to me to try new things, especially when you're young and you have an opportunity for a fresh start." Trey got out of the car and studied the facade of the house Lila had arranged for their first showing. This place was modern without being too sharp. There was absolutely no landscaping—no grass, no trees, nothing to suggest where any of that would go.

And that would be a problem for him, since he had no desire to discover his green thumb at this point.

"First impressions?" Lila asked as she moved to stand next to him.

Trey's immediate answer was that this was not the right place for him, but her hopeful expression stifled it. "Let's see the inside."

Watching her excitement as she hurried to let them inside made him glad he'd postponed the inevitable. As she demonstrated the features, Lila sparkled again. She didn't make any assumptions about what he would do or how he would fill the rooms, but she made sure he saw every single feature that had convinced her this could be the place for him. When she stepped outside, she said, "The only thing we can say about the backyard is that it's large and full of potential. To make it anything special, you'll need some vision." She turned to him. "Do you have a dream backyard in mind? Because you'll have the space for it here."

When she asked, Trey believed she wanted to hear the answer.

And it had been a long time since he'd felt that about anyone, let a woman who glowed like Lila Shepard.

Then he remembered his plan to set some distance between them.

Because he was leaving Horizon at some point and she wasn't.

That plan was failing spectacularly at this point.

"I don't have any daydreams about backyards." He shook his head and tried not to apologize as he watched her shoulders deflate. "The space here is great, but the amount of help I'd need to make it a comfortable place to live is…" He grimaced. "That sounds sad, like 'how is this guy even functioning' levels of sad."

Lila wrapped her hand around his arm and tugged him back inside the house where it was cooler than in the blazing sun without a tree in sight. "Talk to me about where you grew up. If you're nostalgic about the good ol' days, we can use that as inspiration."

Trey shoved his hands in his pockets and strolled around the echoing great room. Vaulted ceilings, no walls and hard flooring meant every step was loud and harsh. Was he going to answer this for her? *How* was he going to answer this for her?

"My dad was in the army, so I grew up in base housing all over the world. What you get there is…fine. Utilitarian. Vaguely 'American' in style, so that you have big appliances and the comforts of home, but nothing unique, either, because you are temporary. Right?" He turned to make sure she was following him, so she nodded. "And then I joined the army, and sometimes it was barracks, sometimes it was boxy apartments, but it was always about…temporary. Since I've been out, I've been focused on the job, so I chose places that were easy commutes. I've picked up a little furniture, photos and things, but the plans are still temporary. For this, to set up a whole house and make it fit me from a blank canvas…" He crossed his arms over his chest. "It's too overwhelming."

"Got it." Lila's eyes narrowed as she studied his face. Then she sighed. "We don't want that. Overwhelming is bad. You have enough to adjust to without adding the stress of all that on top."

Trey wasn't sure what he expected her reaction to be, but he couldn't discern any judgment in her answer. Lila understood what he was saying, and she wanted to help.

What a relief her acceptance was. He didn't feel any pressure to fit in. She was ready to work with him right where he was.

Then he remembered that planning to be in Horizon only long enough to get his career back on track meant this was also another temporary decision.

But he couldn't explain that to Lila, not without the risk of upsetting Rainey if she found out.

And his conversation with Rodriguez and Lila's questions about what home should be had him viewing this decision differently. Even if it was temporary, he wanted more than utilitarian this time.

"This place made some things clearer." Trey followed her back out to the car and watched her fasten her seat belt before she started the engine.

"Like what?" Lila asked as she carefully backed out of the driveway. "Because if you want new or modern, this may be the only choice on the market right now."

"I like landscaping." Trey thought understanding that about himself was a breakthrough. The tiny wrinkle on her forehead convinced him it wasn't much to go on. "Houses with curb appeal."

She glanced at him. "Most people do."

Her dry tone made him smile. "I meant, built in. No green thumb here."

She nodded as she navigated the stop sign. "What else?"

"More walls?" he said uncertainly. Something about the way that great room had amplified every single noise felt off. He didn't want to have this constant reminder of emptiness when he was home.

"Okay," she said firmly. "We're looking for cozy and warm, not sleek and open. I know where we need to go next."

As if his vague comments made perfect sense to her.

Which was a relief, because he didn't want to go into any philosophical explanations of empty rooms or loneliness or being new in town and not knowing anyone to prevent the loneliness by filling up the rooms with noise.

Trey tried to relax in his seat as Lila smoothly navigated these streets that he was still learning. She didn't hesitate, so it was easy to trust that she had a plan. He'd spent so long stepping up, leading teams, that it was a new sensation.

But that was par for the course in Horizon.

Learning a new kind of police work had gotten off to a bumpy start, but he was finding his way. Was Horizon going to teach him other new things, too? He believed the Shepards had life in this town figured out. They appeared to have family life perfected as he observed them from the outside.

Could spending more time with Lila show him what he needed to build a home?

And what would that mean to his plans to get back to the life he'd left behind?

CHAPTER THIRTEEN

As Lila parked in front of Roberta Hale's house for the second time that week, she was hyper-aware of Trey Douglas in the passenger seat. His legs were so long that his knees brushed the glove compartment each time she hit a bump in the road. His hands rested loosely on his thighs. He wasn't doing that annoying thing where he tried to apply an imaginary brake the way her father did when he was forced to ride shotgun.

His cologne or aftershave was light, but every now and then, she got a hint of something citrusy and fresh.

Why was she certain that this was going to be a turning point in their relationship? There was the slightly adversarial Lila and Trey before this house-hunting trip, and there was…whatever they were going to be now that she knew how Trey Douglas smelled.

And he had no idea what kind of home would make him happy. That made her sad and twice as determined to find the answer. Before she'd heard his story, she'd wanted to make sure Rainey understood that she was the best agent around, not just the Shepard representative selling real estate.

But now she had to find Trey the place that wiped his confusion away. When she'd asked for his opinion on the first house, his struggle to answer had gotten her attention. The kind of life that left a person without an anchor, a place they called home, was so foreign to her.

Horizon held a dozen different homes for Lila: the house she'd grown up in, the office she'd built, the spot on the beach she and Bee had claimed as theirs and the condo she'd bought after her first successful year in business. Each one of them contained memories that added up to her picture of "home."

Everyone needed that anchor, didn't they?

Trey deserved to have it.

Panic threatened to well up at how much finding Trey's place now mattered to her, but she reminded herself that this was why she'd chosen this job in the first place.

"Earth to Lila," Trey murmured, his lips twitching as he studied her face. "Are you still with me?"

When she became aware of how long she'd been sitting there, lecturing herself to get a grip, Lila smiled brightly. "This one is older, but it has landscaping built in." She pointed out the trees they could see in the large backyard. "When I added it to the list, I thought you might enjoy having the chance to renovate and put your own stamp on the place. Right now, it's overpriced, but we can get that down to make some room for the changes you would need to make."

If Monica Denis didn't understand the need to negotiate that price, Lila would convince her and Roberta Hale both for Trey's sake.

If he chose this house.

Then she realized she really wanted him to choose it, mainly for that reason. Negotiating the sale of this house after she'd missed out on the listing and for the price she'd proposed would be satisfying. She liked to be right almost as much as Bee did.

Trey paused in front of Monica Denis's for sale sign, but he didn't comment as Lila waved him to follow her to the front door.

Lila's sales pitch on this house was different. Instead of all the bells and whistles, the modern conveniences that had come with the newer build she first showed Trey, she pointed out the history of the house. It had been built in the sixties, and two families had been raised there. It was on the market because the owner had gotten divorced and needed to downsize. The pantry still had a growth chart for two kids—Jennifer and Andrew. Both of them had moved out of Horizon for jobs.

The stray thought popped into her head that Roberta would have been an excellent candidate for another Bay View Tower unit if there were any left.

After brushing the thought away, Lila pointed out the cozy living room with a brick fireplace that would need to be inspected before he started any fires in it, but it had potential for comfortable winter nights. Lila could picture it in December with a Christmas tree on one side and two stockings hung there. She refused to ponder why there were *two* and who the second one might belong to.

The living room led into a dated kitchen. Renovations would be necessary, but there was a lot of space to work with to put in a comfortable, updated kitchen and dining room. New flooring throughout, new paint and some serious updating to both bathrooms would be required. But at the end, he'd have a house that fit his taste, and some history that came along with it.

It was easy to imagine building a life here. She'd been doing it, and it wasn't even going to be her house.

Her pitch was polished. She'd outlined it before she'd sent him the listing. For that matter, she'd started drafting it before she'd knocked on Roberta's door with the contract for the listing in hand. She might have lost the listing, but all the important selling points remained.

They moved into the dining area. French doors looked out over a shady backyard. When she realized he hadn't said a word, Lila asked, "What do you think?"

Trey studied the patio through the window. "It's not hard to imagine a family growing up in this house."

That was true, but he'd never once mentioned the need for a family home. He was fully single as far as she, her mother and any interested parties of Horizon knew.

Did she need to reframe her pitch?

"Needs work," he finally said.

There was no arguing that.

"It is a fixer-upper, for sure. Cross those off the list?" she asked as she made a dramatic slashing motion with her right hand. His eyebrows rose and she decided that it might have been too dramatic, but she didn't want to surrender too soon. "This was a long shot."

He tilted his head to the side. "I'm guessing the first one, the newer build, was what you imagined fit me. What made you go for a long shot with the second choice?"

Lila wrinkled her nose. The only way to answer that truthfully might not reflect well on her, but she wanted to share with him. Maybe it was his explanation of how he'd grown up—Trey had been honest, so she wanted to return the favor.

"You saw the other agent on the sign out front. I wanted you to choose this one so I could go to battle, defeat my enemies and be proven correct and victorious. There is no such trophy as 'World's Best and Rightest Real Estate Agent,' but I wanted to be in the running if one was ever created." She winced. "What a terrible reason to choose a house, right? Not very Shepard-like."

Something about Trey made it easy to confess something she would have never admitted to her family. Every one of her brothers and sisters stood out without breaking a sweat, so having to battle was something she'd keep to herself.

But she would definitely crow over the victory.

"I guess you and Monica Denis have a history," Trey said.

"That sorority I mentioned? She was in it, but we were never friends *or* enemies. Now that she's showing up in Horizon and taking business from me in my hometown…" Lila shifted back and forth. She didn't need to fill in the blanks.

"Enemies is becoming a lot more likely, huh?" Trey asked. "That is a fierce expression. I wouldn't mess with you if I were a real estate agent." His lips curled with what she would label amusement. She shoved her hair awkwardly behind one ear, embarrassed at being caught caring so aggressively but pleased that he was smiling about it.

Then her eyes locked on his. "You're laughing at me. It's silly, right? It's just business. I shouldn't take it so personally."

She expected him to wave her off with something noncommittal. Instead, he answered her directly. "Not silly at all. You take your career seriously. It makes sense that you would fight someone who is threatening your success."

Lila pursed her lips as she considered that. "How can you tell?"

Trey studied her mouth for long enough that she wondered if he'd lost the thread of the conversation.

She fought the urge to call him on it. Accusing him of staring at her lips would take them in a direction she wasn't sure they needed to go.

"Tell what?" he finally asked.

"How can you tell I take my job seriously? I almost turned down your business, remember? That's not a smart decision." Lila wasn't going to mention her deal with Rainey, which had been the only thing to push her into making the right choice.

"You take your family seriously, too. I understand choosing them over me. I'm just glad Bee and TJ and I are ironing things out. We got off on the wrong foot, but I'm happy we're working together." He shrugged. "Sometimes career comes out on top, sometimes family, but I can tell you hustle. You have signs all over town. The billboard. I saw your name listed on the sponsors for the back-to-school night." He motioned at her suit. "I mean, you have the look."

Lila kicked one foot with her yellow sneakers. "Yeah? Do these fit?"

"Absolutely. You're serious about the job but you're still you." Trey froze, color dusting his cheekbones, and she wondered what he was thinking but not saying.

"One thing about hanging out with law enforcement," Lila said with a sigh, "is that they pick up on the details." For some reason, that reminded her of him showing up while she was touring Blue Vista. She and Bee hadn't discussed it yet, but he had to have overheard their conversation. His checking up on her reminded her of the many times her father had done the same.

And how little she wanted someone to notice every little detail or track her movements.

Trey nodded. "You also said 'Shepard-like.' As if it's some measurement. What does that mean?"

Lila instantly wished she'd said less, but his eyes were locked on her face, as if he was searching for clues. She didn't have much hope he'd let this line of questioning go. "My brothers and sisters excel, Trey. At everything. Some of them are way out there in front, leading heroic missions, and some of them are part of the fabric of this small town, but you will not find many people with a bad word to say about any of them."

He sighed. "Good publicity. Must be nice." The twist of his lips made her smile. Then amusement lit his eyes and she had to catch her breath and wait for her heart to slow down. He was devastating when he lightened up. "I don't see the problem. Everyone has told me Lila Shepard has the answer to all my questions."

Lila licked her lips. "As long as your question is finding a place to live…"

He nodded as if that part went without saying.

"Lila can show you houses, yes, but the others can save your life. You see the distinction?" Anxious to get away from the topic, Lila moved over to the French doors that led out to the patio. "Let's finish this tour and move on to the next." When she stepped outside, she tried to give herself a quick, stern lecture about keeping her distance from Trey Douglas, but she was afraid *herself* wasn't listening.

She'd shown him too much. It was terrifying how easy it had been to confess her secret insecurities. What would she tell him next?

LILA WAS CORRECT about his ability to catalog the details of his surroundings, but Trey hoped she didn't understand the extent. After today, he would know Lila was tall enough that her head would rest on his shoulder comfortably, that her shampoo had a light floral scent the made him think of spring mornings, that talking with her about landscaping and college and day-to-day life felt right.

And that hearing her describe herself as being in any way less than her siblings was all wrong.

Alarms immediately blared in his head.

These were not the thoughts of a man who was planning to get back to his real life ASAP.

Not when the woman at the center of those thoughts would never be persuaded to go along.

"I almost had this listing, but I knew it needed work to sell for the price it's listed at. Monica somehow got the listing without expecting the work to be done. So whoever sells this house will either make a bad deal for their buyer or have a battle on their hands. I wanted to be vindicated, but this isn't your war." She kicked a stick out into the yard, full of energy again. "But you need to see this backyard. You wanted landscape. This one has it." She waved an arm as if she was displaying the brick paver patio and shady, deep green yard. The trees were huge. The grass was overgrown but it was easy to imagine it neatly cut.

They each soaked up the shade for a second.

Then he heard it. "How far away is the beach?" He could hear the rush of waves when the afternoon was still. There was a hammock slung between two trees at the lowest corner of the yard, so he stepped off the patio to check it out.

"As the crow flies, it's over there, on the other side of that line of trees." She pointed past the hammock, but the dense greenery blocked any view. "You don't have direct access from here, but if you go to the end of the street, there's a path down to the beach. Not more than ten minutes walking."

As he stopped next to the hammock, the sound of the water was clearer. On impulse, he slid into the hammock, relieved that he managed it without tumbling out the other side. Not making a fool out of himself was always near the top of his list of priorities, but having Lila watching rocketed it to the first position. The hammock swung for a few seconds, but eventually he was able to relax.

Trey closed his eyes. He could hear waves and birds and all the things that he loved so much about his spot at the Needlegrass Motor Lodge. There were no noisy kids, no slamming of car doors from a nearby parking lot. It was easy to picture spending time at the end of the day right here.

He could feel Lila watching him, and he realized there was only one thing missing, one piece to complete the picture.

"I think it will hold both of us." Trey cracked open one eyelid and waited to see if Lila would take the invitation. He ignored the extremely logical voice in his head that was certain this was the opposite of what he needed.

What he wanted was Lila swinging there next to him.

After a pause where he could feel her evaluating all the options, she eased down next to him.

"Wow, I didn't realize we were close enough for the sound to reach us," Lila said softly.

Trey felt her shoulders relax bit by bit and wondered if Lila experienced the same reaction to the sound of ocean waves as he did.

"This is what I'll miss about the Needlegrass—the peace," he said. "I can't see the water every day, but I can hear it, and the birds, and even the people when the beach is busy, but there's something about knowing the ocean is right there that calms my mind."

He managed to contain the wince. No one needed to hear him say anything like "calms my mind," but it was already out there in the world now.

"I've never lived so close to the water," he added awkwardly.

Lila studied his face as she considered his answer. "To the right person, I'm thinking this could add a lot of value. Maybe Roberta Hale's house isn't overpriced at all for that person, even though the inside could use a lot of updating." Her slow smile told him she knew he was on the hook. All she had to do was reel him in.

She'd done the same thing for him that she'd done for Officer Rodriguez and his wife. She'd found the one thing that made all the other inconveniences worthwhile.

"I'm sure you can find closer options," he said as he told himself to be practical about this decision. "You know the chief's days can be long. It makes sense to be near the police station."

Lila sniffed. "If you work like my father, you

will definitely want an easy commute. He was always on call, ready to report at the first sign of trouble."

Reading between the lines, Trey understood that took a toll on his family, Lila in particular. "Hard to enforce boundaries when everyone knows where you live, I guess."

She nodded. "Yeah, but don't you think a little distance might help with that? If you want that, a chance to unplug from the job." She closed her eyes and rested her head against his shoulder. "It seems like this place would give you a strong incentive to take the badge off now and then."

Trey studied the way her hair draped across his arm and decided Lila had identified another secret dream he hadn't known about. A life outside of work, one that made it attractive to leave his desk, suddenly seemed like something he needed.

"I can't buy the second house I tour," Trey said reluctantly. He didn't even know what he didn't know about home improvement. Still, even he could see that the renovations needed here were more than cosmetic.

But it was evident to both of them that his heart wasn't really in the objection.

Lila raised an eyebrow that he read as "Can't you?" but she shrugged. The way her arm slid against his immediately got his attention. "Let's see some more houses, then. There's no need to rush."

"Because I'm the only buyer in Horizon who would pay the price for this house," he said.

She immediately shook her head. "Oh, no, you won't pay this price, no matter how much you love it. You've found the one house where I have no conflict between buyer and seller. If you decide to make an offer, I will not waste my opportunity to make a statement. You will get a fair price."

Her eyes glittered with determination. Why did he find that so attractive?

Then she tangled her fingers through his, and he felt his determination to keep Lila Shepard at arm's length fading away. Sitting with her here, their shoulders brushing as the hammock swung slowly, made it easy to imagine a thousand other days that ended the same way.

Luckily, Lila was still in the moment. "I have one more appointment lined up. Should we get moving?"

Reluctantly, Trey slid out of the hammock and held it while Lila crawled out the other side. Determined to get his head screwed on straight, he searched for a business question. "If I do the work, upgrade the kitchen and the bathroom, you think this will be easy to resell in a few years?"

Lila paused with her hand on the doorknob. She turned the lock and made sure the lights were turned off before heading for the front door. "A few years? Say…five or ten?"

She was watching him closely as he walked out ahead of her.

"Or three…a few years." Since he didn't want to tip anyone off about his plans to get his career back on track much more quickly than that, he nodded. "But yeah, if that's the normal time frame."

Lila paused on the sidewalk, studying him closely.

He had a feeling she was perceptive, good at reading clues, since she'd been surrounded by police officers on all sides, so he did his best to keep his expression clear.

"I do think this is a good investment." She unlocked her SUV. After they slid inside, she added, "Especially when I get you a fair price."

There was not a doubt in her mind that she could do it, either.

He'd known Lila Shepard was beautiful in a colorful way, but this confidence turned up that beauty even more.

As they made their way through the last house, which never stood a chance now that he'd found one with the sound of the sea in the backyard, Lila was thorough. She did the same hard work, pointing out all the features, but when they parked in front of Town Hall, she said, "Sleep on your decision. Let me know tomorrow if you want to write an offer and we'll get this party started." Her grin was contagious, so even though this decision was monumental in his life, he returned it.

Her eyes widened, but she held the grin until he slid out of her SUV.

Trey watched her drive away, stopping completely at the stop sign, using her turn signal appropriately and obeying the speed limit.

Lila was an interesting mix, the police chief's daughter who wanted nothing to do with police business. The town's best real estate agent who was energized by negotiation but still entertained kids at her face-painting booth. She wore that suit well, but it didn't fit her like the bright colors she'd been wearing when they met.

And if she wasn't a Shepard of Horizon, South Carolina, rooted to the place by generations, she could be the kind of woman he fell for before he even knew it was happening. But they were headed in different directions, and he wouldn't be the one to break her heart.

In one afternoon, she'd opened his eyes about what might be possible: a real home and a life with an important job and time to live outside of it. He was grateful for that.

Which made it twice as important that he not hurt Lila.

He'd found the house already. Once they made it through the negotiations, his time with Lila would be over until he was ready to sell it and return to his life. That would be best for both of them.

CHAPTER FOURTEEN

On Saturday night, Lila maneuvered through the crowd gathered around the Sandlapper's outdoor stage with an iced tea martini in one hand and a basket of Charlene's famous shrimp-and-grits puffs in the other. White lights strung overhead were the only illumination other than the waning full moon and the weak glow from the restaurant's windows. The sandy beach below the deck gleamed faintly, and there was a streak of moonlight on each wave that landed on the shore. This atmosphere was hard to distill into marketing copy for tourism web pages, but it was one of the reasons the Sandlapper attracted day trippers and locals alike.

Bee had texted that she was on her way. Lila picked their normal table, a high-top with three chairs in case TJ happened to appear. She eyed an empty seat at the next table because where TJ went, Summer was sure to follow, but she had her doubts the lovebirds would make it out. Their table was situated far enough from the stage at the end of the restaurant's deck that they wouldn't get caught up in the dancing and could still talk, but they also had the opportunity to sing along with the band. The Carolina Waves covered a mix of country and rock, with a dash of South Carolina flair. Bee would bring her own appetizer basket, they would share and Lila thought that would be the perfect end to a really productive day.

Her open house had gone well. Two different couples had come down from Charleston to see her newest listing, and she'd gotten one potential listing that she'd need to follow up on next week. When she and Rainey had met in her office that afternoon, she'd been feeling nearly invincible.

"Hey, Lila," Boogie Howard said as he inched past her, his guitar held high about his head, "good crowd tonight." Horizon's busiest construction expert and lead singer of the Waves pointed at John McEntire, who was moving the mic stands around on the stage. Lila watched McEntire nod and move the stand he'd just placed approximately three inches to the left. She marveled at the way men could silently communicate.

"Yeah, the weather's perfect for some music," she said before sipping her martini. "How's life?"

"Oh, can't complain," Boogie said with a smile. "Sure could use a new renovation project to keep me out of trouble, though." Lila had never known him to be anything but solidly booked. She understood hustling as a small business owner, though, so she grabbed his hand before he could slip away.

"Hey, I might have a lead for you there," she said. "The new police chief is house hunting right now. I figure he'll want to make some changes to the place." Since she was as certain as could be that place was going to be Roberta Hales's fixer-upper, the chief was going to need some professional help.

Boogie wrinkled his nose. "Well, I can't turn down a job, but I appreciate the heads-up."

Lila pulled him closer. "Turn down a job?" What was he talking about?

"I hear he's hard to work with." Boogie bent his head closer to hers. "Everyone in town has a story about his demands." He patted her hand. "But I'm a professional. I can suffer some criticism and still collect the check."

"Testing. Testing," John McEntire said into the mic.

Boogie immediately hugged Lila. "Gotta go." He had jumped up on the stage before Lila had a chance to tell him that he had the wrong impression of the chief.

She slumped in her seat as she wondered exactly how far the gossip about Trey had spread through town in the week since their meeting at the shift change.

"Got here just in time," Bee said with a grunt as she climbed up into the chair and put her basket of golden onion rings on the high-top table. "That is not the face of a woman about to dine on appetizers and loud music. Bad day? Rainey said the two of you had been working on a slide-show all day long." Her eyebrows nearly reached her hairline. "That does not sound like a fun Saturday to me."

Lila sipped her drink again before she answered. "Fun? Absolutely not. Rainey is an absolute tyrant and not nearly as good with PowerPoint as she thinks. But it was productive, and it could turn out to be lucrative if this project goes according to plan."

Bee made the weird humming noise she always did when other people would have whistled. Her sister was tragically unable to whistle. "Lucrative. My little sister is counting her coins. I love to see it."

Since she'd had a rocky start with Rainey on this project, Lila was happy to have her sister teasing her about her business focus. It was going to pay off.

Lila slipped one of the bits of shrimp and grits that had been baked to puffy goodness into her mouth and chewed happily as she considered the Trey problem. "How's work?" His issues with Joe Morgan had made the rounds, no doubt, but was there something else happening at the police department that she hadn't heard about? Was she finally managing to avoid police business?

Bee twirled an onion ring on one finger. "Not bad. I got some cool new software and built these fancy maps that show where calls to Dispatch are coming from over time." She chomped into her onion ring. "The chief was happy with my first attempt. A few refinements and we're going to have something helpful to send out to all the agencies who provide support." She picked up the ketchup bottle, flipped open the cap and squeezed a mound of ketchup onto her onion rings.

Lila stole one from the less goopy side and waited to see if Bee had any other gossip to share. Three onion rings later, she decided Bee was done with her report, and she was no closer to understanding all the news spreading about Trey.

Before she could pick Bee's brain for any other clues regarding the new chief's reputation in Horizon, she saw him walk into the restaurant's outdoor seating area. She immediately realized that it was the first time she'd seen him out of uniform. He was handsome in Horizon's police blues, but tonight he was wearing faded jeans and a white button-down with the sleeves rolled up to expose his forearms.

There was nothing flashy about Trey Douglas, but he would attract her attention in any crowd. He didn't swagger, but he stood there and scanned the crowd…confidently? That wasn't the right word, but she didn't see any hesitation on his face.

There, at the Sandlapper, he drew all the eyes, but not because of how he was dressed. Lila didn't think people were registering his assurance, either. These were covert stares that were way too obvious.

It would have been interesting to watch how the crowd split like he was cutting a path through a hayfield, but she could tell from his expression that he also noticed how people ducked and dodged him. His face grew stonier with each step.

That wouldn't improve his reception in town, either.

"Chief!" Lila called and waved her hand wildly in the air to get his attention. "Join us!"

Bee stopped mid-chew and turned toward her. "Not exactly looking to party with my new boss, Lila."

When Trey turned to cut across the dance floor, Lila copied her sister and picked up her glass to cover her mouth. "If this welcome got any colder, we'd have snow on the ground."

Bee wanted to argue. Lila could see it in her eyes. But Trey stopped two feet from their table and said, "Good evening, Ms. Shepard." Then he turned to Bee. "Officer Shepard."

Then he clasped his hands behind his back as if he was some chivalrous sir inquiring after their health and good fortune.

"We're all off duty here. You're going to have to go with Lila and Bee, Chief," Lila said and ignored the way Bee's eyebrows shot up.

He pursed his lips as he considered her order. His expression was so serious that she immediately wanted to tease him out of it. "As long as I am Trey off duty."

Bee made the weird humming noise again, and Lila stifled a chuckle at the way Trey studied her sister as if he couldn't decide whether she needed help.

"Deal." Lila slid the empty chair toward him with her foot. "If you'll go get an appetizer and promise to share with me, you can pull up a seat."

She was immediately gratified to watch some of the grimness leave his face. His lips curled as he turned to look at the bar. "Any requests?"

Bee smiled brightly. "You can't really go wrong, Chief."

Lila waited to see if Trey would argue over the title, but he moved away, his speed enhanced by the way the crowd melted before him again.

"Spill," Bee said before she took one of Lila's shrimp puffs. "What brought on this warming to the guy when you were threatening to avenge my honor and the family name?"

The way Bee never failed to remember things that Lila hoped she forgot was so annoying. "Rainey applied some leverage, the lucrative deal I just mentioned, to get my promise to find him the perfect house. I did it yesterday. All that's left is writing the offer and then hammering Monica Denis in the negotiations until he gets his fair price."

"Monica Denis, you say? I saw her for sale

sign and remembered how she liked to use occasional French words to add cosmopolitan polish." Bee tipped her nose up. "Like it was never 'have a good night!' but '*bonne nuit*' or '*au revoir*.' Do you remember how often she worked in being descended from one of the original French Huguenot settlers? Then she spent a semester in France, and English was forever déclassé."

As expected, Bee knew more about Monica than Lila could remember, but she did have a vague recollection of asking one of her friends to translate "*bonne soiree*" at the first rush party.

Bee squeezed Lila's shoulder. "I like how this is working out for you. You lost the listing but you're about to win the war. Nice." Bee wagged her eyebrows. "Are you hammering before or after your land deal pitch? Is there a proper way to hammer your competition?"

Lila shrugged. "If there is, Rainey has it down."

Bee nodded. Neither of them doubted that Rainey could navigate choppy business waters.

"So you're…what? Hoping to rehabilitate his image?" Bee asked before she turned to glance over her shoulder to make sure Trey wasn't nearby. "That's a big change for one afternoon."

Lila bit her lip. "You aren't ready to make nice yet?" She'd been hoping that Bee would be supportive because she expected to have more trouble convincing TJ to let it go.

Bee frowned. "At work, I am, but…here? Out

in the world?" She leaned closer and motioned Lila to join her. "What do I even call him? Calling him 'Chief' while he's in uniform is acceptable, but out of it… It feels icky."

"You could try 'Trey' since that's what he asked us to use," Lila said slowly as she blinked at her sister to make sure she understood how silly her question was.

Trey cleared his throat as he set a glass and two baskets on the table. "I got the fried okra and the cheddar cheese straws. I couldn't choose."

Lila and Bee immediately leaned back.

"Trey, you can never go wrong with two appetizers," Lila said. "Right, Bee? You love the okra, too."

Her sister straightened in her seat. "I do, T-T-Trey. You can't go wrong with Charlene's menu." Then she raised her hand and waved at someone across the crowd. "Be right back."

Lila closed her eyes for a second at Bee's extremely obvious escape and hoped Trey didn't notice.

"She wasn't waving at anyone, was she?" he asked. His lips twitched as if he was fighting laughter.

Lila shook her head.

"Running your sister off…" He sipped his beer. "Is that going to be another black mark against my name?"

Lila sighed. Wishing that a police officer wasn't paying attention almost never paid off.

"The trouble she had getting my name out was my first clue." Trey shoved the basket of cheese straws closer to her. "Are we going to eat her onion rings while she's gone?"

The warmth in his eyes delighted Lila. It was like the two of them had their own language. The rest of the world would never believe he was teasing her like this.

"Absolutely we're eating her onion rings." Lila took one and nodded when he selected his own. "She knows better than to leave food unattended. I've been teaching her that lesson my whole life."

Trey smiled and shifted in his seat. "I don't have any siblings. Sometimes I've regretted that, but I will add never losing my snacks to theft to my list of pros."

Lila pursed her lips. "Is it theft? Or is this the ancient common law doctrine of finders keepers at work?"

His low laugh caught Lila's attention. Hearing it for the first time felt like winning something big.

It also caught the attention of the tables around them. She'd been vaguely aware of having an audience, but heads turned at Trey's laughter. Lila sat taller in her chair.

Trey bent closer to her to speak into her ear. "Does being the subject of all this surveillance ever get easier?" The brush of his cheek against hers sent a warm spark down her neck. It landed somewhere in her abdomen.

Since Lila understood exactly what he meant, she was sympathetic. She'd grown up knowing Horizon was watching her, and she'd battled against it. Landing in the middle of all this as an adult must be difficult, especially when he'd spent a lifetime moving from place to place.

But she knew that telling him they were never going to stop watching him would be a mistake.

Instead, she moved closer. "When you realize they'd do almost anything to help you, it lessens some of the annoyance, I think."

He didn't argue, but she could tell he wasn't convinced.

When neither of them seemed able to move away, Lila knew they were going to be adding a new story to the tales about the chief currently making the rounds. Whether this helped or hurt Trey in the eyes of their neighbors remained to be seen.

Since she was also going to have to answer questions about this moment, she had an incentive to get the night back on track.

So she leaned back, even though it was like forcing herself from a cozy nest of blankets on a cold winter morning.

The tug of regret surprised her.

Lila offered Trey her basket of shrimp-and-grits

puffs. "Try these. They're much better warm, but they are delicious at any temperature."

He shook his head. "Shrimp allergy." Then he winced. "Actually, I say that, but I just don't care for shrimp."

Lila's mouth dropped open. The admission was stunning in a way that nothing else he'd shared had been. "No shrimp? How do you live?"

His grin would have knocked her off her feet if she'd been standing. This was what a happy Trey should look like. She wanted to see it again.

"I manage. Living next to the ocean may make that harder, but it hasn't been a challenge so far." Trey stacked up their empty baskets. "I'm going to run these back to the bar. Want another?" He pointed at her empty martini glass and Lila shook her head.

As soon as he left, Bee appeared at her shoulder. "Is this a date?" she hissed close to Lila's ear. "Because it's looking like a date."

Lila narrowed her eyes at her sister. "From your vantage point across the deck, the one you scurried away to at the first opportunity?"

Bee wrinkled her nose. "You ate my onion rings. Let's call it even."

Before Lila could come up with any reasonable explanation for whatever it was happening between her and Trey, he was back. He had two glasses of ice water in his hands, and he slid one across the table to Lila.

"Thanks, but I didn't ask for anything," Lila said, hyperaware of Bee loitering next to the table.

Trey shrugged. "I thought you might need it." He held the other glass out to Bee. "Would you like one?" After a pause, he tacked on, "Bee?"

All three of them blinked in surprise. Her name on his lips didn't sound natural, but it had the potential to.

Her sister pointed over her shoulder with her thumb. "I have a drink. Over there. Where I should return." After a weird wave of her hands around the table, she added, "I'll let you two get back to…it."

Lila and Trey watched Bee disappear into the crowd on the dance floor.

The silence between them was filled with the band's patter as they changed directions for the evening. The Waves always started with a party vibe and transitioned to an easygoing set to end the night.

When his arm brushed hers, Lila was immediately aware of him again. "Don't be obvious, but see the woman standing next to the steps leading down to the beach? Dark hair in a ponytail."

Lila attempted to gaze nonchalantly in that direction and quickly identified his target. "Did you finally meet Belinda from the Daybreak Diner?"

He huffed out a breath. "No, but the cold stare follows me, so I thought I should get a name in case I need to write up a restraining order someday."

Lila waved broadly at Belinda and watched her face transform into a beautiful smile. "Be careful," Belinda mouthed, and Lila rolled her eyes as if the other woman was making a joke.

"She's loyal but not dangerous, I promise." Lila grinned at him and their eyes caught again.

"So," Trey said a little too loudly, then lowered his voice, "I've been thinking…"

Lila snapped to attention. His words and tone had her business senses tingling.

"I want to make an offer on the house—the one with the hammock and the waves," Trey said. He punctuated the statement with a nod, as if he was confirming that to himself.

The surge of adrenaline that shot through Lila's veins was familiar and exhilarating at the same time. She loved this part of the process.

Lila reached over to squeeze Trey's arm. "That's exciting. Congratulations!"

He huffed out a breath. "Is it?" Then he shook his head. "It is. As long as I'm in Horizon, I'll have access to that spot at the end of every day. Even if I have to sign paperwork that says I'll pay on it for decades, I can sell it when I'm ready to move on." His tone suggested he'd been repeating the same thing to himself, but it would take a few more times to be convinced.

When I'm ready to move on. Lila sipped the

water Trey had thoughtfully brought her as she pondered that. The vague sense that he had an idea when that time would come tickled at her brain. Some home buyers wanted a forever home, one that they'd settle into and never leave. Others had time limits. Maybe there was a job assignment that would end, or they had plans to grow a family that would need more space someday. When house flipping was all the rage, she'd worked with one guy determined to make his fortune by buying and selling every year or so. The renovations he'd put in over that span of time were exhausting to think about.

"Do you have a time frame in mind for this moving on?" Lila asked. There was no sense in stewing over his words when she could ask. It wouldn't impact this deal either way, but it mattered to her for some reason she wasn't entirely sure of.

And she knew the answer was three years or less, but she needed to hear him say it.

Trey rubbed his forehead. "Is there any way I can tell you something that won't go back to Rainey?"

Lila hesitated before answering.

She and Rainey had been best friends forever. Other than Bee, there was no one who knew Lila better, but something in her needed to know whatever Trey was going to say.

"I think so," she said, aware that the uncertainty in her voice might not be convincing.

He opened his mouth but hesitated. Eventually he said, "I'm not sure I'm cut out for…this." His vague hand wave could mean dinner at the Sandlapper, sitting across from her or life in Horizon.

Lots of people worried about that, and first-time buyers often got the jitters. His words hinted at something else, another reason he was evaluating his investment in the short term.

Trey was already planning his exit. Gambling that Horizon could change his mind would be risky. Getting closer to a temporary man while she was as permanently fixed here as the statue of Captain Emory Shepard in the center of Battery Park would be foolish.

"If you aren't ready, we'll figure out a way to tell Rainey. I will back you up." Lila squeezed his hand. "From way, way behind you because she will not be happy with either one of us." When he laughed, she squeezed his hand again. Letting go felt wrong, so she didn't pull back. "But think about the way you felt listening to the waves and how hard it will be to let someone else take your spot in that hammock."

He sighed and she knew she had a buyer on her hands. "That is impossible to argue with. Let's put in an offer."

Lila clapped her hands before throwing her arms around Trey's shoulders. Her thrilled hug of congratulations turned into something different when his arms slowly slid around her to rest on her lower back.

But she didn't move away until Trey said, "We're attracting stares."

He eased back, but not so far away that she couldn't see the warmth in his eyes.

"I should go and get you a celebratory beer," Lila said. The need to step away to catch her breath surprised her, but it also made so much sense. She had never expected Trey to affect her this way. He had been rude to her, which was a mistake, but he'd also treated her brother and sister like… Well, he'd acted like he was their boss, which wasn't all that unfair, even if he'd been wrong. He was also a client, and Lila had never been tempted to mix business with romance.

But the fact that her business was exclusively tied to Horizon, where she'd grown up alongside any of the potential romantic prospects, had everything to do with that. By the time any of them were ready to buy a house, she had already dated them once and didn't need to repeat the experiment or there was a good reason she hadn't.

And on top of all that, in his mind, he was leaving Horizon again soon.

The fact that this attraction conquered all those reasons to avoid Trey so easily was scary.

"Actually, I was wondering…" Trey shook his head. "This is such a mistake. I don't know if it's the relaxation of the beer and fried appetizers, or if it's the romantic atmosphere of this crowded deck and musical selection of the Carolina Waves, but would you dance with me?"

He held out his hand.

Lila stared at it. "At least you aren't attracted to me. That would be awful."

Her eyes locked to his as the logical part of her brain was demanding answers. Flirting with him took this unexpected attraction to the next step. That was a dangerous step.

Then she slipped her hand into his and watched his face change. Solemn attention transformed to the gleam of anticipation, and she felt the effects in her abdomen.

"As long as *you* aren't attracted to *me*, I'll recover," he murmured next to her ear as he urged her out of her seat.

Lila was conscious of the way the people who weren't watching her were absolutely tracking their progress as they joined the crowd on the dance floor. Boogie and the band transitioned to a new song as Trey slipped his hands around her waist.

"I wouldn't have guessed Trey Douglas spent a lot of time on dance floors," Lila said nervously because what was she doing? She didn't like Trey…right?

He wrapped his arms more tightly around her. "I don't, but we're shuffling to country music.

How hard can it be?" His crooked smile stole her breath.

When she realized the song was "History in the Making," she considered dragging Trey off the dance floor. Darius Rucker's lyrics about enjoying the moment because it could be one she would never want to forget felt…scary. Overwhelming? Too much.

Then her eyes met his.

Trey pulled her closer.

His lips touched hers in a sweet introduction that she would never forget.

And all the alarm bells faded along with the audience. When he held her in his arms, leading her in a slow circle as he stared into her eyes, Lila didn't care about what her sister saw or what her neighbors said.

She'd never felt that way before.

Everything she cared about was moving with her across the crowded dance floor.

Whatever happened tomorrow, tonight she had this dance and this moment, and she couldn't give it up yet.

CHAPTER FIFTEEN

TREY WAS PREOCCUPIED as he jogged past Horizon's Town Hall on Sunday morning. He'd ventured away from running on the beach near the Needlegrass Motor Lodge in his quest to improve his knowledge of the town's street layout. It also helped him avoid Joe Morgan's glare from the motel office.

Town Hall hadn't been his destination, but somehow he'd ended up there.

Since he'd spent most of his run replaying his night with Lila Shepard instead of scanning the neighborhood, he wasn't sure he'd accomplished his first goal. But at least the run had been free from disapproving stares so far.

He would never forget the way Lila Shepard's eyes had sparkled under the lights strung over the Sandlapper's deck.

The song they'd danced to was stuck in his head—probably because he'd downloaded it when he'd been unable to sleep and had listened to it until it was familiar enough to hum bits and pieces of it while he ran.

Then there was the kiss. He wasn't sure who had moved first, but he knew letting go of Lila when the song ended had been difficult.

Trey tripped over a dip in the sidewalk as he remembered how she'd stared up at him.

He was in trouble.

Maybe watching the waves in the bay would reset his system, firm up his commitment to his plan to keep his distance from Lila. Why did he have serious doubts? He wasn't sure even the ocean was powerful enough to wash that memory away.

Trey crossed over the street to hit the path around the Battery. He would make it to the halfway point and the bench he'd picked out to soak up the view. Then he'd get a grip on this infatuation with Lila.

With this destination in mind, Trey tried to recapture some of his focus. Running had always been about mental health for him. It gave his mind time to work through problems, while Trey put one foot down in front of the other. The rhythm guided his breathing.

It worked to push Lila Shepard to the fringes of his mind, but she never completely disappeared. No one else interrupted his flow, but he was surprised to find he wasn't the only person in the world when he approached his bench.

Tom Shepard was sitting right in the middle of it.

It made sense. The bench was obviously superior in its view of the bay, placement under the shade of the tall oaks and lack of a crowd. The timing was the only element of coincidence.

At that moment, Trey had two choices.

He could raise his hand in a friendly wave and keep running. The bench would be there another day when he could return and enjoy it in solitude, which had been his goal.

Or he could stop and make friendly conversation with the former chief.

Who was also the father of the woman he'd kissed the night before under the moon and the watchful stares of almost everyone in Horizon.

The awkward scale was instantly busted.

The way Tom Shepard watched him approach convinced Trey that the former chief had clocked his options, too, and he was curious to see which way Trey would go.

Trey's steps slowed. Conversation was the braver of the two options, and he had a strong drive to be seen as brave by the former chief.

"Morning, Chief," Tom Shepard drawled as he raised a to-go cup. "Nice day for a run."

Trey propped his hands on his hips. "It is. Even better day to stare out at the ocean."

Tom nodded. "Have a seat. Plenty of room."

The knot of nerves in his stomach surprised Trey. He and the former chief had discussed people they knew in common already. They were acquaintances. There was no way the kiss would even come up. This wasn't a big deal.

He settled on one side of the former chief and stretched his legs out. Fighting the urge to bounce one knee nervously took some concentration.

"Never got into jogging," Tom drawled. "Cool mornings like this are the only ones that could have convinced me to try."

"In my experience, it's a good way to learn the streets." Trey ignored the voice reminding him that it only worked when he was paying attention to where he was going.

The reminder that the former chief's daughter had taken over his brain had Trey hunting for an interesting topic. His brain's refusal to give him one was a problem.

They were silent for a stretch. The crash of waves on the other side of the seawall made that quiet moment peaceful. This was what Trey had been hoping to find that morning.

Then he realized this could be the perfect opportunity to pick the former chief's brain in a low-risk environment. There was no one here to observe them.

"Met with the shipyard security team this week. I didn't know how they were integrated into the police department's operations until Bee mentioned they'd sent an alert about unusual traffic near one of their closed gates," Trey said. "They seem on top of the demands out there."

Tom nodded. “John McEntire’s good at his job. Coast Guard experience, connections with the DEA and South Carolina state police.” At the mention of the DEA, Trey’s interest sharpened. Did he know or work with Dennis Browning? If so, were they still in contact? With all the other issues swirling around him and his position as chief, Trey had almost forgotten to worry about story of the bribery investigation making it to Horizon.

“With a background like that,” Tom continued, “you know he’s watching all the right things to keep the shipyard secure. Rainey recruited him, and I believe she’s got the knack for finding the right people.” He didn’t glance at Trey, so he wasn’t 100 percent sure that he was included at this point. Maybe he was still in a probationary phase.

“He mentioned a disaster preparedness summit. In January?” Trey asked.

Tom nodded. “Has been. That’ll be up to you, of course. All my files on that are in the conference room. Easy to pull when we need to set up a command center in there. The shipyard, the rangers out at Rocky Point Lighthouse, other agencies that cooperate with us—we get together and make sure the plans in place are sufficient to meet current demands. I’ve always been fortunate to have the support I need when emergencies arise. Planning ahead helps.” He sipped his coffee. Trey took that to mean he'd said all he wanted to say about that.

Tom Shepard had built a reputation by planning ahead. Trey could learn a lot from his example. His next step would be to comb through those files, obviously. January wasn't all that far away.

Before Trey could formulate his next question, TJ Shepard asked, "Is this a closed meeting or can anyone join?" He approached with two cups of coffee and Lucy's leash in his hand. The yellow Lab promptly brushed up against Tom Shepard's legs, and the former chief bent down to scratch her ears. The dog studied Trey, but she didn't move until he held out his hand.

Every time he greeted Lucy it got easier, mainly because she was a pro.

As he ran his hand over her head and ruffled her silky fur, he wondered why he'd never had a dog. The quick answer was that pet ownership didn't fit with his mobile lifestyle, not as a kid or a soldier or a law enforcement officer.

But for the first time, here in Horizon, he could meet the schedule a dog needed.

Too bad he wasn't planning on keeping that schedule or this job for the ten or fifteen years a dog would need.

Not that his brain seemed to hold on to that fact for long, based on the way memories of Lila bled into wondering what she was doing at that moment.

"Looks like Belinda didn't know you already had a coffee, Dad." TJ held up one of the coffee cups. "Chief? Want a cup of black coffee?"

Trey was silent until he realized both Shepards were waiting for him to answer. The number of chiefs on the bench had confused him.

"Yeah, thanks." Trey tried to ignore how weird the situation was as he accepted the coffee and watched TJ sit down on the other side of the former chief. When TJ was settled, he bent over to unclip Lucy's leash. The dog flopped down at his feet to watch the birds.

There they were, just three guys and a dog out for a Sunday visit to the park. What a weird picture they would present if anyone else happened to stroll by.

If Trey had been smarter, he would have anticipated where the conversation could go. Would have seen that the connection between TJ and Belinda and the officer's recent visit to the coffee shop all pointed right at an upcoming discussion of Trey's dance with Lila—he'd registered the weight of Belinda's disapproving stare the night before. Instead of preparing for that, he'd been thinking about getting a dog. Horizon was messing with his strategic thinking.

So he was caught off guard when TJ said, "Belinda had some gossip to share this morning. Apparently, Lila was over at the Sandlapper last night, dancing with someone unexpected."

Trey closed his eyes and tried not to grip the cup in his hand so tightly that coffee spurted out the top. Then he realized this was exactly what Lila had been talking about, how she was under constant surveillance in Horizon.

Her father wasn't the chief any longer, but the informants had found a new person to report to: TJ.

And if Lila and Trey were ever a couple and the people of Horizon started to like him, any tales of her misconduct would land on his desk. Her aversion to police business made perfect sense.

"Belinda couldn't wait to see you this morning, I bet." Tom Shepard didn't seem overly concerned about this gossip. He hadn't heard who Lila's partner was yet.

"Anything you'd like to tell us, Chief?" TJ asked.

"Lila and I were celebrating. I found a house here in Horizon. She's putting the offer in tomorrow," Trey said.

The former chief nodded, as if that was a plausible explanation.

TJ wasn't buying it.

"Belinda hit pretty hard on the word 'romantic.' I wasn't there, of course, but reading between the lines, I'm getting more than a dance. She wanted to make sure I warned Lila about you." TJ stared at Trey over his coffee cup. Charming TJ was missing, and Trey had a better idea of how effective TJ would be at interrogation. "I'll have to get more details because I don't know what the warning is exactly. Thought you might help with that."

Lila's father sighed as if he couldn't believe his morning had come to this, but he didn't say anything.

Unless Belinda had a source in Columbia, Trey's best guess was that her warning was connected with her views on how he'd wronged TJ.

But the possibility of the story out of Columbia reaching Horizon had increased now that he understood John McEntire's connections.

"If you'll tell her that I didn't steal the job from you," Trey said slowly, "I will be happy to tell Belinda that Lila and I are working on business, nothing else." Because he couldn't help himself, he muttered, "Then I might stand a chance of getting my full lunch order, too."

TJ paused, mid-sip. "She thinks you stole my job?"

"I don't know where that story started, if it was Belinda or someone else, but when I looked at the apartment next to yours, I heard that many people in Horizon have a problem that I got the job and you didn't," Trey said and he wished he and TJ were having this conversation somewhere else, away from the former chief. He wasn't sure why he felt that, but there was something in the air.

"Well..." TJ said with a quick look at his father. Whatever he might have said floated away in the breeze, and the three of them returned to staring at the waves.

"One word of warning regarding Lila," her father said slowly. Trey thought both he and TJ braced themselves for whatever came next. "She will not welcome the two of you discussing her choices as if you have any say in them. And I'm not sure who was telling whom, if you wanted me to do something in this matter, but I learned my lesson a long time ago. Lila does not appreciate a tattletale or the person who acts on the information." He sipped his coffee.

"Dancing with my boss, the new police chief, is a funny way of avoiding police business," TJ muttered under his breath, but he held up a hand when his father slowly turned his head toward him.

The memory of Lila wondering if she measured up to the rest of her siblings was hard to shake, so Trey said, "She's taking care of her own business in this case, which is selling real estate. And she's as good at it as you are with police work." When he heard how his voice had risen at the end, he regretted not controlling his reaction. If he wanted to convince TJ and Tom that there was nothing to talk about between him and Lila, he should tone down his defense of her.

The former chief turned to study him, and Trey stared out at the water. He had nothing else to say anyway.

Trey lost track of how long they sat there, but

eventually Tom Shepard stood up. "My hour is up. I can go home again, get back to painting the garage." He patted Lucy's head, squeezed his son's shoulder and nodded at Trey. Before he walked away, he said, "If I was still a law enforcement officer here in Horizon, I would be considering what to do about the park rules I see being broken right now. Three citations even as we speak. But I'm not." Then he put his hands in his pockets and strolled away.

Trey and TJ stared at each other until TJ's reluctant laughter ended the moment.

"My mother has instituted required recess hours. He's been retired for one week and already she has mandated time that he has to leave the house, so having all that free time is going great." TJ shook his head as he scanned the park over one shoulder. "That guy fishing is smoking. That's one."

Trey turned in the other direction to stare down the paved paths toward Town Hall. "We've got a drone operator over near the playground, but his son is working the controls. That would be number two."

They both shifted around on the bench to see what was happening behind them.

"I'm not seeing three," TJ murmured. Trey shook his head.

TJ's phone dinged, so he pulled it out of his

pocket and read, "The third one is that your dog is off the leash."

His beleaguered sigh made Trey laugh. The chief didn't make any allowances for Lucy being his son's dog or a law enforcement officer in her own right.

He'd also known that TJ and Trey would feel compelled to identify the citations themselves.

"It's not easy being the chief of police's kid," Trey said as TJ snapped Lucy's leash back onto her collar.

"Yeah, no wonder Lila wants her distance. It absolutely is not easy," TJ agreed as he sat up, "but I wouldn't trade it." He glanced over. "I didn't realize you were getting pushback on taking the job. I thought it was all…" He stopped.

"The consequences of my personality?" Trey asked, to fill in the blank.

TJ winced but didn't argue.

"Those would have been enough," Trey answered because it had taken just a week to realize the size of his error with his first morning briefing. "Although I don't have any regrets about shutting down the overnight pool party at the Needlegrass, the rest of my missteps could have been avoided if my pride hadn't tripped me up."

TJ nodded. "I get that. All you were trying to do was set the tone. No harm in that. Bee showed me her new program. She was excited. As long as you realize what you have in her, you can recover from the rest. Lucy doesn't hold a grudge."

Trey's shoulders relaxed a fraction. He took that to mean that TJ didn't, either.

Then TJ added, "But Lila, she's a new wrinkle in this reconciliation. You are more police business, and she grew up fighting the 'tough being a Shepard kid' the most. I don't see anything romantic between you two working out. What I do see is my sister getting hurt, and I'm not sure I can let that happen if I can help it—even if sticking my nose in where it doesn't belong will upset both Lila and my girlfriend."

Trey frowned. What did TJ's girlfriend have to do with the situation?

"Summer has a real problem with the way I try to solve her problems. And Lila's." TJ shrugged. "And Bee's. I guess maybe I see her point when I list everyone out like that." He sounded both disgruntled and resigned.

Since TJ's warning about Lila getting hurt was what he'd been telling himself, Trey tried not to take that personally. He knew what the correct answer was.

"Once Lila negotiates a fair price for this house, I expect she will be happy to return to neutral corners. She takes Shepard business pretty seriously," Trey said, the gloomy feeling hitting him when he remembered that. After their business was finished, he wouldn't have much opportunity to interact with Lila even at a distance…

"Buying a house is a big step," TJ said.

"Yeah, but Lila found the place that makes that so much easier," Trey replied, and he realized that was true. Before he'd settled in that hammock, buying a house had felt unnecessary, especially since he was already planning his departure.

The memory of how she'd talked about being the only Shepard not in the "family business" popped into his head again, and it was important to reiterate that Lila was as good at her own thing as TJ was with Lucy and Bee was with all the details coming into Dispatch. "Rodriguez told me she did the same thing for his family. She's good at this."

"Spoken like a grateful client," TJ said. "And nothing else."

Trey knew he hesitated too long to agree when TJ's lips curled. It wasn't quite a smile, but his expression made Trey think he understood the internal battle. "Careful, Chief, or you'll have a woman explaining to you that she can fight her own battles." TJ sighed. "When they really ought to realize how much we want to fight for them, that it's a privilege."

It was impossible to argue with TJ. If making sure everyone understood that Lila had worked some magic in his house hunt meant he was fighting in her "Shepard-like" battle, then TJ was correct. It was a privilege.

"Lila's good at taking care of herself, so I'm not going to worry too much about whatever this is, whether it's more police business she doesn't want to be a part of or not. At least, I will try." TJ motioned with his head over at the playground where the father and son were testing their drone. "Now, what's our plan? Are we going to be the guys who interrupt a beautiful Sunday morning with the rules and regulations that govern acceptable behavior in Battery Park?"

Trey exhaled slowly. He understood TJ's question. The desire to look the other way, to get back to his regularly scheduled programming, was powerful but completely at odds with his character.

"We're going to have to. If we don't, we open the door for more next weekend, and then the next we've got a problem that we should have stopped before it made it that far," Trey said reluctantly.

"The old chief would have said the same thing," TJ said glumly. "Big stickler on the rule of law, less interested in being the nice guy." TJ winced. "It's nice to be the nice guy."

"Especially when you move into a new town. Nice guy is the way to go." Trey straightened his shoulders. "The job is the job, the rules are the rules and they exist for everyone's benefit."

TJ sighed loudly. "I heard all that in my father's

voice. Unless we issue citations, what are we accomplishing with speaking to these rascals enjoying the park on a beautiful Sunday morning?"

Trey pulled his cell phone out of his pocket. "Good point. We aren't issuing anything but friendly reminders that the behavior is prohibited in Battery Park. The patrol officer on duty who will swing through after I call Dispatch and ask them to send someone over will issue citations if there's no change." He glanced at TJ. "Fair?"

TJ pursed his lips. "Fair."

"You speak to the smoker, and I'll get the drone," Trey said. That put them both returning the way they'd come in. Logical. "And thank you for the coffee."

TJ's smile was more natural now. "I'll make sure I talk to Belinda, too. Getting your lunch order correct will impact how you feel about the town. If you're getting ready to sign a mortgage, that seems more important than ever."

The offer seemed too close to a favor or a special concession, and Trey wanted to wave it away. Unfortunately, he couldn't ignore the fact that it would be great to be able to walk into the closest restaurant to Town Hall without meeting open hostility.

"Thanks. No hard feelings about the job, then?" Trey asked as he started backing away, heading toward the playground.

"None. Maybe we should have made our

Shepard business more public, but it felt important when I turned down the job to keep it low-key. My dad had his heart set on seeing me step up, talked about it to everyone, so when I didn't want it…" TJ's eyes met his, and Trey thought he could see a man who hated disappointing his father. He could understand that. "Even if it hadn't been you, it wouldn't be me. I'll make sure Belinda knows that." TJ shook his head. "Couldn't ask for a better ex-girlfriend. We met, fell in love and broke up in first grade, and she's been my biggest fan since."

Trey frowned. He had no understanding of a relationship like that. "Your relationship with the veterinarian hasn't caused any ripples in that?"

"Nah, Belinda's been married to her high school sweetheart for years. Loyalty. That's all it is. You'll find it's hard to shake a friend once you've made one here in Horizon."

Trey wondered about that. He'd thought he understood friendship, but he'd been shocked and disappointed at the way it could be forgotten.

"See you in the morning, Chief," TJ said as he led Lucy down the sidewalk toward the man fishing. Trey paused and watched TJ approach him, have a brief conversation, wait for the guy to put his cigarette out and leave. There was no tension in the interaction.

Not that there should be any, because the rules

were the rules, and when they were applied fairly and evenly, they were neither good nor bad.

But pointing out infractions to people didn't always go so unemotionally.

He hit the number for Dispatch as he headed toward the playground.

"Good morning, Chief," the officer said. He thought it was Officer Wheeler, but he wasn't certain.

"Morning, Officer. Could you have the patrol officer assigned to the Battery swing through? We've got a smoker fishing on the seawall at the end nearest to the historic district and some amateurs operating a drone near the playground. Both have been issued friendly warnings, so if they persist, a citation is in order." Trey hoped it wouldn't be necessary. If that father and son turned out to be popular in town, he'd be heaping more disapproval from his neighbors on his own head.

"Sure thing, Chief. If that smoker is Randy Eaton, it won't be his first citation or his last. Got a history of doing whatever he likes, no matter the consequences," Wheeler said. "We'll follow up."

"Thanks, Wheeler," Trey said as he hung up the phone, hoping he'd identified her correctly. Then he waved at the father, who had taken over the controls of the drone, and stepped closer. Explaining the rules to them would be simple. It was also the right thing to do. If they stopped breaking the park rules, there would be no harm done.

If he was smart, he would do the same thing with his infatuation with Lila Shepard. At this point, there was no harm done to either of them. They would finish this house negotiation and return to normal. It was business. There were rules in place.

As it was, Trey suspected he would already have a hard time leaving Horizon without experiencing regret about leaving Lila behind.

Thinking about her eyes, the way she'd sparkled there on the dance floor, her business savvy and the weak spots in her confidence related to her family had to be against his rules regarding Lila. It wasn't too late to do the right thing for both of them.

Rules were good. They protected everyone.

Sticking to them now was a case of better late than never.

CHAPTER SIXTEEN

On Monday, Rainey and Lila made the trip into Charleston with two distinct goals. First, Lila was going to negotiate a solid deal on Roberta Hale's house for Trey. He had found the perfect place for him, and she owed it to him to get the purchase price down. The fact that this also felt like facing off against her own personal Goliath was less important than getting this right for him.

Lila checked her lipstick in her visor mirror and accepted that beating Monica Denis was *less* important but not *unimportant*.

Second, she and Rainey were going to parlay this meeting into a pitch opportunity. If Rainey was to be believed, she knew exactly how to get Monica and her father in the same room at the same time.

Both Lila and Rainey wanted this deal for Horizon.

"I'm telling you, I have my ways," Rainey said as she maneuvered her luxury sedan into a spot along King Street that Lila wouldn't have attempted to parallel park in for all the money in the world.

At that time of day, the traffic on King Street wasn't too bad. The restaurants and boutiques lining one of Charleston's most famous streets would pick up around lunchtime and then grow heavier at dinner, but those were a few blocks away. Rainey had snagged a spot less than a block from the Denis Group's offices in the historic Italianate home that was built in 1859. Lila studied the facade as they walked up the steps to the double doors. Ornate corbels supported the impressive eaves of the three-story building, and the tall windows that lined the front were each crowned with classic pediments. The square tower to the right of the front doors broke up the pure symmetry of the house.

"I have my doubts about the success of this plan, Rainey," Lila said as she brushed sweaty palms over her skirt. "Why couldn't you request a meeting?"

Lila had an appointment to meet with Monica to present Trey's offer. Rainey had decided it was the perfect opening to get to Albert Denis.

Rainey had insisted Lila dress in something bright and fun, so she'd chosen a maxi sundress covered in bright red poppies. It wasn't exactly professional attire, but it was her favorite dress, and Rainey had immediately approved. Lila suspected Rainey was plotting her own business-style twist on "good cop, bad cop." The Denises would lower their guards with Lila, and Rainey would swoop in for the kill.

Whatever happened with "Phase 2: Selling Blue Vista" was secondary to Lila's main goal, "Phase 1: Get Trey's House at the Right Price."

"It would have taken months to get on his calendar. I asked Nevaeh to investigate first, and that was her finding. We don't want to wait that long. I'll be running for reelection again at that point. You meet with Monica, and by the time you have the offer ironed out, I'll be ready for your assistance with the pitch." Rainey picked up the leather portfolio she'd prepared to go along with the slideshow they'd put together.

Lila thought about asking for details on how she was going to reach Albert Denis without an appointment, but that wasn't part of the good cop's job assignment. "All right."

"I love a good belvedere," Rainey said with a sigh as she stared up at the tower. Lila would guess it had at least peek-a-boo glimpses of the ocean. "I wouldn't mind having my own tower like that. Think you can find me a house like this? Something special?"

Blue Vista immediately popped into Lila's head, but if their plan worked, it would no longer be available.

"Do you think you could afford it?" Lila asked. Rainey had good taste, but that didn't mean she could access the millions it would take to make a purchase like this one.

Rainey's only answer was a dismissive sniff before she opened the door and stepped inside.

The interior was as beautifully restored as the exterior. The dark wood staircase that swept up to the second floor was intricately carved and lit by all the natural light flooding in through the tall windows. A domed skylight also brought sunlight in from above.

"Good morning," the receptionist said. "How can I help you?"

Rainey motioned Lila forward with a nod.

Before she could answer, someone said, "Lila Shepard, it's so nice to see you."

Lila turned to see that Monica Denis had entered the grand foyer from one of the rooms off to the side. From the investigations Lila had done to prepare for this meeting, she'd known Monica was still a classically beautiful brunette. She hadn't forgotten how tall Monica was, but she was unprepared to stare up at her.

A fleeting wish that she'd worn heels like Rainey's flickered through Lila's mind.

Then she remembered she would have fallen and broken an ankle—and her pride—if she'd attempted that.

"That billboard does not do you justice," Monica said with a polished smile. "And who is this?"

Lila and Rainey had discussed how this introduction might go, so Rainey offered her hand. "Rainey Blackwell." Under normal circumstances, the rest of her delivery included "Mayor of Horizon."

But before making their pitch, they wanted to know if Monica Denis or the Denis Group had done any reconnaissance on Horizon. Monica's face didn't betray any recognition.

"I'll take a seat." Rainey pointed at one of the two gorgeous reproduction couches. "After I visit the ladies' room."

Since that was the next part of the plan, Lila held up her folder, the one with her headshot that matched the billboard that didn't do her justice. She hadn't forgotten what Trey said. When she realized how much happier she felt wearing the sundress with loud red poppies rather than the stiff gray suit, she decided he had a point. She made a mental note to get pricing on replacing the billboard and take an inventory of how many of these printed folders she had in stock. Maybe it was time to change out the photo. Duke deserved to be on billboards anyway.

"Ready to discuss this offer?" Lila asked.

Monica nodded and led Lila into what had once been the formal parlor. Today it had been sectioned into working spaces, each with gorgeous reproduction wood desks and two comfortable armchairs. The style of the Denis Group's office did provoke some envy. This was the fully realized version of what she was trying to accomplish from her little spot in Horizon. The budget must be a thousand times what hers was. It was easy to imagine working with clients in such an impressive room. The majority of them would have a budget to match.

"You have a beautiful office," Lila said as she settled into one of the seats across the desk from Monica.

"It's been in the family since it was built, but my father's the one who completed the renovation from family home to this," she said. "Before that, it was a drain on the finances. Now? It's a testament to the family business's success."

The mention of the family business reminded Lila how much she had at stake that day.

"I have an offer to present on Roberta Hale's house," Lila said as she slid the folder over.

Monica opened it to scan the offer quickly. "That number is entirely too low. Roberta was clear on the price she'd need to sell. Tell your client to come back with something better."

Lila managed not to roll her eyes, but it was difficult. Monica obviously believed Lila was out of her league. "You're required to present the offer to your client." Lila met her stare and waited until Monica looked away. That was a technique her father had taught her as a girl. Looking away first was backing down. That was true in criminal interrogations or dinner-table negotiations over homework and television time.

She and her father had pitched some epic battles, and she'd managed to win a few. Monica Denis was no match for Tom Shepard or his daughter, so she blinked first.

As Monica reached for her phone, Lila added, "And you and I both know your list price is entirely too high. Any buyer will need to invest time and money in updates. I have a buyer ready to do that, but only when the price is within the market's range. If we can make that happen, we'll set up a quick closing and Roberta can be moving into her new place by the first of next month." Lila crossed her legs serenely. That was another trick she'd learned from her father, and she used it in every negotiation. Maintaining her composure when the other party was leaking emotion, whether it was anxiety in a police interview or exasperation in a business conversation, put her in control. "Would you like me to step out while you discuss this with her?"

Monica shook her head, so Lila listened to one side of the conversation. From what she could tell, Roberta responded as expected, but Monica had seen Lila's logic.

As a successful real estate agent, Monica knew that a sale was imminent if she could help close this gap.

While Lila waited, she tried to hear any conversation from the foyer, but nothing made it through the thick walls and plush furnishings. Money provided the best soundproofing.

Monica picked up a pen and made three notes on Lila's offer. She increased the offer price by ten thousand dollars, crossed out the requirement that Roberta pay Trey's portion of the closing costs and changed the closing period from a month to two weeks.

But she didn't hang up the phone.

Lila took that to mean she expected a quick counteroffer, so she texted him the details.

His reply was immediate.

Go ahead with the counter that we discussed.

Lila contained her smug grin as she took Monica's pen and split the difference on the offer price.

The urge to celebrate was strong because this was going exactly as she expected. She had discussed with Trey the maneuvers Monica would attempt, and it was relief to see that she'd been right. The worry that she might not be able to go toe-to-toe with this Charleston agent with her family business background had been hard to shake. Everything going as planned made it easier to believe she could let that fear go.

Maybe *her* family's business—law enforcement skills passed down by her father—was more important to Lila's success than she'd realized.

His tactics translated to real estate negotiations very well.

When Monica nodded her agreement to Lila's change, she picked up her phone and pointed at the hallway. Calling Trey was only a formality, but it felt good to step outside on the long gallery that lined the front of the Denis House to make that call. It was going to be a warm afternoon, but there was a breeze stirring there in the shade.

"Good morning, Lila," Trey said after the first ring, and she had to lean against the balustrade at the shock through her system. His voice, those words, it was easy to imagine hearing them first thing every day for the rest of her life, and the surprise of that image knocked her off balance. "Do we have an agreement?"

Lila had to clear her throat before she could answer. "We do. She didn't go for covering the closing costs, but we've got a fair price. If you're happy, we'll get the contract signed and you'll own your first home in Horizon."

The hesitation on the line snapped her out of the panicky, fluttery confusion his voice had provoked. "Are you having second thoughts about the house?"

His quiet sigh should have been easy to miss, but she was locked in on his voice.

"No, not the house," he finally said. "Let's do it."

Lila stared down the sidewalk lining King

Street. This was not the time or place to get into deep conversation. Rainey was pulling her strings somewhere in the background, so the clock was ticking on wrapping this up.

But it was too important to let go.

"So, it's the location. You have your doubts about Horizon," Lila said.

His silence was an answer, the confirmation that when he'd been asking about resale, it hadn't been about moving to a bigger place or one that fit any life changes. He was already planning his next move.

And it was going to be out of Horizon.

That happened in real estate. People moved. It kept her in business, in fact.

For some reason, learning that Trey's plans were temporary bothered her.

"This is the right move. Get me that contract, Lila," he said firmly, "and I will take you to the nicest restaurant in Horizon to celebrate, as long as you tell me which one it is."

Lila laughed as he expected her to. "How about coffee at the Daybreak? I'll make sure Belinda is nice to you."

She heard a smile in his voice when he said, "Deal."

They set up a time for him to come by her office to sign the final offer. Then she hung up and stared hard at the street without seeing anything.

She wasn't sure how long she would have stayed there, but her phone dinged with a text.

Wrap it up. Phase two is commencing. Come in and head for the belvedere.

Rainey's directive sounded like movie dialogue, like the orders an action hero would hear through his earpiece before he parachuted in through an improbably paused giant exhaust fan. Maybe that was because it was easy to imagine Rainey in such a scenario.

Lila walked back inside and offered her hand to Monica. "We have a deal. My buyer is thrilled. Horizon's new chief of police is looking forward to moving in."

Monica smiled. "My seller will be happy to have the deal done, too."

When Lila remembered the way Roberta had probed for news about the new sheriff, she wondered if knowing he was moving in would make her happy or not.

"Before I go," Lila said hesitantly. She bit her lip for added believability. "I don't suppose you could give me a tour? I love these old houses, and that tower… I'd love to see it."

Monica paused but eventually nodded. "*Bien sûr*, Lila. We love to show the building off."

If Lila hadn't been trying to guess what she'd find whenever they ran into Rainey, the tour would have been a highlight to the day. Monica sprinkled in family history as they walked through the first floor and up to the second. When they made the turn toward the corner with the tower, they found Rainey and the man who had to be Albert Denis seated in a cozy conversational seating area in front of an office with broad windows on three sides, each with a panoramic view.

She paused to imagine running an empire from such an office and had to remember why she was there. They wanted a tiny, tiny piece of that empire for Horizon.

"Lila's the real estate agent I mentioned. She's contacted the current owners of these properties to gauge their interest. When you and I have a way forward, she'll close the deals." Rainey motioned Lila forward to shake Albert Denis's hand, but Lila thought it was a bad sign that he didn't stand to do so.

She wasn't caught off guard when his handshake included a paternal pat. That matched his slightly condescending expression. "Well now, meeting you, Lila, adds a pretty bow to an unexpected delight for this morning's visit. It's not every day I have surprise visitors, and I know you'll find the right developer for your project." Then he stood. "Monica, you'll see them out?"

Rainey tried to follow him as he headed for his office, but Monica stepped smoothly into her path, almost like she'd done the same a hundred other times.

"Lila, I can't say it has been a pleasure doing business with you this morning, since I'm not sure I came out on top in this deal," Monica said as she held her arms out to herd them back toward the stairs and the front door. "At least I know who I'm dealing with when I go back into Horizon. I appreciate that. But if you want to do business with my father, there are better ways to manage it."

Rainey planted her heels firmly on the bottom step. "I have a better way. Just off the top of my head, selling you on the idea seems like it would lead to success with the Denis Group."

Monica's lips curled in what Lila would call a reluctant smile. "Not guaranteed but it would be stronger than ambushing my father in his office."

"You know what Horizon offers already," Rainey said as she took a step down. "We have land for twenty lots with ocean views situated north of town. All we need is the developer. Lila will handle listing, showing and selling."

As Lila trailed behind them, she understood that Rainey was setting the terms to include her deliberately. If the deal didn't work with Lila's exclusive, it didn't work at all.

And she remembered exactly how much she loved Rainey Blackwell. She would fight for her friends until the very end.

By the time they made it to the bottom of the

staircase, Monica was shaking her head. "Too small. There's not enough business there to draw my father right now. I'll keep an eye on the market, though, when I'm through there to list or sell, and we can circle back around. I see the potential but now isn't the right time."

Lila was ready to argue the case. Monica had been wrong about Roberta's house price, and she was wrong again here.

But Rainey tilted her head to the side before raising her hands in surrender. "Okay, y'all are the experts here. I hope you'll reach out when the time is right. Horizon has all the pieces to be Charleston's next big bedroom community."

Monica opened the front door and held it open expectantly, so Lila followed Rainey down the steps to the sidewalk. They didn't hurry, and Rainey turned back to give Monica a jaunty wave before they walked to the car.

Then she slid inside, waited for Lila to shut her door, gripped the steering wheel firmly and said, "How soon can we get together to come up with plan B?"

Lila buckled her seat belt as Rainey shot out of the parking spot. Luckily, there was no traffic.

"I have time tomorrow morning." Lila inhaled slowly as a stray thought occurred. She took a minute to examine it. "And I already have the beginning in mind."

Rainey slammed on the brakes at a stop sign. "Really?"

"Really," Lila said firmly and told herself not to be offended at Rainey's surprised tone. She pulled out her cell phone, scrolled through the numbers she had stored from previous deals and hit the one for the small firm out of Savannah responsible for building Bay View Tower. Maybe they'd be interested in another condo development with some added amenities to draw the over-fifty-five crowd. It was hard to imagine either her father or the Admiral disapproving of a place that would gradually grow Horizon's numbers.

The land requirement would be smaller for another development like Bay View, so they might also be able to save the original Blue Vista with the right plans.

Based on Rainey's question about finding her a place, "something special," Lila thought she might also have a buyer in mind for Blue Vista. "I will share it with you on one condition."

"Anything," Rainey immediately answered.

"We're also going to brainstorm ways to make sure Monica Denis continues to lose when she ventures into Horizon." Lila had decided that was going to be her chief goal. Horizon was her town, and she had no plans to share it.

Rainey's low chuckle made Lila grin.

"We may not be undefeated, but if anyone can come out on top in Horizon, it's us," Rainey said.

"Don't count this as a loss yet, Rainey. We're still at bat," Lila said before shaking her head. "We don't do sports metaphors."

"But that's clearly our choice and not because we can't." Rainey grinned. "Do you have time to stop for lunch? I'm buying if you do. I've been daydreaming about pimiento cheese and a fried-green-tomato BLT since the last time I came up to Charleston."

"Absolutely. I got Trey the house of his dreams. Lunch is the perfect way to celebrate." She'd have to keep her concerns about how temporary his dream home might be quiet. He deserved to make his own decisions, and Rainey would promptly launch her counteroffensive if she learned he was planning to leave. Lila stared out the window as Rainey made the quick trip to Bay Street and wondered if there was anything she could do to change Trey's mind.

CHAPTER SEVENTEEN

TREY WAS SURPRISED at the anticipation that quickened his steps as he crossed the street toward the Battery on Tuesday afternoon. He'd expected nerves to accompany signing this offer for the largest purchase of his life, but they hadn't kicked in. As soon as he'd talked to Lila on the phone the day before, he'd felt peaceful about this decision. If he was honest with himself, he could admit that a lot of his positive attitude had to do with seeing Lila again.

The kiss remained on repeat in his brain, shut down only when he attempted to remember his plan to keep his distance.

Wrapping up this purchase would help clear his mind.

There would be a few to-do items to complete before the closing, but there wouldn't be much reason to see Lila.

But he had a good reason today.

His only regret was that he'd had to postpone his meeting with Lila to sign the final offer because of a rescheduled meeting with the park rangers at Rocky Point Lighthouse. They'd had some trouble with vandals over the weekend and requested assistance from the Horizon PD. Since he'd been planning to get out to the lighthouse to assess the security needs and readiness anyway, he'd joined Officers Shepard and Roberts for their initial investigation.

Everything about the damage suggested bored kids were responsible. Both of his officers had presented good questions and observed key details, all of which had made it into their initial report. Since that report had landed on his desk right after their morning shift change, Trey could see that timeliness was respected by his officers.

He could thank Tom Shepard for that training.

Shepard and Roberts were good at investigating the scene. The whole department had solid instincts and work ethic. That made his job simple.

Rodriguez had shown him the comments on the back-to-school-night post on the Horizon PD's social media page. They were all positive, even though he was front and center in the photo. Being on social media was a new aspect of police work for Trey.

That the comments were positive had been a pleasant surprise, too.

Bee Shepard had shown him the final draft of the quarterly map they planned to provide local law enforcement agencies. Even in a small town with limited resources, his police department could adapt and accomplish exciting new things.

Being a police officer required both instincts and attention to the details required for reporting and building solid cases. The two didn't always go together.

Paperwork was hated by most law enforcement officers he knew. There was no reason that would be any different even in a small town.

For the first year he'd worked with DEA task forces, he'd been handed every form required for any operation he'd worked on. Dennis Browning had said the same thing every single time. "Rookies write reports." There had been no hesitation in his delivery, either.

That reminded Trey of the text he hadn't answered from the night before. He pulled his phone out.

I've got a job for you. How quickly can you get here?

Browning had given him his first chance to step up to federal cases. Trey had found his purpose there. The work was exciting and made a difference, and he was good at it. Every other time the man had called with a job, Trey had been ready to go. He owed Dennis.

Even now, the urge to ask questions about the assignment bubbled up.

But seeing the suspicion on Dennis's face when Trey had stated his innocence was something he couldn't forget.

Trey hadn't answered this text yet because he wasn't sure what to say. Leaving Horizon at that point seemed impossible but so did turning down an offer to return to the work he loved.

Not even telling himself that nothing had changed in the month he'd been gone made it easier to answer.

Trey shoved his phone back in his pocket and tried to get back a bit of his enthusiasm for the day.

The weather was beautiful.

His new house had an ocean soundtrack.

The bumps at work were smoothing out, thanks in large part to Bee Shepard.

Dispatch had returned to the morning briefings, and no one had remarked on it, even after he'd opened the floor for conversation and Bee reminded everyone that the end-of-summer concert was imminent. After Bee had returned to her spot near the hallway leading to Dispatch, he'd watched TJ Shepard and Sheila Roberts exchange knowing nods. It looked as if they had added Bee's reminder about an influx of bored out-of-towners to their existing knowledge about the vandalism to come up with an answer to who they might be searching for in their case.

Whether or not the upcoming concert had also

occurred to them before the briefing didn't matter much. A lot of policework required being in the room with other smart people. Bee Shepard brought something into the conversation that the Horizon PD needed.

He briefly wondered if the vandals were partying around the Needlegrass Motor Lodge pool and whether he could suggest Shepard and Roberts start their investigation there. The noise and length of late-night parties had not quite reached the preincident levels, but Joe Morgan had not been responding to the ruckus lately, either.

Trey realized irritation was building at the memory of the noise but focused on the fact that he was on his way to sign whatever Lila needed to get this house purchase started. Soon it wouldn't matter how many parties the Needlegrass hosted.

If he was reluctant to rock the boat any more, he could concentrate on his impending move instead.

As Trey crossed the cobblestone street in front of Lila's office, his phone dinged.

He didn't need to check to see who it was. Dennis knew exactly how to get past his defenses. Since the key was persistence, the same weapon Rainey had used to get him to Horizon, Trey resolved to practice saying no…mainly by ignoring the texts. Rainey had had to show up in person. Surely Dennis would draw the line at that.

Lila was seated behind a large desk when he walked in. She greeted him with a smile, and it was like the whole world snapped into focus. At the thought, Trey shook his head but remembered to smile as if he was having a totally normal moment on any average day.

Then the large dog taking up most of the floor stretched slowly and pressed his nose against Trey's hand. He had learned from his mistake with Lucy. The Shepards didn't mess around with their dogs, so he bent to one knee and almost immediately realized that put him at a slight disadvantage with this dog.

But it did make his nametag easier to read. "Nice to meet you, Duke." The dog gave his hair a few careful sniffs, which Trey took to be cautious approval. He raised a hand to scratch Duke between his bushy brows, then moved to sit in one of the chairs. Duke flowed over to lean against his leg, and Trey continued scratching.

Lila's small smile felt like approval. Trey soaked it up.

"The rumors of your dislike for dogs might be exaggerated," Lila said.

Trey nodded slowly. "Absolutely. I never had a dog. That doesn't mean I don't like them. I liked them too much to always leave them behind." He met Lila's stare. "I do that. I leave things behind when I need to move to the next job."

Maybe she had shifted his whole world. That didn't mean she had to shift with him. Warning her about his plans without coming out and admitting them wasn't quite as brave as he wished, but he wanted her help to keep distance between them.

His phone repeated the text alert noise, reminding him that the world might be shifting without either one of them giving permission. Dennis Browning might be moving up Trey's unofficial timeline. Lila could still protect herself, so that when he left, he was the only one suffering the consequences. He could live with that.

She slid paperwork and a pen in front of him. "One of the benefits of home buying, at least in Horizon, is that you will be perfectly placed to remedy that. You can have the time for a dog here, no need to leave anything behind. Jewel at the Shoreline Animal Hospital can help you find the perfect first dog."

Trey scrawled his signature and initialed next to all the spots Lila had marked with an X. "Maybe." The image of TJ and Lucy in the park popped up, and it was hard to deny how much fun a running buddy seemed. The pang of yearning was a surprise. "The learning curve would be pretty steep, though."

Lila dismissed that with a wave of her hand. "The volunteers there are as good at matching pets as I am at houses, so that's saying something. I never had a dog, either. Duke has taught me everything I need to know." Then her face grew serious. "But a dog will need more than three years,

I guess. Wasn't that what you asked for resale options? Where will you be going, Trey?"

She stacked the paperwork neatly while she watched him. Her face was serious. He wasn't sure he'd be able to walk out without telling her his plan to go back to federal task forces and Columbia.

His phone dinged again.

"Is that *police business*? Need to take it?" Lila asked.

Trey pulled his phone out. Browning again.

You won't answer texts, so I'll come to you.

He frowned as he realized that he was going to have to find an answer and deliver it face-to-face. Should he call in Rainey for backup? She might be his only hope to say no and meet his obligations here in Horizon.

Then he realized Lila was waiting for him to answer.

"I shouldn't have kissed you, not knowing that you are part of Horizon and I…" Trey squeezed his phone. Nothing about what he was saying was right.

"And you aren't. Don't want to be." Lila pointed at the paperwork that finalized his offer. "Or are you, Trey? If you want to be, you can. You have the start you need. A good job. A house with the sound of the waves. A dog. What more do you need?"

The fact that she hadn't included someone to take all those pieces and assemble them into a home made him wonder if she had seen herself in this scenario at all.

He hated the confusion on her face.

"Why would you come here without any plans to stay? What was the house hunt about?" Lila asked. She didn't mention the kiss even though he had. He hoped that meant she understood it had been completely uncalculated, the move of a man caught up in a moment.

"This job was a lifeline, a way out of a bad situation. It's also the key to getting my career back on track. I had some trouble in Columbia..." Trey didn't want to go down that track. If Lila believed the worst of him, he wasn't certain he would recover. "Rainey's a friend. I'll do the best job I can while I'm here, and there is no denying that the Horizon Police Department is solid. Your father trained officers here to do good work." Then he leaned forward. "This is police business, right? You stay out of police business." He didn't want to spend more time talking about this. If he left Horizon now, he'd feel like the biggest fraud in the world.

But having Lila believe the worst of him would be unthinkable.

She nodded. "Yeah, I do. My whole life, I've wanted to be far, far away from police business.

I wish I couldn't see more messy police business coming when you go."

"What if TJ is ready for the job then? Imagine how happy Belinda will be to see him seated properly behind the chief's desk." Trey wanted to lighten the mood, but Lila's eyes remained locked on his face.

Her lips were a flat line. "You were planning on a short stay. What is to keep you from cutting that even shorter? What if the right job opens up?"

Since he was ignoring such an offer at that moment, her point was valid. He hated her disappointment.

"I shouldn't have kissed you. That part I regret." He was sincere but also lying. It had to be impossible to truly regret a first kiss that sweet.

"I don't regret it." Lila flopped back against her seat. "In fact, I would like to do it again. Right now."

Trey frowned as he rewound her words in his head. He hit Play and then repeated it twice more to be sure he'd understood correctly. "Even though I'm leaving and you aren't…"

She huffed out an angry breath. "I'm not going to do it, obviously."

His disappointment weighed on his shoulders, but he was also grateful one of them was being smart.

Then he remembered how devastated he'd been

by her confused frown. Tears would put him in the ground.

"Smart. If you did kiss me again, then what? Are you ready to be roped into police business for the rest of your life?" he asked a little desperately. He was weak and he knew it. It was easier to strengthen Lila's resolve than trust his own.

"Honestly, if anyone can help the police chief separate his life from his job, it's me," Lila said, and he wondered if she realized what she was saying. "My mother said that only my father could make it worthwhile to deal with all the headaches, that the man he is makes it worth the tradeoffs required to be married to the chief of police. At the time, I thought it was sweet, but now..." She shrugged. "I guess I understand how that can be true. Maybe not with you, but some other guy who takes over the job." The wry curl of her lips told Trey she was poking fun at herself or him or even both of them.

Trey realized Lila was thinking about more than one kiss.

She was considering a *lifetime* of kisses.

The way his pulse sped up was concerning. Excitement mingled with hope all while he tried to quash it.

"Let's get the keys to this house for now." Trey stood, all his muscles tense, almost as if he was getting ready to run. "Then we can...see."

Lila pursed her lips before nodding. "Said the chicken."

Trey blinked, did the rewind-and-replay thing again. "Chicken?"

She shrugged. "It's okay to be afraid. You're only facing off against a well-run police department that you stepped into without a stitch of local experience, the house that fits you perfectly and the urge to kiss me. I don't think you stand a chance of leaving in three years, but I can't convince you. You'll have to see for yourself."

Before he could assemble a response from the jumble of words bouncing around in his brain, the door opened. Rainey stuck her head in. "Hey, the newest homeowner of Horizon!"

She had her arms wrapped around him in a congratulatory hug before he knew it was coming and then stepped back toward the door. "You guys done? Bee's on her way to the diner. She has some big project she's in a hurry to get back to so she can get the chief his new report."

Trey turned to face Lila and then couldn't look away from her. The pause spun out long enough that Rainey cleared her throat then said, "Mmmkay, I walked into the middle of something, and I'm walking right back out. Meet us down at the diner, Lila."

The bells on the door snapped Trey out of the moment.

"If you aren't afraid that I'm right, come down

with us to the diner. I will introduce you to Belinda and clear the air with her. Then we will systematically convert every one of your haters into neighbors, and by the time you move into your new house, you will wonder why you ever thought you could leave." Her serene smile should have panicked him, but the image was impossibly attractive.

When she moved around the desk toward him, he almost stepped forward to meet her but realized what he was doing half a second before. Instead, he turned toward the door and opened it for her. He wasn't going to meet her or kiss her, but he was also not going to back down. His plan to bide his time in Horizon made sense. It might take a day or two, but Lila would come to see how right he was to keep his distance. Then they could part as friends, and the Shepards of Horizon, South Carolina, would remain cordial acquaintances as he moved up in his career.

"I will follow you. I owe you a cup of coffee for all your help and to congratulate you for defeating your foe," Trey said in what he hoped was a friendly, teasing voice. He wanted to keep Lila in his life, even if they were nonkissing friends. The thought of never seeing the smirk currently on her face again bothered him.

He was reminded of how aware of her he was as they made the short walk down the sidewalk to the Daybreak Diner. He hadn't come back since his first disastrous lunch order the week before, but now that he knew who Belinda was, he realized he should have been prepared.

The brunette behind the counter zeroed in on him as soon as he and Lila entered, but he registered that the diner was in full lunch swing. He spotted Rainey and Bee at the pickup window, waiting for their coffees. TJ Shepard and the veterinarian were seated next to the window. Tom and Kay Shepard had a booth back in the corner.

So literally every person he wanted to impress was already in the diner.

He'd picked a great time to prove he wasn't a chicken.

"What can I get you?" Belinda asked, her narrowed eyes locked on his face.

Before he could answer, TJ stepped up and patted him on the back. "Chief, I wanted to let you know how much I appreciate your hard work. Let me buy your coffee." He leaned closer to Belinda. "And throw in one of my favorite cookies. I know the chief will love the chocolate chunk as much as I do."

Everyone in the diner held their breath, Trey most of all, until Belinda nodded. "Black coffee and a cookie coming up, Chief."

"That's great, and add Lila's drink. I'm buying, though, Shep…" He stopped when TJ widened his eyes. "TJ, thank you for the kind offer, but we are celebrating my new house. I'll be moving in two weeks."

Someone in the back said, "Hey, Joe, there's some good news."

His landlord at the Needlegrass, sitting at a table near the window, raised his coffee cup high in the air.

Trey had to laugh at the way they all turned to see Joe's reaction. Since it was pretty funny, it was easy enough to roll with the punch. "And if anyone knows Sam Pulaski, make sure she knows I won't be upsetting the system at Island Manor, either."

When he turned back to face Lila, he realized that the people in the Daybreak Diner were proving her right. The fact that they were already teasing him made him wonder what life would look like at the end of his self-imposed three years. Rainey had said his police officers would respect him in six months. Would he be able to pull himself away?

Before he could determine whether yes or no was the desired answer to that question, the doors to the diner opened and Dennis Browning stepped inside with John McEntire close behind. Neither man looked surprised to find him there, so Trey guessed they'd checked in at the station to find out where he was. As long as he was in Horizon, there would be no avoiding anyone who wanted to find him.

And he remembered what Lila had told him about how the chief of police was never off duty, not even at lunch, because everyone in town knew how to track him down.

Dennis offered him a hand to shake. “You are a hard man to get in touch with. You’d think I was collecting overdue rent instead of offering you a job.”

Adrenaline kicked in again. The reminder of how he’d looked forward to new jobs was difficult to ignore, but facing Dennis like this also brought the sharp memory of his suspicion.

Now that he had an offer—and there was no guarantee of another one in three years when his self-imposed tour of duty in Horizon was up—what should he do?

The way everything in the diner quieted told Trey that all of his neighbors had heard Dennis’s opening lines.

Lila crossed her arms over her chest as she faced him.

It looked like the time had come to make a decision, and everyone in Horizon was going to be a part of the conversation.

CHAPTER EIGHTEEN

LILA DIDN'T RECOGNIZE the man who announced to the entire diner that Trey's term as chief of police might already be wrapping up, but there was a certain aspect to his expression that she immediately understood. This was one of the other kinds of law enforcement out there in the wide world. Instead of being focused on service to the community like her father, TJ and Bee, this guy liked recognition. He wanted to be the kind of hero that everyone praised. He had made sure all eyes were on him as he backed Trey into a corner.

She moved nearer to Trey without understanding what she planned to do. She just needed to be closer.

"Dennis, this isn't a good time. Let's grab some lunch and head back to my office," Trey said.

Rainey stepped between them. "Oh, I don't know. This could be the perfect time." She held out her hand. "Mayor Rainey Blackwell. Chief Douglas's boss. And you are?"

Lila raised her eyebrows at the coldness in Rainey's voice. Around Horizon, they all had plenty of opportunity to see the charming side of the politician, but Dennis, whoever he was, was about to see a different side.

"DEA Special Agent Dennis Browning," he answered as he shook her hand firmly. "Trey's other boss, the first one, the one who gave him this career."

Lila managed to contain the grimace that wanted to escape at his tone, and one look at Trey's face confirmed he didn't think much of it, either.

"Former boss," Trey said quietly, "and one who didn't seem too worried about making it 'former' when I left."

Dennis Browning scoffed. "Accepting bribes is a serious charge."

Shock made Lila's mouth drop open. Bribery?

She closed her mouth when she realized Trey was watching her closely.

Before she could compose her face, Browning said forcefully, "I was doing my job. You know we practice 'guilty until proven innocent' when we get a whiff of corruption on these task forces." He waved his hands as if he would wipe all that away. "There's a lot of temptation, but this trial should put an end to any gossip. You'll soon be exonerated, and we can go right back to the way we were, rounding up the worst drug dealers and traffickers in the state." He glanced around the room. "Less time for the coffee crew in the middle of the day, of course, but you understand the payoff."

The words "exonerated" and "trial" sent ripples through the room, but Lila noticed that Rainey didn't seem surprised at all. She'd known whatever Browning was referring to, and she'd pursued Trey until he took the job anyway. That was a clear character witness for Lila.

Rainey was certain Trey was innocent of whatever Browning had suspected.

Lila was, too.

But the answer about what she could do to end this confrontation wouldn't come.

Who would ever believe Trey guilty of taking bribes? That officers and agents who had been trained to see through lies and track complex cases believed such an impossible story made Lila twice as angry on Trey's behalf. They should have known better.

Surely no one here could believe it, either. He'd been universally disliked in Horizon for sticking so closely to the rules. There was no way he'd gotten a completely new personality to go with his new position.

Her father cleared his throat, and it was like someone clanged an alarm. Everyone in the room turned toward him, even Dennis Browning.

"Agent Browning," her father said slowly, "we haven't met. I'm—"

"Tom Shepard," Browning interrupted him.

"Yes, I know. I saw you speak at a conference when I first joined the agency. It's a pleasure to meet you, sir." Lila watched Browning scan the room. She wondered if he was trying to find an easy path over to her father's table.

"What was the topic?" her father asked. "Of the panel?"

Lila met TJ's stare across the room. They'd fallen for this tactic a thousand times over the years. Her father was laying a trap for Browning. His mild tone and what seemed like a random question confused his opponents, so they wandered right in.

"Cooperation between law enforcement agencies at all levels, federal, state and local," Browning immediately answered. Lila was impressed if he was pulling that from memory. "I remember it so clearly because DEA task forces rely so heavily on members pulled from a variety of agencies. Your words stayed with me."

Her father nodded slowly and waited for Browning to come around to where he was headed. "Chief Douglas is now a part of that local level. You knew him at a different time and place, but Horizon does not routinely provide federal task force members. It's a small department for a small town, but there's plenty of work to be done here."

Browning returned his nod but with more energy. "I know, but it's easier to replace the chief of a force this size than to find another task force leader like Trey."

Lila studied Trey's face to guess what he thought about that. She had no trouble believing he was very good at whatever he did or that his former boss would track him down to try to bring him back.

"If he's so good, why is he here in the first place?" her father asked. "Did you mess up by letting him go and you need to correct an error, Browning?"

She and Bee exchanged wide-eyed glances because it was rare to see her father escalate. He preferred defusing and problem-solving, but he slowly stood from his chair.

Browning turned to Trey. "Just take the job. We don't need to drag out your past."

Her father faced Trey. "You have anything to be ashamed of in that past, Chief?"

Lila knew there were things that Trey didn't want to discuss. Was her father about to force all that out in front of the lunch rush at the Daybreak? She moved closer to say…what? That Trey didn't have to say anything he didn't want to?

It seemed more important that he do exactly that, tell them all whatever it was that had sent him to Horizon. She wanted him to want to stay. Getting all that out would level the playing field again. Trey met her stare.

She was still wondering whether taking his

hand would help or hurt when he said, "The trial Browning is referring to is an investigation of my former right hand, a longtime member of my team, who is guilty of accepting bribes and derailing a couple of critical investigations. My former boss believed I was involved in the scheme." He shrugged. "At least he did until someone pulled together enough evidence to prove that I wasn't. My word wasn't good enough for him to stand behind me, to support me. Neither was my record or our working relationship."

Browning braced his hands on his hips. "I was doing my job. Due diligence. If you had been patient like I counseled, you'd already be back at work and this whole conversation would have been unnecessary."

Trey glanced around the room. "Let's step outside to finish our discussion." When Rainey moved to follow them, Trey shook his head. Lila was surprised to see that the mayor plopped down in a booth. Then she realized Rainey could keep an eye on the conversation from there.

Once Trey and Browning had left, the room was tense and silent.

Joe Morgan said, "Mayor, seems like you brought in a problem. Did you know your guy's checkered past before you hired him?"

Lila moved closer to the window. Whatever Browning was saying, Trey wasn't buying it. His face was closed, but she could tell by the set of his shoulders that he was ready to argue.

So was Rainey, but that was easy to read on her face. Her eyes were narrowed and locked on Joe Morgan across the room.

"Of course I did, Joe. Do you believe there's something that affects my town that I don't know about?" She smiled but it wasn't a friendly smile. "Like I know you've been thinking about running against me in next year's election."

His mouth dropped open, but he didn't have an immediate response.

"Everything I've said about Trey is true. He's done good work, hard work, for years, and I know he is as committed to serving people as Tom Shepard."

"So these rumors aren't true?" Joe pressed.

A loud snort interrupted their conversation, and everyone turned to face Belinda behind the counter. When she realized she was the center of attention, Belinda flushed a bright pink before clearing her throat. "How anyone could believe that a man who has ruffled so many feathers in such a short time could be capable of accepting bribes to break the law is beyond me. The man has done nothing but rub people around here the wrong way by enforcing rules to an unpopular degree." She waved the towel in her hand. "I should know. I've heard all the tales, large and small. Joe, you've been gobbling up every bit of gossip you can while you're enjoying your daily Sunrise Special, so please do not pretend to be shocked here."

Lila saw TJ point at Belinda and mime a high five, which she returned.

Then her father cleared his throat again, and everyone tuned in to hear his thoughts.

"I had my doubts when Rainey brought him in. I had someone else in mind, but he had other plans for his career." Her father didn't glance at TJ, but her brother concentrated on stirring his coffee. "So I did some checking. I still have a few friends in law enforcement here and there."

Lila smiled as Rainey rolled her eyes. If by "here and there," her father meant in every branch of law enforcement in South Carolina, then yes, he had a few friends.

"I heard the rumors. I heard praise. Then I got to know the chief." He held up his hands as if that's all he needed to say.

And maybe it was. Joe Morgan humphed loudly before waving his coffee cup at Belinda. "I'm going to need a refill."

Was that it? Lila wasn't certain.

Belinda nodded and wound through the tables. "Gonna need to rethink this bid for mayor, too, I'm thinking."

When Belinda passed TJ's table, they exchanged an actual high five and she patted Summer on the shoulder.

"Have we settled this issue, then?" Rainey

stood and pointed at the window. "Because the chief is wrapping things up right now."

Everyone flocked to the long window lining the front of the diner. Lila moved quickly and managed to grab a front-row spot. Trey had finished listening to whatever Browning had to say. Now he had the other man on his back foot, arms crossed, while Trey did the talking, one finger pointing every now and then down at the street and in the direction of Town Hall.

"Whoa, I'm not sure I've ever seen that much… emoting from Trey," Rainey said quietly on one side of Lila.

"It looks good on him," Belinda added from the other side. Then she met Lila's stare. "What?"

"From his biggest hater to…" What? Was she going to be facing off against Belinda now if she managed to convince Trey to settle in Horizon?

Belinda smiled slowly. "Oh, okay, it's like that."

Lila narrowed her eyes. "Like what?"

Belinda shrugged. "Like you're about to be getting absolutely tangled up in police business for the long run."

Rainey raised her eyebrows. Behind her, Bee grinned slowly, and TJ's expression was resigned.

Lila huffed out a sigh. "Too late. I'm already in. But I'm going to need some help convincing Trey that he's staying."

Everyone returned to watching the show outside. Browning was making an angry motion with his hand as he backed away down the sidewalk. Was he leaving? It looked like he was returning to the public parking across from Town Hall.

Lila was preparing a celebratory welcome-back into the diner, but Trey slowly followed Browning, and she wasn't sure whether to trail behind him and beg him to change his mind or to let him go. Luckily, Rainey had no doubts. She slapped some cash down on the table. "Belinda, keep the change." She hurried after Trey.

"She'll give us all the details later," Bee said softly as she wrapped her arm over Lila's shoulder. It was easy to nod because it was true, but it felt wrong to let Trey walk away.

TREY DECIDED THE last place he wanted to be was his office. Everyone in town could track him down there, and he didn't want to make excuses or answer any questions. Instead, he crossed over the cobblestone street into the park and found his way to the bench he'd shared with the former chief and TJ Shepard. He eased down and let the sound of waves calm his mind.

It was a good thing the waves worked quickly because he spotted Rainey out of the corner of his eye about three seconds later.

He stifled a sigh as he stared out over the water. "How bad is the fallout? I should have stopped this before he showed up in Horizon. I'm sorry."

She eased down next to him. "Pretty sure Belinda got it all handled with an assist from the former chief. Joe Morgan doesn't stand a chance of beating me now." He could hear the satisfaction in her voice.

"Beating you?" he asked because that was the part that made the least sense in his head. Then he added, "Wait. You said Belinda handled it?"

He understood each word individually, but when they were arranged in this order, he wasn't following.

"Joe was hoping to fan the discontent about my new chief to stir up some opposition and gather votes in the next mayoral election." Rainey shook her head. "Can you even imagine?"

She obviously couldn't from her satisfied expression, so Trey decided to relax about her election chances.

"I was going to treat this job like a stepping stone to get back to where I wanted to be," Trey admitted because it suddenly mattered that he be honest about everything with her. Rainey had taken a chance, pursued him and brought him to Horizon.

And he had a feeling someday he was going to look back on that decision as the one that changed his whole life.

Seeing Lila's shock about the accusations had shaken him. He'd needed some time to come to terms with the fact that she was going to need answers. That was discouraging. He'd hoped she could see his character.

"Did you think I didn't know you were plotting to leave ASAP?" Rainey asked.

He turned to face her. "I never said it."

She rolled her eyes. "You didn't have to. You made yourself miserable trying to hold on to it. I had to pry your fingers loose to get you here, and you have held yourself apart from everyone in this town as best you could." The corner of her mouth curved up in what he would label an evil smirk. Other people might just call it a smile. "Lila Shepard is Horizon's secret weapon. In so many ways."

Trey stretched his legs out as he considered that. "Yeah, you hear a lot about the Shepards as the new guy in town, but Lila surprised me."

"I bet she did," Rainey said in a low voice. "She surprised me, too. Together we're about to bring something big to Horizon."

"The subdivision she told me about?" Trey asked and realized he hadn't even asked how the presentation went. He let his head fall back and stared up at the leafy canopy overhead. He was as bad as the rest of her family, treating her as an afterthought.

"No, they said no. While I was reeling from the shock and considering my lunch order as a consolation prize, Lila was already on the phone, putting together a new pitch for a better deal that fits Horizon perfectly." Rainey shook her head. "On top of that, she also forgave me for the nearly fatal error of even thinking of working with an outsider. That was a rookie mistake."

"And we don't make rookie mistakes, do we?" Trey asked in the same tone she'd used with him on his first day as chief.

"Not if we can help it." She smiled at him. "And if we do, we fix them. You have been doing that so well that your friends defended you while you weren't even in the room. That's real friendship. Can you find that if you go back to Columbia?"

He knew the answer, of course. His friends in Columbia hadn't defended him while he'd been standing there next to them. There was no doubt what had happened when he'd been absent.

"I wish..." He swallowed the rest of the sentence, but Rainey scooted closer.

"You wish...what?" she asked.

"Lila seemed pretty shocked." He shrugged. "I wish she'd been able to dismiss the claims as easily as you did."

Rainey groaned. "Oh, please."

Trey frowned at her. Sympathy had never been her strong suit, but this seemed about as far from sympathy as she could get.

"Think about this..." She gripped his arm. Hard. "What if the difference is that you told me, and Lila got to hear it from the skunk you used to work for? There's no way she believes that you had anything to do with taking bribes. Trust me."

Trey squeezed his eyes shut.

Because he was doing it again, jumping to conclusions without enough information. He'd talk to Lila and get everything out in the open.

Just as soon as he wrapped his head around settling, for now, in Horizon.

If the offer to step back up to leading a task force came from someone other than Dennis Browning, Trey wasn't sure what his answer would be even now. Telling Browning to leave Horizon and lose his phone number had been satisfying. Staying here was the right answer for today, but he wasn't certain about tomorrow.

"What if this still isn't forever?" Trey asked. "Are we going to be okay?"

Rainey gave him a true smile this time. "We're going to be okay."

"But you aren't worried about finding a new chief anytime soon, are you?" Her smile widened into a grin, and some of his anxiety drifted away on the ocean air.

"Nope." Rainey patted his shoulder. "All you have to do now is get those house keys and convince Lila to take a chance on more police business. Think you can do it?"

It was easy to picture Lila's face when she'd said she wanted to kiss him again, when she'd floated the idea of a future of kissing him even though he was the chief and brought a whole lot of police business with him. "Yeah. I can do it."

He would find a way to make it happen.

Demonstrating that he was going to be a new kind of chief with a new way of doing police business was the key.

"I'm glad to hear it." Rainey thumped his shoulder, and he realized he'd gotten lucky when Rainey Blackwell had decided he was one of her people.

"But you gotta tell me about this turn of Belinda events." Trey needed some time to figure out what he wanted to say to Lila.

And listening to how these new neighbors of his had settled the issue of his guilt or innocence with less struggle than his old friends and coworkers reinforced his certainty that he was on the right track. Finally.

CHAPTER NINETEEN

On Friday evening, Lila surveyed the crowd that had gathered in Battery Park for the final concert of the season. It was a beautiful evening, with a cool breeze blowing in off the water to remind them that the summer was transitioning to fall. The change in the air was exciting.

The open green space between the playground and Town Hall was packed, which had to be thrilling Rainey wherever she was. She'd invited the builders of Bay View Tower to come to Horizon, so she and Lila had spent a few hours that afternoon walking the land around Blue Vista.

Nothing had been signed, but Lila's business senses were telling her that construction would be starting on Horizon's newest complex in under a year. None of the details were set, but Marc Jackson's quiet "whoa" as they'd stepped into the clearing to take in the view had been satisfying.

Rainey's immediate grin convinced Lila that her business senses were on the same page.

They had an appointment scheduled for Monday to discuss next steps, and Lila had written a few notes as soon as she made it back to her office. She would make some adjustments to their original plans and exclude the actual Blue Vista house with an eye to selling Rainey on a unique fixer-upper.

Cousin Mike would be pleased to keep the house in the family, she thought.

Lila and Duke had brainstormed a list of amenities that would be especially attractive to the over-fifty-five crowd. The new tower would not be limited to those buyers, but Lila had plans to spread the word far and wide to bring them into Horizon.

And all of this preparation was setting her up perfectly to stipulate that she be the exclusive listing agent for all the units in the tower.

Monica Denis could cry in her *bière* about it.

From her spot, Lila could see three different signs advertising her services at this end-of-summer celebration. She'd decided not to set up a booth, but replacing her boring professional headshot with the more casual one of her and Duke together was inspired. No one could ignore her distinguished gentleman, and once he got their attention, her name should stick.

Business-suit Lila wasn't who she was. Trey had been right about using a photo of the real her. She had to be dancing, singing Lila Shepard, and her clients in Horizon would adjust.

Skipping the booth and embracing her new

business philosophy meant Lila felt pretty free that evening. It was a good night to celebrate a great summer.

She shifted the camping chair—which she'd carried out from her office—on her shoulder and evaluated her choices for the best view of the stage.

Bee was volunteering in the police department's booth.

Her parents were hovering near it, but it appeared as though her mother was preparing to tow her father closer to the stage. TJ and Summer were already seated front and center.

Instead of attaching herself to any of them, Lila threaded carefully through the blankets and groups of chairs, nodding and speaking as she went, until she was near the back of the audience. The number of rowdy college kids ranged around the stage meant a little distance would be good.

As she set up her chair, Roberta Hale marched up. "Well, I guess you're pretty pleased about how this whole deal turned out, aren't you, Lila?"

Off balance, Lila pasted a smile on her face as she tried a few different answers in her head. Eventually, she said, "Ms. Hale, I am very pleased. I found the perfect buyer for your house. It is everything he didn't even know he wanted. His love for your house got you the very best price, too. This is the perfect match for both of you. That's hard to come by."

And she wasn't even going to say "I told you so" even though she had. The satisfaction of making the sale made it easier to take the high road.

That and actually being so very right.

Roberta pursed her lips. "Good answer." She shook her head. "I had my heart set on more, of course, but I can't deny that you proved yourself to be equal to or better than Monica Denis."

Equal to or better... She'd take that. It was intensely satisfying to hear this from Roberta, but Lila lectured herself not to gloat.

"I hope you'll keep me in mind whenever you're ready to buy or sell again, Roberta." Lila cleared her throat. Using her first name instead of the polite address she'd been raised with was uncomfortable, but she only needed practice.

Roberta pointed with her chin. "The new chief sure does look different out of the uniform, doesn't he?" Her confrontational tone had softened, which caught Lila's attention.

She turned to see that Trey had stopped at the police booth. He had a chair like hers hanging on his right shoulder, and in his casual T-shirt and jeans, he appeared to be an average citizen of Horizon. He might even blend in with the college kids, but not if they were partying after midnight around the Needlegrass Motor Lodge's pool.

As she watched him talk and Bee laugh in response, Lila wondered whether her father would have shown up to one of the biggest tourist nights of the whole year in street clothes when he was chief. She didn't think so. For events like this, he'd always scheduled more shifts, more officers, to help with traffic, crowd control and safety.

And when her father had asked for more from his officers, he'd always been the first in line, on duty, in his uniform. She'd spent a lot of time blaming the people of Horizon for her father's schedule, but she owed a little of that blame to him. She was glad Trey was doing something different.

"Did you know he's the person buying your house?" Lila asked.

Roberta sighed. "I did, but I did not know how handsome he was. That little tidbit didn't make it into the stories circulating through town." She shook her head as if she was disappointed at how other people had failed her.

As they watched Trey move through the crowd in their direction, it was easy to understand Roberta's disapproval of the town gossip. On the list of things people could say about Trey Douglas, how good-looking he was should land at the top.

Lila hadn't seen him since he'd walked away from the diner, but both Bee and Rainey had promised her that he was not leaving. He'd texted her twice, answering questions about the closing she had set up and accepting the results of the inspection. Both texts had been extremely unsatisfying to Lila, so she waved her hand and pointed at the empty grass next to her chair. If he ignored her invitation, she was going to have to get proactive.

Because if the rumors she was hearing were true and Trey Douglas had changed his mind and dug into Horizon, she was going to get another kiss.

Soon.

But first she needed to know what had taken him so long to find her. If he'd decided to stay a while in Horizon, what was his issue?

When he met her stare across the crowd and then turned away from her, the irritation he'd provoked that first day in the squad room bloomed in Lila's chest. When Roberta raised her eyebrows, Lila decided the irritation had made it all the way out to her face, too.

Lila watched him weave through the crowd to the edge of the stage. Boogie Howard bent low. The two men shook hands, and she hoped Boogie had gotten the memo that Trey was correcting his early mistakes. The two of them were going to have to work together on Roberta's house.

When Boogie nodded and clapped Trey on the shoulder, she decided whatever the conversation was about, it made them both happy. Trey's expression had changed when he turned back to face her.

This time, there was no doubt he was headed her way.

Lila vaguely registered that every head in the crowd turned to watch him go. He was still slicing right through any barriers, but this time it was because he was focused solely on her.

Roberta intercepted him ten feet away, and Lila had to fight to keep the scowl off her face. She met Bee's stare across the crowd, and her sister smiled slowly. Lila hoped that meant Bee was excited to see what came next, not that Lila was betraying her high level of annoyance.

"Chief, I hear you'll be moving into my house," Roberta said as she crossed her arms over her chest. "I do hope, now that you'll be settling in town, you can do something about the noisy traffic outside my new place. It's over by the high school and the way those kids blast their radios is a scandal."

Trey paused, a courteous expression on his face, which Lila took as a positive sign of his commitment to making a good impression now. A glare would have fit her mood at that moment.

"Ms. Hale, that is police business." He pointed to the police booth. Lila saw Bee quickly duck her head as if there was no way she'd been watching the drama unfold. "You see I'm off duty, not wearing a uniform. But those officers will be glad to take down any information you'd like to share and write up a report. I will take a look at that first thing on Monday when I'm back at my desk."

Roberta was ready to argue, but Trey turned his back on her and closed the distance between them.

He stopped in front of her as Boogie said, "Let me be the first one to welcome you all to Horizon's final concert of the season. Most of you know us. We're the Carolina Waves, and we normally like to get the show started with some party music." Boogie turned to look at his band over his shoulder. "But tonight, I've got a special request from the new chief of police. He has some important business to discuss with Lila Shepard, so we're gonna play his favorite song, 'History in the Making.' I don't know if it's Horizon's hometown real estate agent's favorite song, but the chief seemed to think she'd like it. And the chief and I agree that it's always the right time to make a beautiful woman smile."

Lila was excruciatingly aware of every pair of eyes locked on her in that moment.

This was like that first morning in the squad room times a hundred, but the feeling in the air was completely different.

"No police business tonight?" Lila murmured as she smiled up at him.

He shook his head slowly. "Not when I'm out of uniform. That's going to be one of my new rules. We have enough officers on duty to handle whatever comes up, and Tom Shepard trained them all well."

She understood that he was making a statement for Horizon with the street clothes.

But he was speaking directly to her, too.

Whatever happened between them, he wanted to mark the line between his job and his life outside of it, and she thought that was exciting.

She could do what her mother had done if she was facing a lifetime as the chief's significant other, but she would never be able to do it as gracefully.

Trey was trying to show her she wouldn't have to.

When the music started, Trey offered her his hand. Lila took it and stood slowly. Just behind Trey, she could see Roberta Hale had clasped her hands in front of her mouth as if she was overcome with emotion.

"I thought you didn't spend a lot of time on dance floors," Lila said as she stepped into his arms.

"I don't, but you make me want to try new things…repeatedly. And we're just shuffling to country music. How hard can it be?" Trey's hand slipped around her waist as he tugged her closer.

Lila raised her eyebrows as relief settled over her. They'd had this conversation the first time they danced, but it felt completely different tonight. She didn't need him to promise he was staying in Horizon forever, but she desperately wanted him to try doing Horizon with her.

"What took you so long to find me?" she asked. Her voice was soft, and it was impossible to ignore that the nearer she was to Trey, the less whatever he had done to irritate her mattered.

He bent his head closer to hers. "I wanted all this mess in Columbia settled, so I drove over after work on Wednesday, packed up whatever I could from my storage unit and first thing on Thursday morning, I visited Dennis Browning and the agents investigating my report."

Lila stared up at him. "How did it go? I can't believe anyone could imagine you had anything to do with shady police work for a second."

His slow smile nearly wiped all of her brain processes out, just static, but she shook her head to clear it.

"I'm satisfied I made my case clear. Dennis understands I'm not coming back." He tightened his hand on hers. "I've got a new plan now. I have a home here, and I'm going to be the best small-town police chief in South Carolina someday."

Lila pursed her lips as she wondered what Tom Shepard or his fans would say about that.

"If anyone can, it's me. I am going to be working with the best who were trained by the best," Trey added.

Then he pulled her close enough to rest against his chest, and as they danced, he sang the words of the song next to her ear. Lila wanted to freeze time so she could run around and make sure everyone was watching, that all of the people who had repeated tales of his bad behavior got a front-row seat to what had to be one of the most romantic experiences of her life.

But she didn't want to let him go.

"How do you know the words?" she asked and pressed her forehead to his shoulder.

"I downloaded the song as soon as I made it back to the motel that night. I've been listening to it ever since." Trey squeezed her closer. "Anytime I wondered what I was doing in Horizon, I hit Play. I've got them down now. I won't ever forget them."

Lila knew what he meant. Some things were impossible to forget, like facing off against Trey Douglas for the first time or kissing him under the twinkling lights on the Sandlapper's deck.

Or hearing him say he was going to stay in Horizon.

This dance would be another sweet memory, too.

And she couldn't wait to see what came next.

EPILOGUE

One month later

TREY SIGHED HAPPILY as he stretched out in the most expensive hammock he ever wanted to see, but it was his for the low, low price of a mortgage payment every single month for…as long as he wanted to stay. He owned this incredible spot in this lush backyard with the soundtrack of ocean waves. Only one thing could make it more perfect.

He closed his eyes but almost immediately felt the weight of someone watching him intently. The heavy breathing near his ear was the only clue he needed to solve the case.

"Duke, is that you, buddy?" he asked as he cracked one eye open.

The Great Dane resting his head next to Trey's grinned, and his tongue lolled out to one side. He was seated on the ground next to the hammock. He'd claimed it as his spot. Trey reached over to scratch between his bushy eyebrows the way Duke liked best and peered over his shoulder. Where Duke was, Lila would follow.

And he'd missed her.

It had been almost six hours since he'd seen her last over lunch at Palmetto State Pizza.

Since then, Lila had been working on a business deal with Rainey, and he'd been unpacking the few boxes he'd moved up from the storage space he'd been renting in Columbia. It wouldn't take long to empty them all, but he wasn't in any hurry.

He and Duke stared into each other's eyes while he waited for Lila to appear. They had spent important moments like this every night since he'd moved in, just him and the dog hanging out at the hammock, listening to the waves, and Trey thought it might be the most peace he'd ever felt.

"Don't let me interrupt," Lila said before shaking the cup in her hand. The rattle of the ice triggered his immediate response.

"I'll take that," Trey said as he held out his hand for the lemonade.

Lila grinned as she slid in beside him. "Want me to tell you yet?"

She'd asked the same question every time she'd handed him the lemonade. Knowing where to get this lemonade for himself would ruin her surprise.

He answered the same way he had every time. "No, it wouldn't taste as sweet without the delivery."

She sighed and rested her head against his shoulder. That was another critical piece of this hammock experience, Lila Shepard cuddled up next to him.

"I brought you something else, but I left it inside after I watered it," she said and tilted her face up. "Rainey and I had to drive down to Savannah to talk to Marc Jackson about the offer he wants to present to the shipyard's board of directors for their part of the land parcel we need. We walked by this plant store with an amazing window display, so I got you a houseplant. It's an ivy in an adorable birdcage. It's going to look great on your bookshelf."

Trey slowly grinned. "I don't have a bookshelf."

"Yet." Lila patted his shoulder. "You don't have a bookshelf yet, but I got the name of a fantastic thrift shop in Charleston from Summer. Hank and Hattie Brown furnished the shelter's office from there. I thought we could go up next Saturday after my open house on Duneside." She studied his face as she waited for his answer.

"Great plan," he said as he had to every single suggestion she'd made. That made him think of Kay Shepard suggesting that Lila would be able to turn his house into a home. She was doing it, one piece of furniture at a time, and removing every bit of the pressure he might have felt about filling the place.

Would he have ever decided he needed any houseplant, much less one in an "adorable" birdcage? He doubted it, but there was no question in his mind that it would fit on his eventual bookshelf perfectly.

"I liked it so much that I got a matching one for my office," Lila said. "I already have a bookshelf."

Trey squeezed her closer. Why did having the same plant and planter she had feel so sweet? It was like the home decor equivalent of matching sweaters, and he loved it.

He would never have said he needed Horizon.

Or a job leading a small-town police force.

Or neighbors who knew every single step he made and felt entitled to give him advice.

But needing Lila Shepard made sense. There was no reason to worry himself over it, either. She was a force of nature like the waves in the distance.

When she shifted against him, as if she was about to sit up, he hummed the chorus of the song they would dance to every time the Carolina Waves played it and watched her smile light up her eyes.

"This is another of those moments, isn't it?" Lila asked. "We're going to want to remember this."

Trey turned to his side and held her as the hammock swung gently side to side. "The first time I saw you in the squad room, it was your eyes that caught me. And at the back-to-school night, your smile was magnetic. And then we danced, and I knew what it was like to hold you in my arms.

Here, I understand what it means to belong to a place, a time and a person."

She pressed her forehead to his chest. "Are you trying to make me cry, Trey? Because I'll do it."

He laughed and pressed a kiss against her lips. "Because of you, I know what it's like to come home."

"Think you'll be happy doing that in Horizon?" she asked.

Trey nodded. There was no doubt in his mind. Whether it was this house or another, wherever Lila Shepard was would always be home.

* * * * *

Don't miss the next book in Cheryl Harper's A Lowcountry Heroes Romance miniseries, coming February 2027 from Harlequin Heartwarming.